UNHINGED

UNHINGED

A
Home Repair Is Homicide
Mystery

SARAH GRAVES

B A N T A M   B O O K S

UNHINGED

A Bantam Book / January 2003

Library of Congress Cataloging-in-Publication Data
Graves, Sarah.
    Unhinged / Sarah Graves.
        p. cm.
    ISBN 0-553-80229-1
    1. Tiptree, Jacobia (Fictitious character)–Fiction.   2. White, Ellie (Fictitious
character)–Fiction.   3. Women detectives–Maine–Eastport–Fiction.
4. Dwellings–Maintenance and repair–Fiction.   5. Female friendship–Fiction.
6. Eastport (Me.)–Fiction.   I. Title.

PS3557.R2897 U54 2003
813'.54–dc21

2002025559

Published simultaneously in the United States and Canada

Bantam Books are published by Bantam Books, a division of Random House, Inc.
Its trademark, consisting of the words "Bantam Books" and the portrayal of a
rooster, is Registered in U.S. Patent and Trademark Office and in other countries.
Marca Registrada. Random House, New York, New York.

PRINTED IN THE UNITED STATES OF AMERICA

BVG   10 9 8 7 6 5 4 3 2 1

UNHINGED

Chapter 1

Harriet Hollingsworth was the kind of person who called 911 the minute she spotted a teenager ambling down the street, since as she said there was no sense waiting for them to get up to their nasty tricks. Each week Harriet wrote to the *Quoddy Tides,* Eastport's local newspaper, a list of the sordid misdeeds she suspected all the rest of us of committing, and when she wasn't doing that she was at her window with binoculars, spying out more.

Snoopy, spiteful, and a suspected poisoner of neighborhood cats, Harriet was confidently believed by her neighbors to be too mean to die, until the morning one of them spotted her boot buckle glinting up out of his compost heap like the wink of an evil eye.

The boot had a sock in it but the sock had no foot in it and despite a diligent search (one wag remarking that if Harriet was buried somewhere, the grass over her grave would die in the shape of a witch on a broomstick) she remained missing.

"Isn't that just like Harriet?" my friend Ellie White demanded about three weeks later, squinting up into the spring sunshine.

We were outside my house in Eastport, on Moose Island, in downeast Maine. "Stir up as much fuss and bother as she could," Ellie went on, "but not give an ounce of satisfaction in the end."

Thinking at the time that it *was* the end, of course. We both did.

At the time. My house is a white clapboard 1823 Federal with three full floors plus an attic, forty-eight big old double-hung windows with forest-green wooden shutters, three chimneys (one for each pair of fireplaces), and a two-story ell.

From my perch on a ladder propped against the porch roof I looked down at Ellie, who wore a purple tank top like a vest over a yellow turtleneck with red frogs embroidered on it. Blue jeans faded to the color of cornflowers and rubber beach shoes trimmed with rubber daisies completed her outfit.

"Running out on her bills, not a word to anyone," she added darkly.

In Maine, stiffing creditors is not only bad form. It's also a shortsighted way of trying to escape your money troubles, since anywhere you go in the whole state you are bound to run into your creditors' cousins, hot to collect and burning to make an example out of you. That was why Ellie thought Harriet must've scarpered to Vermont or New Hampshire, leaving the boot as misdirection and her own old house already in foreclosure.

From my ladder-perch I glimpsed it peeking forlornly through the maples, two streets away: a huge Victorian shambles shedding chunks of rotted trim and peeled-off paint curls onto an unkempt lawn. Just the sight of its advancing decrepitude gave me a pang. I'd started the morning optimistically, but fixing a few gutters was shaping up to be more difficult than I'd expected.

"Harriet," Ellie declared, "was never the sharpest tool in the toolbox, and this stunt of hers just proves it."

"Mmm," I said distractedly. "I wish this ladder was taller."

Shakily I tried steadying myself, straining to reach a metal strap securing a gutter downspout. Over the winter the downspouts had blown loose so their upper ends aimed gaily off in nonwater-collecting directions. But the straps were still firmly fastened to the house with big aluminum roofing nails.

I couldn't fix the gutters without taking the straps off, and I couldn't get the straps off. They were out of my reach even when, balancing precariously on tiptoe, I swatted at them with the claw hammer. Meanwhile down off the coast of the Carolinas a storm sat spinning over warmer water, sucking up energy.

"Ellie, run in and get me the crowbar, will you, please?"

Days from now, maybe a week, the storm would make its way here, sneakily gathering steam. When it arrived it would hit hard.

Ellie let go of the ladder's legs and went into the house. This I thought indicated a truly touching degree of confidence in me, because I am the kind of person who can trip while walking on a linoleum floor. I sometimes think it would simplify life if I got up every morning, climbed a ladder, and fell off, just to get it over with.

And sure enough, right on schedule as the screen door swung shut, the ladder's feet began slipping on the spring-green grass. I should mention it was also *wet* grass, since in Maine we really only have three seasons: mud time, Fourth of July, and pretty good snowmobiling.

"Ow," I said a moment later when I'd landed hard and managed to spit out a mouthful of grass and mud. Then I just lay there while my nervous system rebooted and ran damage checks. Arms and legs movable: okay. Not much blood: likewise reassuring. I could remember all the curse words I knew and proved it by reciting them aloud.

A robin cocked his bright eye suspiciously at me, apparently thinking I'd tried muscling in on his worm-harvesting operation. I probed between my molars with my tongue, hoping the robin was incorrect, and he was, and the molars were all there, too.

So I felt better, sort of. Then Ellie came back out with the crowbar and saw me on the ground.

"Jake, are you all right?"

"Fabulous." The downspout lay beside me. Apparently I'd flailed at it with the hammer as I was falling and hooked it on my way down.

Ellie's expression changed from alarm to the beginnings of relief. I do so enjoy having a friend who doesn't panic when the going gets bumpy, although I suspected there was liniment in my future, and definitely aspirin.

"Oof," I said, getting up. My knees were skinned, and so were my elbows. My face had the numb feeling that means it will hurt later, and there was a funny little click in my shoulder that I'd never heard before. But across the street two dapper old gentlemen on a stroll had paused to observe me avidly, and I feel that pride goeth before *and* after the fall, like parentheses.

"Hi," I called, waving the hammer in weak parody of having descended so fast on purpose. The sounds emanating from my body reminded me of a band consisting of a washtub bass, soup spoons, and a kazoo.

Some were the popping noises of tendons snapping back into their proper positions. But others—the loudest, weirdest ones—were from inside my ears.

The men moved on, no doubt muttering about the fool woman who didn't know enough to stay down off a ladder. That was how I felt about her, too, at the moment: ouch.

In the kitchen, Ellie applied first aid consisting of soapy washcloths, clean dry towels, and twenty-year-old Scotch. A couple of Band-Aids completed the repair job, which only made me look a little like Frankenstein's monster.

"Yeeks. All I need now is a pair of steel bolts screwed into my skull." The split in my lip was particularly decorative and there was a purplish bruise coming up on my cheekbone.

"Yes," Ellie said crisply, putting the first-aid things back into the kitchen drawer. "And you're lucky you *don't* need bolts."

Responding to her tone, my black Labrador retriever, Monday, hurried in from the parlor, ears pricked and brown eyes alert for any unhappiness she might abolish with swipes of her wet tongue.

"You could have killed yourself falling off that ladder, you know," Ellie admonished me. "I *wish* you'd let me—"

Wriggling anxiously, Monday threw a body-block against my hip, which wasn't quite broken. Monday believes you can heal almost anything by applying a dog to it, and—mostly—I think so, too.

But next came Cat Dancing, a big apple-headed Siamese with crossed eyes and a satanic expression. "Ellie, I'm fine," I said, trying to sound believable. "I don't need a doctor."

Except maybe a witch doctor if Cat Dancing kept staring at me that way. She was named by my son Sam for reasons I can't fathom, as the only dance that feline ever does will be on my grave. She wouldn't care if I died on the spot as long as my body didn't block the cabinet where we keep cat food. We'd gotten her from my ex-husband Victor, who lives down the street and is also reliable in the driving-me-crazy department.

"Right," Ellie agreed. "Why, you're just a picture of health." *Picktcha:* the downeast Maine pronunciation.

When Ellie's Maine twang gets emphatic it's a bad time for me to try persuading her of anything. Fortunately, just then her favorite living creature in the world padded into my kitchen.

"Prill!" Ellie's expression instantly softened as she bent to embrace the newcomer.

A ferocious-looking Doberman pinscher, Prill sported a set of choppers that would have felt right at home in the jawbone of a great white shark. But the snarl on her kisser was really only a sweet, goofy grin. Prill was an earnest if bumbling guardian of balls, bones, dishrags, slippers, hairbrushes, and cats.

Especially cats. Squirming from Ellie's hug, Prill spied Cat Dancing and greeted the little sourpuss by closing her jaws very gently around Cat's head. Then she just stood there wagging her stubby tail while the hair on Cat's back stiffened in outrage and her crossed eyes bugged helplessly.

"Aw," I said. "Isn't that cute?"

Cat emitted a moan keenly calculated to warm the heart of a person who has just pushed the cat off the kitchen table for the millionth, billionth time, and that was about how many times I'd done it just in Cat's first week here.

"Prill," Ellie said in gentle admonishment. Days earlier she and I had found the big dog alone and tagless on the town pier, gamely trying to steal a few mackerel heads from the seagulls. No owner had yet claimed her, and I doubted now if anyone would.

Cat's moan rose to an atonal yowl as Sam came in with his dive gear over his shoulder, wearing his new wristwatch which read out in military time. It was, my son had informed me happily, the way the Coast Guard did it. In love with all things watery, this summer he'd signed up for an advanced diving-operations seminar so risky-sounding, I disliked thinking about it.

But if he was going to be in and on the water for a living, as seemed inevitable, I guessed as much supervised practice as possible was only prudent. Now he dropped his gear beside the buckets of polyurethane and tins of varnish remover I'd put out a few days earlier. Besides the gutters, I was also refinishing the hall floor that spring.

"Wow, where'd you get that big shiner?" Sam asked with the half-worried, half-admiring interest of a young man who thinks his mother might have been in a recent fistfight. At nineteen, he had his father's dark hair, hazel eyes, and the ravishing grin—also his dad's—of a born heartbreaker.

"Oh, no." I rushed back to the mirror, finding to my dismay that Sam's assessment was correct. An ominous red stain was circling my right eye; soon my face would be wearing two of my least favorite human skin colors: purple and green.

And *speaking* of green . . .

A bolt of fright struck me. "Ellie, come and hold my eyelid out, please, and look under it. I think when I landed I shoved a contact lens halfway into my brain."

One blue eye, one green; oh, blast and damnation. But just as I was really about to panic, Sam's girlfriend Maggie arrived with a tiny disk of green plastic poised on her index finger.

"Did you lose this?" Maggie was a big red-cheeked girl with clear olive skin, liquid brown eyes, and dark, wavy hair that she wore in a thick, glossy braid down her plaid-shirted back.

"I spotted it on the sidewalk," she added. It was Maggie who'd bought Sam the military wristwatch, shopping for it on-line via her computer.

Then she saw me. "Jacobia, what *happened*?"

Well, at least the lens wasn't halfway to my brain. "I was testing Newton's law. The demonstration got away from me." I popped the other lens out. Suddenly I was blue-eyed again. Both eyes. "I'm okay, though, thanks."

Actually parts of me were hurting quite intensely but if I said so, Ellie would insist on taking me to the clinic where Victor was on duty. And rather than submit to my ex-husband's critical speculations on how my injuries had happened, I'd have gone outside and fallen off that ladder all over again.

"I guess I can't be in your eye-color experiment, though," I said. Like Sam, in the fall Maggie would be a sophomore at the University of Maine. "I don't think I should put the lens back in right away," I explained.

The experiment, for a psychology-class project, was to see how long it takes a person to get used to a new eye color. If my own reaction was any indication, the answer was *never*. It was astonishing how jarring the past week had been, seeing a green-eyed alien with my face looking out of the mirror at blue-eyed me.

Disappointment flashed in Maggie's glance, at once replaced by concern. "Oh, I don't care about that silly experiment," she declared.

But she did. She had designed it, proposed it, and with some difficulty gotten it approved, to get credits while staying in Eastport—where Sam was, not coincidentally—for the whole summer. It wasn't easy getting people with normal sight to wear the lenses, either. I was among the six she'd persuaded, the minimum for the project. "It's you I'm worried about," she added.

The girl was going to make someone a wonderful daughter-in-law someday. But it wouldn't be me if Sam didn't hurry up and get his act together. Other mothers fret if their kids get romantically involved too fast, but my son's idea of a proper courtship verged on the glacial.

Luckily in addition to her other sterling qualities Maggie was patient. "You should put something on it," she said. "A cold cloth or some ice."

"That," Ellie interjected acidly, "would mean she'd have to sit still. And you're allergic to that, aren't you, dear?"

Dee-yah. Catching the renewed threat of a clinic visit, I sat down and accepted the ministrations she offered: aspirin, a cloth with cracked ice in it. If I didn't, she might hog-tie me and *haul* me to Victor's clinic. She could do it, too; Ellie looks as delicate as a fairy-tale princess but her spine is of tempered steel.

Also, I'd begun noticing that something about Newton's law had hit me in a major way. Sunshine slanting through the tall bare windows of the big old barnlike kitchen wavered at me, and the maple wainscoting's orangey glow was shimmering weirdly.

"Oh," I heard myself say. "Psychedelic."

"Jake?" Ellie said in alarm, reaching for me.

Then I was on the floor, Prill's cold nose snuffling in my ear while

Monday nudged my shoulder insistently. Faces peered: Sam, Maggie. And Ellie, her red hair a backlit halo, green eyes gazing frightenedly at me and even the freckles on her nose gone pale.

"Okay, now," I began firmly, but it came out a croak.

". . . call the hospital?" Sam asked urgently.

"Lift your feet up," Maggie advised.

So I did, and felt much better as blood rushed back downhill to my brain again. Newton's law apparently had advantages, although if my brain planned depending on gravity for all of its blood supply, I was still in serious trouble.

Which was how things stood when my husband, Wade Sorenson, walked in. Tall and square-jawed, built like a stevedore, with brush-cut blond hair and grey eyes, he surveyed the scene with an air of calm competence that I found hugely refreshing under the circumstances. And while Sam asked again if he should phone the hospital and Maggie insisted I put my feet up higher and Ellie was all for summoning an ambulance right that instant, Wade said:

"Hey. How're you doing?"

He doesn't freak out, he doesn't screw up; he's the only man in the world into whose arms I would trustingly fall backwards.

Or forwards, for that matter. Crouching, he assessed me, smelling as always of fresh cold air, lime shaving soap, and lanolin hand cream. He'd already noticed that I was breathing and had a blood pressure. The dogs backed off and sat.

"Your pupils are equal," he commented mildly. Meaning that I likely did not have the kind of brain damage that would kill me. Or not right now, anyway.

Victor would have scoffed at the notion of Wade assessing anything medically, but guys who work on boats learn how to eyeball injuries pretty accurately, reluctant to forfeit a day's pay for anything but the probably-fatal. And as Eastport's harbor pilot, guiding freighters safely through the watery maze of downeast Maine's many treacherous navigation hazards, Wade works on boats pretty much the way mountain goats work on mountains.

Eager to lose my invalid status, I sat up. Not a good move. "Hey, hey," Wade cautioned as the room whirled madly. "Take it slow."

"Okay," I said grudgingly. That Newton guy was beginning to be a real pain in my tailpipe. But I was *not* lying down again.

Ellie was just waiting to bushwhack me into the clinic, Sam resembled a six-year-old who wanted his mommy, and Maggie—

Well, Maggie looked solid and unruffled as usual, for which I was grateful since I had an idea I'd be needing her, later.

For one thing, I'd planned a special dinner in honor of the tenant who'd moved into my guest room that morning, an aspiring music-video producer filming his first effort here in Eastport.

For another, somewhere between the ladder and the ground I'd had an important epiphany. Harriet Hollingsworth wasn't just missing.

She was dead. And she'd probably been murdered.

"She had no car, no money. No family as far as anyone knows. So how did Harriet drop off the earth without a trace?" I asked a little while later, sitting on the edge of the examining table at the Eastport Health Clinic.

The clinic windows looked out over a tulip bed whose frilly blooms swayed together in the breeze like dancers in a chorus line. Across the street, a row of white cottages sported postage-stamp lawns, picket fences, and American flags. Beyond gleamed Passamaquoddy Bay, blue and tranquil in the spring sunshine, the distant hills of New Brunswick mounding hazily on the horizon.

"Well?" I persisted as Victor shone a penlight into my eye. "Where'd Harriet go? And how?"

The clinic smelled reassuringly of rubbing alcohol and floor wax.

But years of marriage to a medical professional had given me a horror of being at the business end of the medical profession. Ellie had brought me here while Wade finished the gutters, knowing that otherwise I'd go right back up the ladder again; if you let any element of old-house fix-up beat you for an instant, the house will get the upper hand in everything. And although I wasn't graceful or surefooted I was stubborn; so far, this had been enough to keep my old home from collapsing around me.

Victor snapped the penlight off. He'd tested all the things he could think of that might show I was *non compos mentis,* which was what he thought anyway. When I came here from New York and bought the house he'd had a world-class hissy fit, saying that it showed my personality was disintegrating and besides, if I moved so far from Manhattan, how would he see Sam?

I'd said that (a) at least I had a personality, (b) if mine was disintegrating it was under the hammer blows he had inflicted upon it while we were married, and (c) as it was, he hadn't seen Sam for over a year.

That shut him up for a while. But not much later he'd moved to Eastport, too, and established his medical clinic.

"Normal," he pronounced now, sounding disappointed.

"A person needs money to run," I reminded Ellie, "even when money trouble is why they are running in the first place."

"She scavenged, though," Ellie countered. "Cans, returnable bottles. Over time, Harriet could have gotten bus fare to Bangor from that."

"Then what?" I objected. "Start a new life? Harriet was barely managing to hang on to the old one. And what about all that blood at her house?"

"Nobody reliable ever saw any blood," Ellie retorted.

After her boot was found, a story went around that a lot of blood had been seen on the top step of Harriet's porch. By whom and when was a matter of wild speculation, and when I'd gone to see for myself it hadn't been there, so I'd discounted the rumor. But now . . .

11

"Ahem," Victor said pointedly. He had dark hair with a few threads of grey in it, hazel eyes, and a long jaw clenched in a grim expression. Partly this was his normal look while ferreting out illness and coming up with ways to knock its socks off.

Also, though, it meant I was not regarding him with sufficient awe. "Could you," he requested irritably, "pay just a little more attention to the situation at hand?"

Reluctantly I focused on him. This took some doing, a fact I'd failed to mention when asked about symptoms; blurry vision, I understood, could mean Something Bad. But I was determined not to become a patient if I could help it, and I *had* just taken out the contact lenses . . .

"You might have a mild concussion," he pronounced at last.

"That's all?" Ellie questioned. "She seems quite shaken up."

She was complicating my exit strategy: find the nearest door and scram through it, lickety-split. I rolled my eyes at her to get her to pipe down; the room lurched, spinning a quarter turn.

"The simplest possible explanation is usually correct," Victor intoned. " 'Shaken up' is as good a description as any."

"So I can go?" I slid hastily off the examining table. If it meant getting out of here right now, I'd have hopped off a cliff.

Which, it turned out, was just exactly what getting off that table felt like. Somewhere were my shoes, making contact with the tiled floor. They seemed far away and not entirely reliable, as if connected to my body by long, loose rubber bands.

Feets don't fail me now, I thought earnestly. If I had to, I would take floor-contact on faith.

The way, once upon a time, I'd taken Victor. "Someone would remember if Harriet took the bus," I told Ellie.

Victor frowned. He feels everyone should keep silent until he finishes giving *his* opinions. And as he will finish giving *his* opinions a day or so after his funeral, mostly I ignore him.

But now we were in the land of traumatic head injury, where Victor is king and all he surveys is his to command. He'd gotten reeducated for country doctoring, but back in the city Victor was the one you went to after all the other brain surgeons turned pale and began trembling at the very sight of you.

So this time I listened. "Twenty-four hours of bed rest," he decreed. "Watch for headache, disorientation, and grogginess."

Breathing the same air as Victor made me groggy. We'd had a peace treaty for a while, but now Sam was away at college most of the time and without him to run interference for us, Victor and I were about as compatible as flies and flyswatters. And guess what end of that charming analogy I tended to end up on.

"Great," I said glumly. It wasn't enough that I looked like I'd gone nine rounds with a prizefighter. My X rays were clear but my face was a disaster area, and the click in my shoulder had gone silent, probably on account of the swelling.

But I *couldn't* lie down. I had *things* to do: dinner guests.

And Harriet's murder. First, I had to convince Ellie that it had happened. I had a pretty clear idea of how to do that, too; Harriet hadn't owned much, but she had possessed *one* thing . . .

"Well, maybe not actual bed rest," Victor allowed. "But if you won't take it easy," he added sternly, "I'll admit you to the hospital for forty-eight hours of observation."

An odd look came into his eye, and I realized he could make good on this threat if he came up with dire enough reasons. Wade might believe Victor, if he sounded sincere; Ellie, too.

And Victor was good at sincere. "I will," I vowed, "take it easy. Um, and is it okay to put the contact lenses back in?"

Because if I could, Maggie's project might get saved. Victor looked put-upon.

"Oh, I suppose," he replied waspishly. "It looks bad but the orbital processes were spared, the swelling's minimal, not *in* the eye at all, and you have no signs of neurological dysfunction."

Never mind if your face looks like roadkill; if you can follow his moving finger with your eyes and touch your nose with your own, you're good to go. "But why in heaven's name are you participating in amateur-hour science?" he wanted to know.

"Thank you, Victor," I cut him off. It's yet another of his talents, making me feel like a rebellious child.

Leaving Ellie to settle up at the business desk I made for the exit before he could decide to prescribe a clear liquid diet. Maybe I'd learn later that I'd knocked an essential screw loose and it needed replacing right away, before my brains fell out.

But I doubted it. And I doubted even more that the gleam in his eye had been benevolent, when he realized that if only for an instant there, he'd had me in his power.

Again.

So I was getting the hell out of Dodge.

My name is Jacobia Tiptree and once upon a time I was a hotshot New York financial expert, a greenback-guru with offices so plush you could lose a small child in the depth of the broadloom on the floor of my consulting area. I was the one rich folks came to for help on the most (to them) important topics in the world:

(A) Getting wealthier, and

(B) Getting even wealthier than that.

Everything was about money. Fallen in love? Break out the prenuptial agreements. Somebody died? The family is frantic not with grief for the dearly departed but because the old skinflint stashed his loot in an unbreakable charitable remainder trust.

Loot being the operative term; most of my clients were so crooked their limousines should've flown the Jolly Roger. But I didn't care, mostly on account of having started out with no loot whatsoever, myself. Until I was a teenager my idea of the lush life was glass in the windows, shoes that fit, and not too much wood smoke from the cracks in the stove chimney, so I could read.

At fifteen I ran from the relatives who were raising me, trusting in my wits and a benevolent universe to pave my path, which is why it was lucky I turned out to *have* a few wits about me. Getting through Penn Station I had the sense I'd have been safer in a war zone; men sidled up to me, crooking their fingers, weaving and crooning. With my pale shiny face and hick clothes, lugging a cheap suitcase and in possession of the enormous sum of twenty dollars, I must've looked just like all the other fresh young chickens, ready for plucking.

Fortunately, however, all my cousins had been boys. Something about me must have said I knew precisely where to aim my kneecap, and the nasty men skedaddled. Before I knew it (well, a couple of weeks after I hopped off the Greyhound, actually) I was living in a tenement near Times Square where I'd found the best job a girl from my background could imagine: waitress in a Greek diner.

My feet were swollen, my hair stank of fryer grease, and in the first couple of days I learned thirty new ways to buzz off a lurking creep-o. Meager wages and no tips; Ari's Dineraunt wasn't a tipping kind of place, except on the horses. But it was all-you-could-eat and most of the other girls didn't enjoy the food. Too foreign, they said, turning up their well-nourished noses.

Which left more for me. Short ribs and stuffed grape leaves, moussaka and lamb stew; ordinarily the owner was tighter with a dime than a wino with a pint of Night Train, but for some reason Ari Kazantzakis thought it was funny to watch me shoving baklava into my mouth.

Maybe it was because he had enough family memories of real hunger to know it when he saw it. Ari had a photo of Ellis Island behind the counter, and one of the Statue of Liberty in his fake-wood-paneled office. The tenement where I lived was just like the one his parents had moved into when they got here. Or exactly the one.

Whatever. Anyway, one day Ari's accountant didn't show up and the next day they found him floating in the East River, full of bullet holes. Suddenly it wasn't all sweetmeats and balalaikas at the Diner-aunt anymore. More like hand-wringing and sobbing violins until I said I was good at math and that when I wasn't slinging hash I was taking accounting courses. By then I'd gotten a high school equivalency and talked my way into night school.

I'd figured it was the only way I would ever get near real money, which was true but not in the way I'd expected. Two days later I was carrying a black bag, the one the accountant had been expected to pick up and deliver. That was how I got to know the men at the social club, several of whom later became my clients.

They thought it was hilarious, a skinny-legged girl with big eyes and a down-home accent running numbers money. But they didn't think it was so funny a few weeks later, when every other runner in the city got nabbed in an organized crime crackdown.

All but me. Like I said, I'd had boy cousins, and if there was anything I was good at besides math, it was evasive action. A few years later when I'd finished school, gotten married, begun solo money management, and had a baby, one of the guys from the social club came to my office.

He wore an Armani suit, a Bahamas tan, and Peruggi shoes. The diamond in his pinky ring was so big you could have used it to anchor a yacht. His expression was troubled; they always were on people with money woes. And this guy's familiar hound-dog face was the saddest that I had ever encountered. But when he saw me behind my big oak desk, he started to laugh.

Me, too. All the way to the bank.

And there you have it: my own personal journey from rags to riches. Victor's another story, not such a pleasant one; first came the hideous coincidence of our having the same uncommon last name. At the time, I regarded this happenstance as serendipity. And I'll admit I was still full of bliss when our son Sam appeared. But soon enough began the late-night calls from lovelorn student nurses whom I informed, at first gently and later I suppose rather cruelly, that the object of their affections was married and had a child. And in the end I got fed up with the city, too.

I'd thrived in it but when Sam hit twelve it began devouring him: drugs. Bad companions. And our divorce half killed him. So I chucked it all and bought an old house that needed everything, on Moose Island seven miles off the coast of downeast Maine.

It's quiet: church socials and baked-bean suppers, concerts in the band shell on the library lawn when the weather is warm. There's the Fourth of July in summer, a Salmon Festival in fall, and high school basketball during the school year, of course.

But that's it. Not much out of the ordinary happens in Eastport.

Unless you count the occasional mysterious bloody murder.

Chapter 2

Outside the clinic, Ellie assessed me. "Death warmed over," she pronounced. "How do you feel?"

"Oh, great," I replied, wincing. "If Victor hadn't X-rayed my neck and shoulder I'd think they were broken, too. But at least I'm not dead. And trust me on this, Ellie: Harriet is." My ears were still ringing. "And not by her choice, if that is what you're going to say next. Suicides don't hide. They *want* people to find them."

Across the street, a seagull stood like a living weather vane atop the painted brick chimney of Weston House, one of Eastport's many charming bed-and-breakfasts; 150 years earlier, John James Audubon had stayed there on his way to Newfoundland. Beyond it across the water I could just pick out Franklin D. Roosevelt's summer place on Campobello Island, its emerald lawn sloping down to the rocky shore of the bay. So my eyes still worked, anyway.

"But I still don't get why you're so sure," Ellie said as we crossed the parking lot. Behind a cedar fence, the white shingled spire of the Congregational Church soared loftily to a massive old clock, its face overlooking the grammar school and town hall.

The tower clock chimed twelve as we got into Ellie's car. I pulled the visor mirror down, very carefully inserted both of the contact lenses, and blinked experimentally.

"Harriet had," I repeated, "no family to go to. Or anyone to help her that we know of. And we would know, wouldn't we?"

"Definitely." Ellie started the car. In Eastport, half your neighbors know who your next of kin is, and if you were born here the other half *are* your next of kin. And since Ellie had been my friend since practically the moment I'd arrived here five years earlier, I knew, too.

Although in Eastport there's always more to learn, even for Ellie. "But Harriet did have enemies," I went on, startled again at the change the green lenses made, like the special effects in a horror movie when the vampire's eyes glow. "The letters she wrote to the paper describing what she saw people doing when she watched through her binoculars," I added.

Ellie looked unconvinced. "The *Tides* never printed most of her letters."

"Doesn't matter." In Eastport, if a pin drops at one end of town you hear it at the other. "Everyone *knew* about them."

"No one took her seriously," Ellie persisted.

But I still thought someone had. "Let's go to Harriet's," I suggested. "Have a look around. First, though, how about a drive downtown? I need a dose of scenery before I become a shut-in."

She glanced at me. "You're following Victor's advice?"

Horrid thought. But crossing the parking lot had taken every ounce of my concentration due to the ripple the ground kept developing under my feet, and the contents of my head were still shifting around inside my skull like wrecking-ball rubble. Back in the bad old days when Sam and his pals couldn't find other drugs to ingest, they'd huffed paint thinner; now the gongs in my ears rang as if I'd sucked up a whole tin of the varnish remover that was waiting for me back at the house.

"Ellie, I'm not sure I've got a choice."

She nodded silently, turning toward Water Street which is Eastport's main drag, running parallel to the waterfront, and when we got there she pulled into the parking lot overlooking the fish pier and Passamaquoddy Bay.

When people come to Eastport it's the first thing they see, that paint-box blue water stretching pristinely from the harbor, dotted with boats. I feasted my eyes on it, breathed in the tart mingled smells of salt, seaweed, and creosote.

Ellie switched off the ignition. "Okay, let's see if I've got this straight. You're going to lie down, which means you're an inch or so from falling down."

"Yup." Across the water Campobello Island wiggled and glowed like a radium-green snake until I closed my eyes, whereupon it kept doing the very same thing on the backs of my eyelids. I felt sure Victor wouldn't have regarded this as a good sign. And I was equally sure I wouldn't tell him.

"I'll just give it a couple more hours," I told Ellie. "I only had the wind knocked out of me."

Or maybe it *was* the lenses. But Maggie was depending on me, and I hated letting her down. I felt our family had let her down enough, one way and another; sometimes I thought witnessing the war between Victor and me had messed Sam up so badly, that rakish grin of his might always promise more than it could deliver.

Out past the pier three fellows on maintenance detail washed windows, swabbed decks, and polished the brightwork on the two biggest boats in Eastport's working fleet. The *Pleon* and *Ahoskie* were tubby, unglamorous vessels, but Wade made sure the crew kept the tugboats shipshape.

20

"All right. But you won't lie to me," Ellie insisted. "You will tell me if you feel worse and you'll tell me in time to *do* something about it. Deal?"

"Deal." In Eastport it's wise to plan medical emergencies in advance. Even Victor didn't do major surgery here. If you needed a brain surgeon, you also needed a Life Star helicopter. Which I hoped not to; after Harriet's house, I planned to get horizontal and stay that way for the rest of the afternoon.

But what somebody said about the best-laid plans went double for me that day. "Look," Ellie said, pointing, and when I obeyed the world only spun a little bit.

Across Water Street, three young fellows with deep tans and aviator sunglasses were emerging from Wadsworth's Hardware store. All three wore T-shirts, khaki hiking shorts, and blond hair tied in ponytails. They hustled purposefully up the sidewalk past the old redbrick and wood-frame storefronts comprising Eastport's business section, their arms loaded with purchases.

"Music-video guys," Ellie sized them up swiftly.

"What else?" Their boss Roy McCall had moved his stuff into my guest room at seven that morning—the town's motel rooms and bed-and-breakfasts were all full—and dashed out again to begin work. A music video, I gathered, was a labor-intensive project.

McCall's three minions strode down Water Street to their rented headquarters in the old Knights of Columbus building and went in, just as a truck with a big square cargo compartment began backing slowly around the corner. In red with black shadows the truck's lettering read *Top Cat Productions*.

It stopped and a crew began unloading equipment: light bars, microphone booms, film cameras, musical instrument cases, massive amplifiers, and mountains of coiled cable and wires.

"Wow," Ellie said, easing onto the street away from the truck whose crew was working so fast, the cargo compartment was nearly empty.

Only a wooden crate and some wires remained in it. I craned my neck, pleased to find my vision had cleared. The ringing in both my ears had dropped to a hum, too, though the left one still sounded static-fritzy.

Ellie slowed to speak to Purlie Wadsworth, who stood in the brick arched doorway of the hardware store watching the action. "So what do you think?" she called. "Is Eastport ready to be the command-and-control center of a major music production?"

Because that was what Top Cat had been promising us since back in February. In return for permission to block off streets, erect stage sets, replace public signage, and generally take over the place, Top Cat had promised jobs, paid-in-advance tenancy of several vacant down-town rental properties, local purchase of any and all needed supplies, and a bonanza for every lodging place in the area, this being one reason every one of them was now full.

Purlie nodded contemplatively. A tall, rawboned man with pale hair and a faraway look in his eyes, he didn't play music in the store or blow it from the sound system of his pickup truck. Nor did you hear it coming from the windows of his house, should you be passing. Once, Purlie had worked in a gravel pit; now peace and quiet was just what the doctor ordered.

Unless something else brought good business into the hardware store. He bounced gently on the heels of his work boots as a pair of Top Cats emerged from the truck's cargo box. Across the street two more technicians had already set up a big camera.

"What the heck are they doing?" Ellie wondered aloud as the crew threw what looked like a net over the entire truck, tying it at the bottom so that the vehicle was entirely, although loosely, enclosed. The net's strands glittered metallically in the sun.

"Ready," one of them called to the camera operators.

"Rolling," the operator called back.

Which was when I noticed suddenly that except for us, no one was on the street. While we were parked, big yellow sawhorses had been put up at both ends, closing off access. The wooden crate still sat in the truck's cargo compartment rear, looking oddly familiar; where had I seen one like it before? Also, the plate glass windows of the storefronts all had paper tape plastered across them, as if . . .

Something *ping*ed in my memory. The Top Cat crew backed away from the truck. The net was good. I understood the net. But . . .

"I say, let 'em come," said Purlie, who had been in charge of blasting at the gravel pit. "Make the durn video, spend their money, give us all a boost and may the devil take the . . ."

Down the street, a Top Cat crew member produced a handheld radio controller. With a flourish he pressed a button on the device. And as he did so, my memory produced the following information:

The button closed a circuit inside the radio controller, and sent a signal to a receiver in the crate in the cargo compartment. The receiver closed its own circuit, whereupon a battery in the crate began producing electrical current. The current jumped a gap, creating a spark that fired a blasting cap lodged in a larger amount of less volatile, more powerful material. This sequence of events is called "lighting the candle."

With a bright white flash and a concussive *boom!* the truck's cargo compartment exploded. The net over it billowed briefly as if inflated, then collapsed.

". . . hindmost," ex-gravel-pit-blasting boss Purlie Wadsworth finished, not turning a hair.

Me, either.

"How could you just sit there?" Ellie demanded moments after the blast. "You didn't even flinch."

Kids raised in mining towns think explosions are the sound of food falling onto the table and school clothes showing up in their closets.

"Ellie, when they weren't digging coal my uncles blew up stumps with black powder and fertilizer from the feed store. One of my cousins set off a charge in the privy behind the parsonage. When the smoke cleared he'd demolished the whole church."

Actually I had even more history with explosives than that: the fact was, my mother's family romance with anything that could be made to explode was what got my father interested in her in the first place.

But now wasn't the time to talk about it. Instead we drove to Harriet's past the redbrick Frontier Bank building, the Happy Landings Café with its colored umbrellas out on the deck, and the Motel East perched on a bluff overlooking the water. Beyond the motel you could see all the way down the bay, to the bridge over the channel to Canada. Out past the span the fog lay on the water like a strip of grey wool, the first sign of changing weather.

"Well, I don't care how used to it you are," Ellie complained, which was unlike her. But it *had* been a big explosion; my ears were jangly again. "That thing nearly scared my heart out of my throat."

Actually, no time was the time to talk about it. We drove up Shackford Street between front lawns studded with snowdrops and grape hyacinth. The lilac leaves were out but their blooms were still purple-grey nubbins as tight as tiny fists.

"They netted it to keep stuff from flying around and hurting someone," I told her. "Reinforced the cargo box, too, by the looks of it afterwards." Remarkably, the truck had appeared undamaged.

"All they want from a blast like that is the flash. It was a fine job," I concluded, "of keeping everything contained."

The music video was called *Shake It Till You Break It,* and even before witnessing the blast I'd worried that's what it might do to us. But these guys were good: their competence—I thought at the time—a favorable sign.

Ellie harrumphed as she pulled the car over and we climbed out. Harriet Hollingsworth's house looked even sadder and shabbier in close-up than it had at a distance. And there was something new about it, something different I couldn't quite put my finger on.

"And they did it right away because they wanted to get it done," I added, "get the worst over right off the bat so there'd be nothing else for anyone to complain about."

This I'd gleaned from talking to the fellow who'd held the radio controller. After running around forewarning the Water Street shop owners, all the crew wanted was to get the deed done before word spread any further. A crowd of onlookers would have spoiled their shot, and they hadn't noticed Ellie and me when they were putting up the sawhorses or they'd have shooed us out of the area, too.

"I wish Harriet *were* still here," Ellie fretted. "She'd have plenty to say about setting off a bomb downtown."

"Harriet never minced words," I agreed distractedly. Then: "Ellie, what's so different about this house?"

The porch leaned drunkenly, one end on concrete blocks and the other on a tree stump. The steps were a death trap promising a broken ankle or worse. The windows sagged, the walls bowed, and the roof resembled the aftermath of a major hurricane.

All that, though, was normal, as were the heaps of rusting scrap metal, old plastic toys, and boxes of magazines poking from the tangled weeds. What puzzled me was what was missing. There'd been something else in the yard and it was gone now. But I couldn't quite remember . . .

"Hello." A man's voice came from behind me; I jumped about a foot just as I realized what the absent element was.

The "for sale" sign was gone.

"Sorry if I startled you." Then he saw my face, more of a shambles than the house. "Are you okay? Can I get you a glass of water or something?"

He was mid-fiftyish or a little older, attractive in an ordinary-guy way, with crinkled brown eyes and greying hair clipped short. He held a box brimming with old kitchen stuff in both work-gloved hands.

"I'm fine," I replied, ignoring Ellie's glance, so full of unspoken Maine twang it could practically have tied itself in a knot. "Had a little accident earlier, that's all."

"Sorry to hear that. Well, I'm Harry Markle. From New York. I just bought this old place from the bank."

He grinned, showing white, well-kept teeth. "Guess I've got my hands full. Getting it back in shape'll keep me busy a while."

I smiled in return; this guy had no idea how busy he was about to be. Just not drowning in his bed when it rained would be a project, by the looks of that roof.

I got my wits together, or what was left of them after a concussion and a bomb blast. "I'm Jacobia Tiptree," I recited, "I live over there in that big old white house. This is my friend Ellie White. Welcome to Eastport."

"Thanks." His handshake was papery-dry despite the glove he pulled off. And minutes earlier he'd heard a blast that must've suggested nuclear attack.

But no comment came from Harry Markle. A cool newcomer, I diagnosed. He went on enthusiastically.

"Wonderful town. I'd been moving around all over the country for a year or so. But when I got here I just fell in love with it as soon as I saw it. And with the house."

I understood; it had happened that way to me. You may cross the long causeway that leads here from the mainland meaning only to spend a few hours sight-seeing, but unless you hightail it back before Eastport captures you, you can end up here for life.

"So what'll you do here, Mr. Markle?" I asked.

Besides keeping his house from falling in on him, I meant. He shrugged. "Make it Harry. I've got a feeling folks don't stand on ceremony, this far downeast."

"You've got that right." But he hadn't answered my question.

So I said nothing, which is a little-known but tremendously effective method of getting other people to say things, instead. Seeing that I was still waiting, Harry continued, "I guess first I'll clear out more living space, set up some sort of work area, a place I could get a few things done from."

Again, not exactly an answer. He wore a navy T-shirt, jeans, and a very nice, newish-looking pair of rubber-soled boots. "Want to come in, see what I've done so far?"

City accent; Brooklyn with the softening that came from time away from the old neighborhood, talking to lots of people.

"Harry," Ellie began, "it's very nice to meet you. And we'd like to see the house, but right now I think we ought to . . ."

Lie down, she was telegraphing sternly at me. *Fall onto the sofa and stay there until I say you can get up.*

That plan still seemed prudent to me. But I wanted to go inside even more now that I saw Harry was getting rid of things.

"Please?" He looked from one to the other of us. "I do need someone to say I wasn't crazy to buy this old wreck."

"You're on," I replied heartily as we picked our way up the steps and over the death-trap porch.

"Phewie." Ellie wrinkled her nose when we got inside. "Dust. And what's the other smell?"

"Forty years of eating out of cans, and keeping the cans," Harry replied somberly. "Rinsing them wasn't a specialty, either. This," he waved around, "is an improvement over when I got here."

Cracked linoleum curled up from the slanting floor; on it rested an old white-metal sink unit with most of the porcelain chipped off. Loops of once-bright wallpaper festooned in greasy ringlets over the stove, a crusted horror. The ancient plaster ceiling was disintegrating; gritty bits of it crunched under our feet.

"I gather the previous owner was . . . unusual," Harry said carefully.

"Don't worry," I said. "We knew she was off the deep end. I guess you're living in there?"

I pointed at the dining room. Its formal character and the fact that it's used least makes it the last room to get seriously ravaged in many old houses.

"Yep," he replied. "I think she did, too. Live in it, at the end. I've cleaned it up a little better."

We followed him down a hall between stacks of, apparently, every issue of every newspaper ever published: tabloids, special editions, even the *Sporting News,* many with bits clipped out.

"I need to get a recycling truck over here," Harry said with a wave at them. "She seems to have been quite the news junkie."

"And a junk junkie." Pails filled with ancient, mummified chicken bones gave me a start. In the gloom they looked like tiny human skeletons. Everything was covered with a thick, feltlike coating of dust, glued down I imagined by decades of Harriet's sour, increasingly suspicious exhalations.

Then I peered into the dining room, caught my breath in surprise. "Oh, Harry! This is . . . This is fabulous."

As if someone had waved a magic wand, the old hardwood floor shone, smelling of lemon wax. The hearth gleamed, brass andirons polished and laden with birch logs. An elegant little chandelier twinkled prettily, its crystal pendants ammonia-fresh.

"Not too shabby?" Harry beamed with justifiable pride. He'd set up a bedstead, a table and chair, and a bench on which he had laid out some books and a lamp. A radio stood on the newly wiped sill of one glittering-clean window.

Something else stood there, too.

From Harriet's window you could see straight into many other houses in town. When she wasn't reading newspapers she'd probably sat right in this room writing letters about what she'd observed. And although I'd expected to find her most treasured possession sooner or later, coming upon it now made my heart lurch.

"Oh," Ellie pronounced comprehendingly, seeing it with me:

The one thing Harriet wouldn't have abandoned. Because even if she ran off and started a new life, somehow—

Well, what could life possibly be to Harriet Hollingsworth without her binoculars?

When I first came to Maine and bought an old house I learned the most important part of do-it-yourself fix-up: knowing when not to. Unfortunately I learned this by falling through a floor I'd been trying to reinforce; even more unfortunately, what lay beneath it was a whole civilization of spiders, silverfish, and a particularly nasty species of centipede: big, smart ones.

I swear they had roads, aqueducts, even little schools going on down there in the darkness, and if I hadn't fallen in on them they probably would've developed nuclear weapons. In the end, the only thing that got reinforced that day was my dread of anything having so many more legs than I do.

But as my old New York friend and mentor Jemmy Wechsler said when he discovered the Mob had a contract out on him just because he stole several million of their favorite dollars: Live and learn.

Not that I went right out and found out how to fix old floors; that came later when the centipedes decided that life *under* the floorboards might not be all that they had wished for, and I woke up one night to tiny eyes gleaming balefully at me from the foot of my bed. Instead what I got from that unhappy episode was the ability to delegate the really big jobs, born of my resolve that the next time somebody fell into a squirming mass of insects, it wouldn't be me.

So when the ell needed a new roof I hired a local mother-and-daughter team who called themselves the Shingle Belles. Fast, fearless, and efficient, those two didn't fall into masses of insects or anywhere else as they scrambled over the roof tossing tools to one another, cursing cheerfully.

Likewise, discovering that the foundation of my old house was crumbling, I balanced the cost of hired help against the cost of the back surgery I would need after hauling the big old stones out of the cellar myself. Then I engaged another expert.

And when Ellie and I got home from Harry Markle's that day, the expert was standing in the side yard gazing pensively at my ladder. From the way it was lying on the lawn you could figure out what had happened, especially if you factored in the little drops of blood sprinkled artfully across the sidewalk. Wade was absent, drawn downtown, I guessed, by the lure of the explosion.

"Hello, Mr. Ash," I said, making my way across the lawn to the helper I'd hired. "Don't worry about that ladder, I'll put it away."

He straightened, his pale-blue eyes softening as he saw that I wasn't badly injured. But he frowned at the mess of my face.

"Ice on the lip," he suggested gravely, putting out a bony finger. Somehow his touch didn't make me flinch the way Victor's had. "Beefsteak on the eye," he added.

His work-roughened hand sketched the suggestion of a caress in the air alongside my head, drew back chastely. "Yeah," I said, "but you should see the other guy."

At that he chuckled, a lean man in his late fifties, wearing blue coveralls, a faded red flannel shirt, and old leather boots. For a guy who worked on basements and crawl spaces he was very clean, smelling sweetly of concrete dust and something else I couldn't identify, sharp as an old penny.

"Going to put some crampons into these ladder feet for you," he said, watching me climb the porch steps.

Notched clamps, he meant, so the ladder wouldn't slide. To hire Mr. Ash I'd put a note up on the bulletin board at the IGA, looking for a stonemason. And the very next morning Lian Ash's ancient pickup truck was out in the driveway as if he'd been just waiting around for me to need something from him.

"I guess you'll be climbing this ladder again, will you?" he inquired mildly. "Not put off heights any worse'n you were?"

I hate heights but I hate waiting even more for other people to brave them for me. "Yes, Mr. Ash." His benevolent figure seemed to turn the tide on what had been, so far, a dreadful day. "I'll go back up there again."

His face remained impassive but a small, protective smile twinkled in his eyes, under a shock of hair as fine and white as milkweed silk.

"Well, then. Guess we'd better fix it." He turned away.

"Mr. Ash," I called, really wanting to go inside now; the aspirin Ellie had given me earlier was wearing off big-time. "Was there something else you wanted? I mean, that you came for in the first place?"

Probably by now the whole town knew Jake Tiptree had fallen off another ladder. But I hardly thought Lian Ash would hotfoot it over here just on account of that.

"Nope," he replied. "Lookin' over the job. Need to talk about all o' this work. Costs, materials. Make some decisions."

He got into the truck, a beat-up little vehicle with Bondo patches, mismatched tires, and a new heavy-duty bedliner that was probably holding the whole thing together.

"But we can hash that over later," he added. "After that, we start taking the old cellar wall apart an' bracin' 'er up."

I could have used some of the braces he'd be using, big cast-iron ones built to take the weight of houses. I gripped the porch rail as he slammed his truck door and backed out of the yard.

"Come with me," Ellie said firmly, taking my arm in a gentle grip that nevertheless managed to imply how much force might be exerted if I were foolish enough to resist. For this reason, and because the world had again begun spinning gently as if the rotation of the earth were being demonstrated especially for me, I followed Ellie meekly into the parlor and sank into the only piece of furniture not currently occupied by a household animal.

"*Wuff,*" said Monday, thumping her black Labrador tail at me from her place on the sofa.

"*Mmmph,*" uttered Prill, wagging her short, stubby one as she settled herself more comfortably in the easy chair.

"*Meeowrowyowowl,*" Cat Dancing commented from the recliner, observing through crossed blue eyes the sad fact that I was still not dead.

Kicking my shoes off, I lay down carefully on the settee and pulled up the comforter Ellie had crocheted for me the previous Christmas. And while she brought aspirin and ginger ale to take it with, and Sam and Wade returned, working together at hauling the downspouts bumpingly up the ladder, I picked up the latest issue of the Eastern Maine *Examiner*.

Besides ads for truck parts and all-terrain vehicles and notices of births, weddings, and funerals, it printed news from all over the county, not skipping the juicy stuff. Bar fights, bad checks, boundary disputes, and arrests due to the possession of illegal substances were grist for the *Examiner*'s mill, along with house fires, vandalism, and the locally popular car-versus-moose encounters, with photos if the moose won.

This week's riveting lead story had to do with a young man caught trying to evade the Canadian border patrol with a bag of illicit pharmaceuticals. But soon I drifted into a half-sleep watched over by the animals. Ellie delivered a cold cloth for my head; she'd have brought me a beefsteak, too, but I vetoed that.

I already had the smell of blood in my nose: Harriet's. Someone had gotten rid of the body but made a mistake, I mused drowsily, by losing her boot in that compost heap.

Around me the parlor's old gold-medallion wallpaper glowed dully, the sunshine through the antique, wavery-glassed windows slanting slowly to late afternoon. Then I did sleep, not waking until Ellie asked in the gloom of dusk if I felt like getting up for dinner or wanted it in my room.

Dinner upstairs while the company laughs below isn't as bad as being sent to bed with nothing at all, I feel, but it's close. Voices were already mingling in the dining room as I struggled upstairs to change clothes and wash my face before hobbling down again.

And all this—my tumble from the ladder, Victor's clinic, the explosion, Harry Markle, the binoculars, the guests, and my growing certainty that Harriet Hollingsworth had been murdered—

—was why it never occurred to me to wonder how Mr. Ash knew I disliked heights.

An old wooden house on an island in Maine needs about as much regular scraping and painting as your average battleship. But over the years Harriet Hollingsworth's house hadn't gotten any at all.

"Pressure hose?" Harry Markle tossed the suggestion out and looked around the table for comment. Ellie had kindly invited our new neighbor to dinner, and the conversation had turned to the repairs he meant to do around Harriet's old place.

"Uh-uh." Ellie's husband, George Valentine, shook his head at the notion of removing paint with a high-powered stream of water. "Soaks the wood."

George was a compactly built man in his thirties, with dark hair, the milky-white skin that runs in some old Maine families, and grease-stained knuckles. In Eastport, George was the man to call if your plumbing failed, your lights flickered, or your car began unexpectedly trailing a banner of blue smoke.

Which reminded me: "George, can I borrow your circuit-alert tester? There's a ceiling light fixture out upstairs."

He rubbed the bluish five o'clock shadow that was always on his jaw. "Dunno. You aren't going to be climbin' any ladders with it, are you?"

He unclipped it from his belt: a dandy device that looked like a pen, but if you got it near a live wire it buzzed and flashed red warning lights at you.

I tucked it in my sweater pocket, wishing again that the fuses in my old house correlated a bit less whimsically with its actual physical areas. Some wiring was new, some the old knob-and-tube variety, all installed piecemeal over the years after the waning of the gaslight era. The only way to be sure you'd shut off all power in a room was to shut down the whole fuse box, wreaking havoc on the activities of everyone else: Wade in his workshop, Sam at the computer, me with my power tools, and the animals in the TV room watching cartoons.

But with George's gadget you could test the wiring itself, avoiding the fuss, bother, and mess of accidental electrocution. "You pressure-hose an old house, you'll never keep any paint on again," George added to Harry Markle.

George's quick, sharp glance always seemed to be expressing some smoldering resentment, so that despite his diminutive size, George was a fearsome figure until you got to know him. He was getting along with Harry, though.

"Better use a grinder," he offered, taking a potato from the platter being sent around. The platter matched the plates and cups Ellie had bought at a yard sale the summer before; in blue and white they depicted stylized scenes of life in China, where a century ago the plates had been loaded on a schooner, ballast for the return voyage to Eastport.

"Paint'll crumble off," George added, "you put friction on it with a paint grinder."

"Great," Wyatt Evert commented sourly. "Put a little more of the old lead paint into the environment, too. Just what we need."

George speared himself a piece of baked salmon stuffed with bay leaves, lemon slices, onions, and peppercorns, served with new peas and buttered potatoes sprinkled with parsley. Ellie and Maggie had done themselves proud.

Seated across from George, Wyatt was a fortyish, balding beanpole of a man with leathered skin, thin liver-colored lips, and a facial expression that suggested he had just bitten into one of those lemon slices. He was the leader of the other group currently visiting Eastport, nature buffs here to see the eagles nesting at the Moosehorn Refuge thirty miles to our north.

"You had your way," George said to Wyatt, "folks'd live in mud huts. That is, the folks you decided were fit to go on living at all."

I glanced up curiously but Wyatt didn't react to the odd comment. "People resent the inconvenience I cause," he sniffed, "when I talk about their environmentally incorrect activities."

"Ayuh," George agreed again. "There's that, too."

This time Wyatt did open his mouth to retort, displaying the biscuit he was chewing. Beside him at the table sat his assistant Fran Hanson, a polished young woman wearing professional-looking makeup, her blond hair clipped short around her elfin features.

Fran always looked as if she'd visited Elizabeth Arden about twenty minutes ago. But her manner didn't match her aggressively stylish look; she wasn't about to interrupt her boss.

Roy McCall had no such hesitation, however. "A few guys on my video crew won't have much to do for a few days," my new houseguest told Harry. "You could hire them to start the scraping."

Roy was perhaps twenty-five, with curly black hair and the sweetly rounded face of a cathedral-ceiling cherub. Tonight he wore a green cashmere sweater, grey slacks, and Armani loafers. He drank some of the wine he had brought as his contribution to the dinner, a lovely California cabernet the color of rubies, and as expensive.

"Just make sure they put down tarps," Wyatt Evert instructed Harry sharply, wagging a finger at him. "To catch the paint chips."

George rolled his eyes. By all rights he should have hated Roy, who made the rough-hewn George look like a bumpkin. Despite his plain manner, George was sensitive to such things. But in the coming weeks Top Cat Productions would spend north of a million dollars in Eastport. So George was cutting Roy a *lot* of slack.

"I'll get the environment police on you if you don't," Wyatt went on meanly. "Get *canvas* tarps, not junk from around here."

"You can buy canvas tarps here if you want them," I piped up. "In fact there's an ad for them at Wadsworth's right now, in this week's *Quoddy Tides*."

Not listening, Wyatt guzzled Roy's good wine without tasting it. Roy averted his gaze politely while the rest of us cringed, and when I got up to take plates to the kitchen, Roy joined me.

"I'm so sorry," he said, once we were out of earshot. "He started talking to me downtown and just followed me home."

I rinsed a platter. Two glasses of the excellent cabernet he had brought were suiting me admirably. Victor would have *plotzed*, I supposed, but Victor—tra-la—wasn't here.

"Never mind," I told Roy as I rinsed another platter. I felt *much* better. "It's not the first time Wyatt's cadged a meal off me, *and* brought his little helper, Fran."

Wyatt's idea of good environmental protection was *him* being protected from picking up a restaurant check or cooking his own dinner. I'd have sent him packing but his crack about calling in the cops was no idle threat.

"Don't run afoul of him," I warned McCall. "Wyatt informed the state once on a fellow who let some apprentice carpenter students tear down his old shed for practice. Turned out there was asbestos in the shingles. The guy came close to paying a ten-thousand-dollar fine on account of his good deed."

Roy looked impressed, and even more contrite than before. "I wish I had cold-shouldered him, then," he declared.

"No. It's smarter to keep tabs on what Wyatt's up to. But his social skills verge on the nonexistent at the best of times, and he's worse than usual, lately."

Roy tipped his head in a question. "A member of one of his nature groups had an accident a few weeks ago," I explained. "He drowned. I guess Wyatt's still upset about it."

"Really? How'd that happen?"

I turned off the faucet. Back in the dining room, Maggie and Sam had turned the table talk to a happier topic: Prill's rescue from a diet of mackerel heads.

"Nobody's sure," I told Roy, who had cleverly opened a third bottle. He poured us each a glass. "They were at Moosehorn Refuge with cameras and binoculars. Wyatt brings a group a few times a year to go on elaborate nature walks. Charges them a bundle, but from what I gather he gives good value. And it's not as if they can't afford it."

Roy sipped wine delicately, pausing to savor it. I'd tried not to sound too judgmental in my description, but he'd caught my drift. "And?"

"Well, we get quite a few ecology buffs around here and most of them are pretty harmless. But Wyatt's groups are . . . different."

"Yeah," Sam put in, coming in with some plates. "And most of us think the wrong group-member got himself drowned."

"Sam," I reproved him. "He can hear you."

"No, he can't. He drank most of one of Roy's bottles and now he's got his head down on the table, snoring."

Sam grinned, returning to the dining room where Harry Markle had apparently fallen in love with Prill. "Good dog," I heard him telling the animal delightedly.

She was, too. But two dogs were too many for my household. A few moments later Maggie repaired to the parlor where she began tuning her banjo. Soon she and Sam were singing their own version of an old Gordon Lightfoot tune:

37

"They took a big ship on a terrible trip, it was cold, it was dark, it was scary . . ."

"Anyway," I went on as Maggie's voice lilted. "Wyatt's folks are always dressed in brand-new clothes that cost the earth, and driving too fast in their gas-guzzling SUVs."

"Which," Ellie put in, checking the coffeemaker, "I don't get. You'd think fuel economy would be tops on his hit-list."

". . . so I wrote down this song, it's a million words long, and I used up the whole dic-tionary," Sam chimed in with Maggie.

"Meanwhile, they're all always shooting off their mouths in the stores and restaurants, about how fishing and logging and so on are ru-ining the environment," I explained.

Roy nodded, getting it. Fishing and logging and so on were how people made their livings around here, and they didn't like know-it-all strangers—people from away, the locals called them—coming around telling them they ought to quit. Or worse, that they should be *made* to quit.

"Wyatt's fat-cat clients could dump arsenic in the water supply and he wouldn't say boo, as long as they kept paying him," George said, coming in to fetch cups and dessert plates.

We were having a berry pudding with fresh whipped cream and coffee with a blackberry brandy that George had distilled three au-tumns earlier, after Ellie and I had picked the blackberries.

George made a face. " 'You mean I can't get today's *New York Times* today?' " he mimicked Wyatt's nature-watching customers.

"Wyatt arranges the whole thing for his clients," I told Roy. "Books the rooms, has the drinks and meals catered, plans the nature-watching, and gives lectures. On eagles, for instance."

Roy got dessert spoons from the silverware drawer without being asked to. I already thought that as a houseguest he was the cat's paja-mas, so easy to get along with, you'd have thought he'd been living here forever. And just before dinner when he took me aside to pay for his room, he'd ignored the sum I asked for when we made the arrangement.

Instead he'd estimated what the same room would cost in Los Angeles and added thirty percent. "For the inconvenience," he'd said charmingly.

"Water's deep in that marsh right after the snowmelt," I went on. "And from what got reported in the *Tides,* it seems like one of the group got separated from the rest."

Ellie took up the story. "By the time they thought to look for the poor man he'd been missing for a couple of hours."

Sam and Maggie harmonized, "*. . . the water was deep and the waves they were steep; the captain and crew started drinking . . .*"

"They found him in the marsh?" Roy McCall's face was still.

I nodded, getting out the electric mixer. "They think maybe he slipped, stepped in a hole where the water was over his head. And at this time of year that water's cold."

"*. . . but booze on the lake is an awful mistake and especially when you are sinking!*"

"Brr." McCall shivered. A moment of silence: *sinking!*

"Hey, Mom?" Sam came in as I finished whipping the cream. "Maggie and I are going to skip dessert. She wants to take the boat out, see if she can navigate by the stars." He cuffed her sturdy shoulder as she appeared in the doorway behind him.

With wisps of dark hair escaping her thick braid and her costume as usual a medley of denim, flannel, and double-knit, Maggie seemed the opposite of the polished, blade-slim Fran Hanson. "Kid takes an astronomy course and all of a sudden she's Bosco Diorama," Sam added teasingly.

Maggie cuffed him back. "That's Vasco da Gama, you booby." Sam had a disorder that had turned out to be different from and worse than dyslexia. He played it for laughs, mostly.

"I only took astronomy," she said, "so I could bail you out when *you* got in trouble writing the term paper, and . . ."

She stopped, went on in another tone. Besides hours when she did little but help Sam with schoolwork, she played endless games of Scrabble and anagrams with him, to help him develop his verbal dexterity.

"Anyway. You owe me a moonlight sail," she finished.

I disliked seeing her treat him so tactfully; she never used to. It let me know she sensed the ambivalence of his feelings for her. But my son didn't seem to notice.

"Yeah, yeah," he replied cheerfully. "Hey, it's past nineteen hundred hours, we want to get going." Whereupon they went out to try to get Sam's car started; I kept insisting he needed a newer one but he was about as quick to spend money as he was to pursue romance. Fortunately the trip to the boat basin was a steep downhill ride.

Back in the dining room I found the pudding and cream eaten, George's blackberry liqueur bottle nearly emptied, and the party ending. But Harry Markle couldn't get Prill's muzzle off his knee.

"Looks like *somebody's* fallen in love," Ellie observed with a glance at me; I'd confided to her my worries about Sam.

Prill sighed, gazing soulfully up at Harry. "Did you have pets in the city?" I asked him, pouring the last of the liqueur into my coffee. What the heck, I was already going to have the mother of all headaches in the morning.

Harry shook his head, fondling Prill's ear. "Wanted to. But in an apartment . . ."

He raised his free hand, let it fall. "Too hard on the pet. Besides, with my schedule I didn't think I could take the right care of one."

"What schedule would that be?" Roy McCall asked, just making conversation. Beside him, Evert continued to snore softly.

"I was a cop. NYPD, downtown," Harry replied pleasantly. But not in a way that encouraged further questions about this work.

"Oh, then you must know all my old haunts," I said. "Ciro's, on

Lombardy Street? And Dorian's Grill?" In the city I'd gotten in the habit of checking stories. My clients would lie to me about the silliest things, to save face or to keep me from being able to testify about their businesses, later.

Or they would until they got to know me. Harry Markle waded right in. "Yeah. Good old Ciro's. I know Dorian's too, but it wasn't my kind of place."

Harry rose. Prill, too; stubby tail wagging, her head tipped eagerly as if to say, "Let's go, boss!"

Harry looked at her, trying to decide whether or not to say something. "You found her?" was what he finally came out with.

"Yes, Harry," I said. "And we're stuck with you, aren't we, Prill? Unless," I went on slowly, "you want her? She does eat a lot and she needs plenty of exercise," I added hastily.

It would be awful if he took Prill, then broke her heart by not keeping her. "A dog like this, you have to really be sure . . ."

"I'm sure," he said. "I'd meant to get a dog as soon as—"

Suddenly I knew I couldn't have found Prill a better home if I'd designed it for her myself. I doubted she would ever let him out of her sight from now on, she was so smitten with him.

Even though he was, as I had just determined, a stone liar. "Come on," he told her, "let's get you settled in for the night."

"Wha'?" said Wyatt Evert, raising his head from the table as man and dog exited.

Wade took one of Wyatt's arms, George took the other, and together they got the drunken man on his feet.

"We'll get him to his room," Wade told Fran, who watched tight-lipped before leaving on her own; I'd scarcely heard a word from her all night. Instead she'd cast speculative looks at Roy McCall, who'd returned them in a way I thought might bode interestingly for Fran in the future.

Between the two men Wyatt stumbled in winey befuddlement as

from the other side of the house I heard a roar: Sam's old car starting at last with a bang of backfire and then a clattering of valve-chatter as it headed downtown.

"Thanks," Harry told me, opening the door with Prill hugging his leg. From the first, she'd positioned herself at his side as if to keep anyone else from getting near him.

Overhead, the stars twinkled with unusual brilliance, their light amplified by the first hints of storm-fueled humidity.

"Don't mention it," I said, and was about to say something more. Something on the order of:

Don't lie to me. I've been lied to by the best.

But from down the street I could still hear Sam's car, its engine howling. The sound, as of somebody trying to go fifty in second gear, was not among those I'd come to think of as normal from the old vehicle.

"Ellie," I called, pierced by a premonition. "Catch Wade and George."

Maybe if they got there in time they could stop whatever was happening; hold it off, get in front of it somehow.

But by now they'd have heard it, too, the whole town alerted by that ghastly scream of metal-on-metal protest.

Sam, I thought, standing there frozenly. *Maggie.*

Then came the crash.

Chapter *3*

"My fault," Harry Markle told me in the hospital corridor.

After the sirens. After the ambulance.

After the Jaws of Life.

I wheeled on him. "What're you talking about? You didn't have anything to do with it, you weren't anywhere *near*..."

But then I stopped, because Harry had a look on his face and I'd seen that look before. The guy wearing it had been sitting in my office making a will, two other guys waiting for him outside. He'd called the two guys in to witness it so I could notarize it.

After that, no one ever saw him again. A favor, it had been, to my guy: letting him make a will. A sign of respect from better times. But times change. And my guy had known it.

Harry, too. "Come on," he said now with quiet intensity, indicating a sign on the wall near the recovery room: CAFETERIA ->

43

Sam and Maggie were sleeping off the anesthesia. Sam had a broken clavicle. Maggie needed surgery to find and fix abdominal bleeding. But both kids had been wearing seat belts and both, the surgeon—not Victor—assured me, would be just fine.

At the crash site, things had been different. A vivid mental snapshot of an ambulance technician's fist rising into the air kept making me feel short of breath. A fist rising and slamming down on Sam's chest, because his heart had stopped.

"It was an accident," I said numbly again, pulling a plastic chair from a cafeteria table.

The place was deserted at three in the morning, fluorescents humming overhead but the coffee urn producing only a sour black liquid. "They say Sam's heart's fine now, though."

The surgeon, a pleasant Pakistani gentleman with enough credentials to float a barge from here to his homeland, had told me that broken collarbones healed so readily, you could put the two pieces at opposite sides of a room and they would still knit back together almost immediately. And in a young man Sam's age, the surgeon had continued kindly, even such a blow to the chest was not a thing to be overly troubled about. All would be well.

"But you lied," I added to Harry Markle, anger piercing the fog as I swallowed the bitter stuff.

"There's no Ciro's on Lombardy Street," Harry agreed, "and I don't know of any Dorian's Grill. But was I supposed to say so right then, let everyone know you were trying to catch me out?"

"Huh." I stared at my hands cupped around the cup. "It would have been awkward, wouldn't it?"

He shrugged. "Don't worry about it, I do the same thing. Cop habit: you get so you don't believe anything anybody says. So you check."

Then he took a deep breath and threw me the curveball, the one I couldn't have seen coming in a million years.

"Listen. This probably isn't a good time to say this. But I know about your father."

I nearly choked on the coffee. "How . . ."

But of course: when Harry Markle became a cop, my dad would have been a fresh entry in New York police lore. Jacob Tiptree, the fumble-fingered moron who blew up a Greenwich Village house while trying to rig an anarchist bomb, was a famous old radical villain.

The blast broke windows for blocks, leveled the town house, killed six co-conspirators plus his young wife, Leonora. The lone survivor was Tiptree's daughter, Jacobia Lee. It's how I ended up in hill country being raised by my mom's relatives.

But sitting there in the hospital cafeteria I didn't see how any of it could be linked to Sam, as Harry was implying.

The steering column of Sam's car had broken off on impact. The force of it had stopped his heart, and only the quick-thinking ambulance technician had known how to restart it:

She'd hit him again. Hard, with her fist, while I'd struggled unsuccessfully to make the people at the crash site let me near. He'd flopped like a fish when she slugged him, I saw that much.

I forced my mind from it. "If you've got something else to say, Harry, say it. I'm too exhausted to play twenty questions."

He sighed. "I was going to tell you, anyway. Because if you found out, you'd wonder why I didn't. Like with the restaurants."

"Uh-huh." I gazed at him, dumb with fatigue and the remnants of fear, waiting for the punch line.

But I wasn't ready for that either. "See, back then I was on the task force trying to catch him."

The *only* survivor: me.

"He didn't," I said carefully through a throat thickened by sudden emotion, "live. He and my mother and their friends—"

"Yeah," Harry agreed. "That was the official story, that no one got out except the kid. You. But some thought different."

He leaned back in the chair. "I was a new young guy, but I'd been top of my class at the Academy. I was getting groomed. So as a rookie I was put on as errand boy to some biggish operations."

"One of them was to catch my father." I couldn't absorb it. So I defaulted back to the situation at hand: "But you still haven't said what that's got to do with Sam, with his accident."

"It's complicated. Or was." A look of pain creased his face.

I must have made a sound of impatience.

"Your dad was never found," he told me. "We spent a long time searching. I even met you again a few years later. Remember?"

I remembered men coming to the house. Strangers; not a good sign in the hills. I didn't remember Harry. But that didn't mean anything; by that time a man in a suit, clean-shaven and wearing shoes, might as well've been from Jupiter.

A tired-appearing woman in nursing garb came in; my heart lurched, but she wasn't looking for me. She tried the coffee urn, sighed, settled for hot water and a tea bag before going out again.

"Anyway, the task force finally ended. I'd made detective. And not so long ago I got assigned to another case. A nut job who specialized. The victims were cops' wives, husbands, or significant others. Remember?"

I nodded. It was the kind of sensational story that got into the news loop, even way up here in Maine, and I recalled it now because it had happened in Manhattan, in my old stomping grounds. I'd followed it in the back pages of the *Bangor Daily News*.

And then I'd forgotten all about it. "But I don't—"

"You will, in a minute." Harry's eyes said I wouldn't be happy with it, either. But by now of course I had to hear the rest.

"I also didn't catch *that* guy," he said grimly. "Instead, he caught me. Here." He pulled a folded newspaper clipping from the breast pocket of his worn leather jacket. "This sums it up."

The date inked on the clipping said it was three years old but the events popped out of it as if they were only yesterday, the kind of occurrences you imagine only happen in nightmares.

Or you hope so. "Jesus," I said when I finished. There was a lot more detail in the clip than the *News* had picked up from the wire stories.

"This guy found out you were after him? He killed your wife *and* your . . ."

He winced. "Yeah. I had a girlfriend. I'm not proud of it, but that's the way it was."

"And he found out about them, somehow, and he killed her. I mean, killed them both."

"Right. But there's more. Final act: the guy suckers me to a rooftop by the river. He's got a woman up there, he's holding her hostage at knifepoint. The woman is a hooker, addict, well-known skell. In other words, she's trash."

My turn to wince. "I mean," he said, "from the way they spun it, the tabloids. Not from my point of view. Never from mine."

He took a deep breath. "So anyway, he's got a mask on, so I can't identify him, and he's got the woman at the edge. Ten-story building. And he's dancing around up there, daring me to take my shot."

"And?" Had the *News* named the cop involved in what it had called a hostage situation gone wrong? I couldn't remember.

He continued steadily. "This is a guy who has killed people I love, people my friends love. I don't know why I didn't charge him, take the three of us off the goddamned roof."

"But you didn't. And you didn't shoot."

He dropped his gaze. "No. He kept holding her so I'd have to shoot her, to get at him. I'd put in a call for backup and I was waiting. But before they were even in position, he spotted them. It was like *he* was waiting for *them*."

The fluorescent lights set into the ceiling tiles made an insectile hum, flickering just at the edge of my awareness like the light in a bad dream. "Waiting for . . . ?"

"Witnesses," Harry said flatly. "Cop witnesses, who'd know how badly I had screwed up, going up there alone. And the reporters who'd heard the radio traffic on the call, so everyone else was going to find out about it, too. Once he had them arranged . . ."

I caught on. "He was taunting you. You could've shot him but he was betting you wouldn't shoot an innocent woman. Innocent at the time. Beside him, she must've looked like an angel."

Harry Markle's eyes gazed into the middle distance. "Yeah. Like an angel. But when he pushed her, she couldn't fly."

He looked at me. "Didn't," he said, "fly." Suddenly my son in his hospital bed seemed safe as houses.

"He scrambled down a roof door," Harry recited, "locked it inside, got clean away. And that was the end of my cop career."

Wade came to the door with a copy of *Working Waterfront* in one hand. The big front-page story was about an old lobster boat fitted out like an emergency room, to bring health care to island towns even more remote than Eastport.

Wade made an A-OK sign with his thumb and fingers, waited as Harry went on: "I got put on desk duty, finally sent to a shrink, which by that point I needed. I kept seeing the woman's face."

"I can imagine," I sympathized, then wished I hadn't.

Because I couldn't imagine. Not really.

"But it was also all *they* needed, the bosses, to get rid of an embarrassment. Me."

He looked up. "I traveled. Now I'm here. Decent retirement package, I had my years in. They did what they had to do, get me to go without a big fight. So I buy an old house, get a dog, live a life. Such as it is."

None of that had been in the papers, of course. "Harry, that is terrible. I'm so sorry. But–"

A grin twitched his lips: not a nice grin.

Not at all. "But you still want to know what all that's got to do with you, Jacobia? Or with Sam? Think about it."

So I did, and what I came up with made my stomach do a queasy roll. "Harry, you're not telling me you believe—"

"Not *believe*," he interrupted harshly. "I *know.*"

Wade came to the table, his grey eyes narrowed protectively. "Harry, are you saying someone did this deliberately to Sam?"

"It had to be an accident," I insisted. "That old car . . ."

But Wade was frowning. "George towed it over to the garage. Sam was awake when he got here, he said the brakes just went out."

"I heard him say that, too," Harry put in. "That's why . . ."

I shook my head dumbly. "The brakes? You mean completely?"

Wade nodded, his face grim. Another thought struck me as my mind danced away from the notion of someone trying to hurt Sam.

"Harry. You said you'd met me *again*. After I'd gone to live with my aunt and uncle."

He smiled almost pityingly. "The first time? I don't think you'd remember that. The blast blew you out of the house into the yard. A piece of sheet metal landed on top of you. Other wreckage, like bricks and so on, piled on that."

Dimly, I did remember: not the details, specifically, but a tremendous sound, the smell of the smoke, a soaring sensation and screaming that I later understood must have been sirens.

And me. "A man came," I recalled slowly. "Dressed in blue. He looked into my eyes. He said everything would be all right."

It wasn't, but never mind. "A young cop. He pulled me out." I looked at Harry. "Was it you?" I whispered. "You saved me?"

Harry nodded slowly, his eyes glistening. He swallowed hard, his throat working before he could speak.

"That was me. And it's great to see you doing so well, Jake. But I've brought something. *Someone.* I didn't know . . ."

His voice broke wretchedly. "I'm sorry, Jacobia. So sorry."

A tear slid down his cheek.

The next day when my panic over Sam had faded I could sort my thoughts better, but the result didn't feel like improvement. Harriet Hollingsworth had been murdered; I remained quite sure of that.

But now there was a new wrinkle. The guy living in her house was a blast from my past, and he believed Sam's accident wasn't one. That instead it had something to do with *him*.

"Well," Ellie said, frowning, "what he told you checks out."

We'd let the answering machine take phone calls, getting the incoming numbers from the caller ID box and noting them down for later callbacks. Everyone we knew wanted to be told Sam was all right and reporters from the *Tides* and the *Examiner* had called, too. But I hadn't felt like talking to anyone.

Instead via the Internet on Sam's computer we had confirmed most of the details of Harry's tale, the ones that were publicly available, anyway. Newspaper archives of *The New York Times* gave the NYPD's version of the story Harry had told me the night before.

Chillingly, the on-line articles delivered no photos of any police officers. They'd appeared in the print editions, a sidebar noted, but were later judged inappropriate for electronic versions in case a cop's face caused him or her to be targeted by what one quoted officer termed colorfully, "a fruitcake from afar."

The phrase was funny but the message behind it wasn't: that someone had spooked even the cops of the NYPD. Ordinarily the devil himself couldn't scare one of them, I mused as I marched downtown with Monday frisking along beside me.

I strode past the Top Cat truck, parked in front of the Peavey Library. Two production workers were eyeing the massive old Revolutionary War cannon on the lawn as if wondering how to fire it. I could have told them they'd have to get the log out of its throat, first. During the War of 1812 the cannon must have looked sufficient to the soldiers at Fort Sullivan on the hill over the harbor. That is, until they spotted the British flotilla sailing up the bay and knew they were outnumbered hundreds to one.

Which went to prove something, I supposed, but I didn't know what and at the moment, I didn't care. Twenty-four hours earlier my only worry had been fixing a gutter.

Now I had an injured son who might not have gotten that way by accident, a missing woman who surely hadn't, and a new chapter in my own thoroughly lousy history, starring a father who instead of dying in a bomb blast might instead have callously abandoned me.

On Water Street the shops gleamed with freshly washed plate glass, new paint, and tubs of red geraniums; sidewalks bustled as the shops' proprietors readied for the coming tourist season. I passed the Quoddy Crafts store, its front window filled with the gorgeous stuff people around here kept busy making all winter: finely worked earrings of silver-wrapped beach glass, sweetgrass wreaths intricately braided with colored silks, white ash walking sticks incised with Native American glyphs, stained glass panels glowing with jewel colors.

And much more, but I didn't stop to admire it. Down on the dock, past the massive grey granite building that housed the Customs office and the Coast Guard, a wooden hut called Rosie's sold hot dogs and onion rings. Near Rosie's stood the pay phone from which a dock worker had called 911 after Sam's crash. I ignored that, too, as I entered the wooden storefront that housed the Eastport Police Department.

"Thanks," I told Eastport's police chief, Bob Arnold, as Monday flopped down on the floor by Bob's grey metal desk. I'd called him hours before, and he'd agreed to make some inquiries for me.

"Early retirement," Bob confirmed now. On his desk lay fresh copies of the Ellsworth *Union-Leader*, the Portland *Gazette*, and the *Examiner*, plus several more I wasn't familiar with.

You never saw him reading one, but by the end of the day Bob would have absorbed the contents of them all. According to Bob, there was nothing a crook liked better than a cop who hadn't yet cottoned on to the capers the crook had been pulling elsewhere.

"Under a cloud, like he said," Bob went on, meaning Harry. "Union got him his pension, hadda fight for that. And they never caught the creep he'd been after, either. Once Harry Markle was out of the picture, this bad guy he'd been chasing stopped doing bad deeds like someone shut off a switch."

Bob was pink-cheeked and balding, with big blue eyes that looked innocent until you peered more deeply into them. "Like maybe it was what the guy'd had in mind in the first place, hurting Markle," Bob observed thoughtfully.

"An old enemy of Harry's?" That hadn't occurred to me. "But all those deaths, isn't that an awful lot of . . ." I faltered.

"Overkill," Bob agreed dourly, gazing out the window. "That's why I don't buy the idea, myself."

Ellie and I could research a lot, but some questions you had to be a cop yourself to ask effectively. And I wanted them asked, never mind if some of the answers knocked me for a loop. I didn't enjoy being blind-sided by the past.

Or anything else. "But it's not just Harry's facts that are accurate?" I pressed Bob. "His spin on it is true? Someone in the city really was victimizing cops, by killing their loved ones?"

Out on the water a little black-and-red scallop dragger was puttering into the harbor. But most of the town's boats were in the boat basin getting extra bumpers thrown on for what locals predicted would be a gullywhumper.

"Yeah. Nobody in the series not connected to the job."

The string of deaths Harry had been investigating had begun about five years earlier. They were bad ones, the killings ritualistic. The papers hadn't printed the gory details but you didn't have to work too hard to imagine them. "A real mess," Bob added unnecessarily.

To distract myself from the mental images I fixed my eyes on the horizon. The storm was in the mid-Atlantic states now, raising hell all over the place; state of emergency on the Jersey shoreline.

"Thing like that, you ask yourself," Bob said, "what's the point? But in this case, you look at the big picture, seems like knocking off a whole lot of people *was* the point."

I turned back to him. "What do you mean?"

He shook his head sorrowfully. "The cop connection made it special, and maybe there was some grudge-type reason somewhere in the past. Somebody targets cops, it's 'cause they don't like cops. But when people *keep* killing people, bottom line it's usually 'cause they like killing."

Brr. He peered at me. "Looks like someone had a poke at you, too, Jake. Or are you working on your house again?"

"House," I confirmed tersely. No need to add to my already stellar reputation by detailing exactly what had happened.

Bob got up, gazing across the street at the concrete barrier that I gathered Sam had crashed into; the night before, it was on Bob's orders that I'd been kept from the scene until Sam was revived. The barrier bore dark blue car paint and white scars from the impact, its orange reflectors smashed, shining bits of them littering the street.

"Kid's lucky," Bob commented, hitching up his belt which was burdened with baton, sidearm, and cuffs. Bob was the kind of guy who expected the best but always prepared for the worst. "He's going to be okay? And Maggie?"

"Uh-huh." Just thinking about it again made my heart do a buck-and-wing. "We went back to the hospital before breakfast. Sam said all he thought of when the brakes went was making it around the corner."

Or they'd have ended up in the water. The howling I'd heard was Sam desperately trying to slow the car with the transmission. But the Key Street hill was too steep for engine braking, and the attempt had failed.

"They're agitating to get out today," I said. "Sam might but Maggie probably not. She took a harder hit."

He'd been chipper, no more cardiac monitor, requiring only codeine to be comfortable. Maggie looked pale and in pain despite stronger pills, but she'd had her game face on, working to get up and into a wheelchair and already suggesting word games she and Sam could play while they remained in the hospital.

"They'll be fine," I said again, mostly to reassure myself. I'd wanted to stay but Sam was clearly mortified at the thought of being watched over by his mother. When I'd left, Maggie had been urging him to concentrate on homonyms: "quail" and "quail," et cetera.

"Victor's there with them, and so is George."

"Good. Listen, Jacobia," Bob said uncomfortably as a breeze through the open door riffled his sparse hair.

With his slow, face-saving way of handling trouble, people joked Bob ought to have his motto, "All in good time," stenciled on the cop car. Bob gave a guy room to consider his options, have an apology ready when the moment of truth finally arrived and Bob stood toe-to-toe with him, radiating moral authority. "This story Harry Markle is telling now, about this guy following him," Bob went on doubtfully.

We went outside. At one end of Water Street the Top Cat crew was loading big equipment onto a pickup truck: lights, cameras, I don't know what all else, only that there was a lot of it.

At the other, in front of the Motel East, people in safari garb climbed into Wyatt Evert's van. They carried cameras, backpacks, all the gear they would need for a day out observing nature, plus lunches Wyatt had had packed for them.

"Hope they've got plenty of bug dope," Bob observed.

Wyatt, looking rocky after his evening of appreciating fine wine at my house, got behind the van's wheel and peered into its oversized rearview mirror. His assistant Fran Hanson was in the passenger seat, staring straight ahead.

"Blackflies out at the Moosehorn are so big right now, they could stand flat-footed and look right over the barn at you," Bob added wryly, watching the van pull out.

Then he turned back to me. "Thing is, Jacobia, Markle seems okay. Got his work cut out for him with Harriet's house."

I hadn't said anything about what I thought really happened to Harriet. An abandoned pair of binoculars, however convincing to me, wasn't going to cut much ice with Bob; I needed more. So I just listened as the breeze blew in, smelling of sea salt and the storm that was out there, past where we could see.

"But back in New York, Markle's got a reputation as a loose cannon," Bob said, getting down to brass tacks.

"Fellow I talked to," he went on, "said Markle was the kind of guy, wouldn't let go. Thing'd go cold, Harry wouldn't give up on it. He would work on his own time and put other people in danger, plus himself."

"That's not good." But it fit, actually; going up on that roof before a backup team was in position, trying to be a hero. "Thinking it was personal, all about him. He still thinks so."

Bob looked at me, and I got the message: *don't make the same mistake.* But at the moment, it *felt* personal.

A big old blue work truck, its muffler belching and its bed piled high with lobster traps, trundled past on its way to the boat basin. The men liked to be on their boats, even just tied up at the piers, puttering and trading gossip. And there was work to do before the boats got blown, as George would have put it, nine ways from Sunday.

"Did your friend say anything more about the last case Harry was on, specifically?" The ghastly one: targeting cops.

"Ayuh." Bob eyed me unhappily. "Says before Markle finally took his retirement he already had the idea the bad guy was stalking him, had it so he couldn't think about anything else. He got counseling but that didn't help him."

The psychiatrist Harry had mentioned. "And there was some other thing he was working on, some old case he couldn't seem to accept a closing to, that it was over and done with," Bob said.

I had an idea maybe I knew what that one was. But it wasn't important now. "So, Bob, you think Sam's accident really *was* an accident?"

Bob eyed the length of the street again, taking it all in with practiced casualness. He could spot a guy with a baggie full of illegal pills so fast, the guy would be off the breakwater and into the lockup before the first startled flurry of denials and excuses finished escaping his lips.

And to that kind of guy Bob gave no leeway for apologies. "I don't want to swear to it. But Sam's car was a clunker. Rust gets started over the winters, salt and so on. Year after year. Eats through."

"Can't someone tell for sure if it was rust?"

I hadn't examined the car; I'm no mechanic and I didn't want to look at it, anyway. Seeing the scraped and broken barrier was bad enough.

Bob shook his head, following my gaze. "That's not what Sam hit, Jacobia. The barrier's just what he scraped by, going fast."

He pointed. "*That's* what he hit."

"Dear god." There wasn't very much damage to it, so I hadn't noticed. But about forty yards past the barrier, a granite boulder marked the far corner of the Neptune Fish Company parking lot. A *big* boulder.

"Whole front end of that car's a shambles, no one's ever going to know what happened for sure, there was just too much damage from the impact," Bob said.

He turned to me. "Mechanical problem's the simplest answer, though. And in my experience, simplest is correct."

Which had been Victor's comment, too, in another context. "I am just saying," Bob went on, "you want to look at what Markle says from all angles, 'fore you go acceptin' it as gospel. People who know him say his imagination's his whadyacallit."

"His Achilles' heel." The Top Cat Productions truck rumbled toward us.

"On the other hand," Bob cautioned, "if Harry Markle *did* have an old enemy following him—"

"Not someone whose radar you want to be on," I agreed. But with Bob not seeming to give the notion much credence, it seemed more remote to me, too; comfortingly so.

Too bad I couldn't dismiss the rest of what Harry had said. "What else did you find out about him, anything?"

"Just that he's got a girlfriend already. One of the dancers in that video they're making, name of Samantha Greer. Not local," he added.

People from away could behave like a hutch full of bunnies for all Bob cared; he didn't have to attend town meetings with *their* parents. "Jake. About the binoculars."

So he knew that Harriet hadn't taken them with her. Around here, if a sparrow fell Bob knew it before the feathers quit fluttering.

Knew, and did something about it, too, if necessary.

All in good time.

I hoped.

My old house stands on a granite foundation each block of which was quarried miles away on the mainland, dragged to the water, barged over the channel, and hauled by oxcart to the site where it was mortared in by someone who knew how. The house's first owner, Captain Jeremiah Loundsworth, survived a long career of dangerous, extremely lucrative commercial voyages only to perish by shipwreck in a storm while carrying soldiers to the Civil War.

Sometimes in the house late at night I could almost hear the weeping when the word came: that the captain was lost. Or possibly it was cheering at the news that the old tyrant had finally drowned.

I'll never know; the walls cannot speak. But they can fall down, and they were doing it very convincingly when I returned home.

"Sorry," Wade said, throwing an arm around my shoulder as I gazed at the clapboards lying where they had fallen onto the back lawn. A row of them had smashed the pretty trellis Ellie and I had built the previous summer to support the Concord grapevines.

"Guess we bumped them too hard with that ladder," Wade added ruefully. "Gutters and downspouts are all on straight, though."

I managed a chuckle. The rotted clapboards were bad enough. But the real disaster was why they'd fallen; the framing beneath them was rotten, too. And that meant . . .

"Leak," I diagnosed grimly. "Bad flashing, snow and ice on top, water ran inside." I should have let the Shingle Belles do the whole roof, not just the actively leaking portion on the ell, as they had advised.

But it was too late now. The hole where the clapboards fell resembled a spreading patch of leprosy. And it would act like one if it didn't get repaired, as Sam would've put it, *soot tweet*.

"I'll order the materials today, by Friday I can have new clapboards painted," I said, adding and subtracting in my head.

Mostly subtracting. The job would take hundreds of dollars' worth of clapboards, as hideously expensive as skin grafts. And it would need oil-based paint, which is the very devil to work with. But here on the island in the damp salt air, latex exterior paint is about as durable as a dusting of powdered sugar.

"Turpentine," I recited. "Sprayer nozzle—"

The way to paint clapboards is *before* you nail them up: two coats of primer, two of paint. I was certainly not going to paint them with a brush, and the paint-sprayer nozzle had a clog in it.

This being yet another do-it-yourself home-fix-up rule: *The paint-sprayer nozzle always has a clog in it.*

"The storm will be past by then. And," I went on recklessly, gazing at the bare spot which was a good ten feet higher than I'd ever climbed before, "maybe I can put the clapboards up myself. I could rent scaffolding, or borrow a longer extension ladder."

Wade's head moved against my hair in a way that I had learned meant he was trying hard to keep from laughing outright. "What's so funny?" I demanded.

"You." He wrapped me in a bear hug. We hadn't yet discussed the previous night's revelations about my father. Now I leaned on him, feeling the tight metal clamp around my heart ease momentarily.

"A longer ladder," he marveled at last. His hands smelled like gun oil; when not piloting big cargo ships in and out of Eastport's shipping dock, he was a well-known gunsmith with a workshop upstairs in the ell of the old house. "Don't you think you should give that face of yours a break from slamming it into stuff?" he added, eyeing my bruises.

"Maybe you've got a point." Wondering what else could go wrong, I followed him inside with Monday trotting behind me. The day's only bright spot was that I'd been able to put the contact lenses in again that morning, adding yet another unnatural color to the ghastly panorama that was my face.

"I called the hospital," Wade went on, pouring me a cup of coffee. "Talked to Victor. Sam's coming home after another set of X rays."

The coffee was fresh. Maybe Victor would set up a catheter so I could infuse some into my brain. "How'd he sound?"

Wade grinned. "Like Victor. Trying to figure out some way it could be your fault, but he couldn't because it isn't."

A clatter hammered up from the cellar but I was so tired I barely flinched, just raised a querying eyebrow at Wade. "What's going on?"

"That's Mr. Ash," he replied as if this explained enough noise to raise the dead.

But Lian Ash had said he would be over to discuss the work, not to begin it. We hadn't even talked about costs or materials, and now he was ripping 200-year-old stones out of my walls with, it sounded like, a jackhammer.

Wade rinsed his cup, tied a red bandanna around his head to keep sweat from dripping while he worked on a Harpers Ferry rifle he was restoring for a client.

"George'll bring Sam home," he added. When he finished the rifle he planned to reload some shotgun shells, a chore that always made me nervous because it involves compressing explosive powder. But Wade said it was safe and that it was a waste of a good shotgun shell not to reload it.

A muffled oath rose from the cellar. "Son of a bore," it sounded like. Moments later a puff of mortar dust preceded Lian Ash into the kitchen.

"There," he uttered, wiping his hands on his trousers. "Now I see which way the wind blows. Next I'll get jacks up, keep the house from fallin' down while I pull out the bad areas."

Dust ringed the outline of the respirator he'd been wearing; his blue eyes gleamed out from a coating of 200-year-old grit.

"Won't you need some help?" Wade asked. "Big operation."

"Yes, sir, I will. But not," Lian Ash added, "with taking old stuff out. Too many men on that, 'fore you know it one of 'em's pullin' out somethin' you haven't braced yet. Somethin' you have not entered into your calculations. *Then* you've got problems."

He turned a serious gaze on me. "Speakin' o' problems, I'm sorry about that young feller of yours. Heard he took a weave and a bobble, last night. Glad he came out of it all right."

Somehow just having the old man around made me feel better. "But

Mr. Ash," I added when I'd reassured him again about Sam's welfare, "I need an idea of what you are going to charge for the foundation project, before you begin. An estimate, so I don't get in too deep."

"Ah, yes. Getting in too deep. A situation to be avoided if possible. Though sometimes it isn't," Lian Ash finished wisely.

He ran himself a glass of water and stood drinking it at the sink. "Chlorinated water. Wonderful invention. Quenches thirst, replenishes the cells, and kills germs on contact. Ahh," he said appreciatively, setting the glass down.

Wade shot me a wink, vanishing back upstairs to work on the rifle and reload the shells, and when I turned again Mr. Ash was scribbling numbers on a pad of paper.

"This is the materials. This other number," he poked at the pad with the stubby end of his pencil, "is the labor. Add it all up," he poked at a third number, "you've got your estimate. Ten percent over or under."

I looked at Mr. Ash and then at the number again, lower by half than what I had feared would be the result.

"This seems very reasonable," I managed, expecting him to add some caveat: that when he got into the job things might change or that he might need more help, or more equipment.

He didn't. But: "Mr. Ash, I don't mean to be intrusive here. There is one other thing I need to talk to you about, though."

His pale blue-eyed glance flickered alertly at me. "Where've I been all your life?"

"Well, yes." I'd liked him so much, I hadn't asked him for references when I'd hired him, and now I was sorry. "You see . . ."

He nodded slowly. "Man does his work, minds his business, no one cares where he comes from till there's trouble. Like last night."

Oh, dear. Now I'd offended him.

But when I looked up he was gazing at me without resentment. "It's all right," he said. "Things happen, you get nervous and want to make sure you've covered all your bases, is all."

"That's it exactly," I agreed. It was this sense of immediate sympathy that had let me skip the references in the first place.

"I kicked around a few years," he began slowly. "Fetched up here last winter, found a little house on the shore road needed fixing."

Omitting any mention of how he had paid for the house on the shore road. But I didn't need his financial *vitae*.

"Wasn't it lonely?" Out there in winter, I meant. Eastport offers plenty of chances for social interaction, but if you take advantage of them you'll be seen at them. And he hadn't been.

"Not to me. I read a lot," he explained. "Newspapers. And biographies. Did you know Frederick the Great wasn't the warrior born an' bred that most people think he was?"

As he spoke he drew idly on the notepad: bricks, a curving path in the jack-on-jack pattern. Simple, elegant.

"Young Frederick was a poet and composer," he went on, "all he wanted to do was hang out and play music with his friends. But his father was cruel. Had a blood disease that all those royals had back then, all over Europe. Painful, and it made him mean."

"Porphyria," I supplied. I read a lot, too. In the old days I even read the *New England Journal of Medicine*. But this wasn't what I wanted to discuss.

I quelled impatience as he went on with his story.

"Frederick got to be a teenager, him and a friend ran off. They got caught on account of a mix-up, a soldier mistook 'em for somebody they weren't and arrested 'em. Fred's father punished 'em both."

Actually, it wasn't quite like that. It was a misaddressed letter that tripped up young Frederick and his buddy, got the pair caught. But even as I remembered this I heard my own old New York pal Jemmy Wechsler, commenting in my head:

Quiet, youse could learn—something. That was before Jemmy moved uptown, took lessons with a speech coach so he could attract a better class of suckers.

Mr. Ash went on: "The friend's punishment was, he got beheaded. Fred's was, he had to watch. Right then, I figure Fred decided if anybody had power it was goin' t'be him. Cuts way down on the lopping-the-heads-off-the-friends action, y'know."

Power. It's the name of the game, all right. I noted, too, how neatly Mr. Ash had turned the conversation away from himself.

But then he surprised me. "How I got started on reading was, I spent a stretch of time in the lockup. Was back in my drinking days, not around here, and not lately. You might say I've turned over a new leaf."

I guessed he'd just needed a little time to get around to this in his own way. He went on agreeably: "Past few years, I'd been working in Portland. One day I took a ride, ended up here in Eastport." He twinkled at me. "Saw the water, streets, and houses laid out like a postcard from the good old days. Sound familiar?"

Oh, of course it did. To a person of the right persuasion, finding Eastport was like falling down the rabbit hole in *Alice in Wonderland*. I still expected to find little bottles marked Eat Me and Drink Me on the shelves of the IGA.

"But," he added, "fact is, you're my first job here. If that makes you nervous, y' want to get someone else to bid on this . . ."

He paused. Time for a decision: I could bring the whole job to a screeching halt while I scrutinized Mr. Ash's background.

Or not. Jemmy used to say one way to decide if you could trust a guy was, the guy wasn't offended if you didn't trust him. Another was that the guy told you the bad stuff up front.

"No, Mr. Ash," I said firmly. "Thanks for offering, but if it's all the same to you I think we'll go on as we've begun."

He moved away from the sink, heading for the cellar door: a clean man with china-blue eyes, white hair, and knobby knuckles on his powerful, liver-spotted hands. "Well, then. In that case, I'll just go down and finish the tear-out."

In other words, exactly the kind of man you want working for you, slammer or not. Back in the city if I had worried about jail time, I'd have had to cut my client list by half.

"You got your own project started, I see," he added, nodding at the ell. "Saw it yesterday, so I brought you a little something I thought might come in handy."

Let's see, now: my ongoing spring projects included the gutters, the foundation, the hall floor, the siding, and . . . oh, right, the insulation under the ell floor.

The fact, I mean, that there wasn't any, so the floor sucked the warmth right out of your feet when you went out there in the winter. But you couldn't *fix* it in winter; if you opened a floor up then, you might just as well hook the furnace to it and pump warmth outdoors, not bothering to try heating the house.

The ell floor had slipped my mind completely in the recent chaos— so many disasters, so little time—but he must have seen where I'd begun tearing up the carpet over it, days earlier. Now he waved at a row of brown bags in the hall next to the cans of polyurethane and varnish remover.

"No sense buyin' a whole roll of insulation for one spot," he explained.

In the bags were strips of thick pink fibrous material, remnants from someone else's insulation project: just what I needed.

"Come to think of it," he allowed, "now'd be a good time to talk to your man, too. Something I've been wanting to ask him."

So Lian Ash went up to Wade's workshop, and the conversation must have been successful because not much later I heard him in the cellar again, his footsteps accompanied by the patter of old mortar falling and the creak of floor jacks being deployed. And I was just sitting there over my cooling coffee, kidding myself into thinking the day might actually be improving, when Ellie came in and made the comment that turned everything on its ear again.

"**Harry decided too** fast," Ellie said, "that Sam's crash was deliberate."

"He said he'd heard Sam say the brakes failed," I replied, gathering tools. A funny thing happens when I work with my hands; my brain kicks in, running in the background until it has solved whatever is worrying it.

Or it tries. "It was both brakes going that made Harry feel so suspicious," I said. "Still, it *was* an old car and things happen to them. George drove *his* old truck until a rear wheel fell off," I reminded her.

"That's not my point." Ellie followed me to the ell. A shedlike structure added after the main house was built, its shelves held a motley collection of Sam's dive gear, Wade's hunting gear, and the light summer clothes I wore one month out of every year.

"But Harry only met us a few hours earlier," Ellie argued. "It isn't sensible to believe Sam's crash was deliberate *and* that it was connected to Harry's old troubles." She gestured as emphatically as she could with insulation material in her arms. "It's too big a leap, someone's hurting Sam on account of Harry."

On my knees at the spot where the carpet met the wall I slid the box-cutter's triangular blade from its slot and began sawing, using a metal ruler for a straightedge and working from the area where I'd already begun to tear up the carpet.

"So I think," she concluded decisively, "we should ask Harry about it all again."

With the box-cutter, I cut an oblong of carpet and lifted it out. Later I planned to coat the undersides of the carpet pieces with white glue, smear a similar coating of glue onto the plywood floor, and press the carpet pieces back down again where they had been.

"We might as well accuse Harry of causing the crash himself, then," I told Ellie. "Because if it's too big a conclusion to jump to afterwards, the only other explanation is that he must've known about it before-hand."

I cut another carpet oblong. It wasn't a solution any home-repair professional would have approved, but the carpet's random pattern would make the fix unnoticeable.

"I'm not *saying* Harry's responsible," Ellie shot back. "I'm not even saying it was anything *but* an accident. All I'm saying is that either Harry's a fruitcake nuttier than Harriet ever was, or there's more to the story. More than he told you."

God, I hoped not. I'd reported to her on the jack-in-the-box aspect of the conversation, my dad's possible survival jumping out like the face on some startling, unbenevolent toy.

"Sam'll be home soon," she pointed out. "Don't you want this set-tled before he gets here?"

I sighed, still wielding the razor-knife. "Ellie, there's nothing to set-tle. If Harry didn't have a bee in his bonnet over his own career crash, he wouldn't be saying this stuff about Sam's accident in the first place."

That, anyway, was the simplest explanation, that Harry's outburst had been triggered by his feelings, not by the facts. And until I had some *other* explanation, I intended to stick with it.

"All right, dear," Ellie replied equably. "Suit yourself."

Dee-yah: the woman was relentless. Removing the final carpet sec-tion, I glanced around to make sure I'd brought along a keyhole saw; the way I felt, I could have mistakenly grabbed a chain saw.

"Here," Ellie said, passing me the sledgehammer instead.

Time to put a hole in my floor. I used the drill and a quarter-inch boring bit to make holes at the corners of the plywood section I planned to remove. Ellie took the drill from my hand and replaced it with the keyhole saw; I slipped the blade's tip into a drill hole and be-gan sawing.

"If we talk to Harry again," she went on, "and it really does sound as if he's just sort of . . ."

"Flying on one wing?" I repositioned the tip of the keyhole saw blade, slipping it into the second drill hole, and cut toward the wall again. "Obsessed by the idea that someone's still out to get him, but not realistically?"

"Exactly," Ellie said. "Then we probably don't have to worry about some crazy unknown person getting up to something else."

"Yeah," I retorted. "Instead we can worry about a crazy known person: our new neighbor." I got up; the room tilted.

"Jake?" Ellie said worriedly.

"I'm fine." I shook my head, clearing it. The plywood piece had come free just as I'd planned. Pleased, I lifted it out.

Immediately, a dank gust blew from the crawl space beneath; there shouldn't have been any airflow at all down there. Peering down, I spotted a telltale shaft of light angling from outdoors.

"Damn. Another break in the foundation." I got up again.

"So your thought is, if Harry's obsessed with his past but gives us no real reason to believe someone from his past is *here*—"

My ears roared; I'd stood up too quickly.

"*Then* we can feel safe," she confirmed. "Jake, are you sure you're okay?"

The roaring faded. "Will you please stop fussing over me? I said I'm fine. And open one of the bags, too, please. I'd like to get this job done while I'm young enough to remember how."

The hole in the outer wall was an unexpected obstacle; I'd have to get Mr. Ash to look at that. But I could still insulate this area of floor, eliminating a spot so frigid that a person risked frostbite just walking out here on a December morning.

"And," I gave in, mostly because if I didn't she would never quit, "then we'll find Harry."

Some ancient wooden lath pieces stretched under the floor joists. I figured I'd just tuck all the insulation strips around those. "Maybe hearing what he says will set your mind at . . . *gah!*"

One minute I was reaching into the hole, groping around to gauge how much insulation to stuff in there and wondering if Mr. Ash had brought enough. The next I was yanking my hand back with a shudder as a spider the size of an aircraft carrier skittered up my arm and onto my shoulder.

"Where is it?" I demanded.

"I don't see it."

"What do you mean, you don't see it? It's a *spider* and it's *on me somewhere.*"

"Hold still," Wade suggested, appearing from upstairs.

"No problem," I managed through lips clamped rigid in case the spider got any additional horrid ideas.

Wade held an empty jar in one hand, the lid in the other. "Keep," he said conversationally, "still."

You betcha. I felt a prickling sensation as of a leaf caught in my hair: a *moving* leaf.

"Wow," Ellie said, glancing at the floor where more of the creatures were emerging from the hole: big, brown ones, impressive and to me immediately recognizable.

"Gotcha," Wade pronounced, closing the jar's lid. The violin mark on the creature's underside was visible through the glass.

I let my breath out. "Thank you."

Brown recluse spiders were common in the warm climate where I'd grown up. Their bite, though rarely fatal, could have made me quite ill had I suffered it; back there, they lurked in woodpiles or in the dark corners of sheds. But not here. Not in Maine. The brown recluse was a warm-weather species, one I'd been delighted to leave behind when I'd moved northeast to Manhattan.

"You know, Ellie," I said, watching Wade deftly capture the rest of the creatures, "maybe we do need to talk to Harry again." Because my small carpentry job—and all those spiders—had indeed kicked my brain out of neutral.

Ellie was right. Whether or not Sam's crash was an accident, Harry's suspicions about it made no sense unless he had more reason for them than he was telling us. Also—and in the press of recent events this fact had escaped me till now—Harry's arrival in Eastport coincided rather neatly with Harriet's departure.

Too neatly. And those spiders: warm-weather spiders.

Spiders from away.

Chapter 4

Top Cat Productions had rented the Danvers' house on Blaine Street, high on a hill overlooking the causeway and the mainland. It was an avenue of professionally restored old homes with wide, landscaped lawns and garages rebuilt out of the original carriage houses.

"I just want an answer: did he have a solid *reason?*" I said as we quick-stepped up the hill. The breeze off the water was like a chilly kiss, sweet with spring but still smelling faintly of last winter's snow. "Or was all that somebody's-still-after-me stuff just Harry, self-dramatizing?"

"Right," said Ellie, to whom I'd repeated Bob Arnold's sum-up: that Harry had taken his police work way too personally.

"*And* I want to know why *we'd* be targets," I said. "All the other victims Harry thinks Sam's crash is hooked to were *close* to cops, not just casual acquaintances."

"Also, ask him if his enemy ever used spiders before," Ellie suggested. "Poisonous spiders."

I looked at her. She was serious. And the spiders had come from somewhere. "Okay. That's simple enough."

But when we got there, it wasn't. A few calls around town had told us where we should look for Harry; word was that his new girlfriend was in today's video shoot. When we arrived, the big white house swarmed with activity.

"Keep it steady!" a T-shirted young man yelled to two others who were operating a pump just outside one of the cellar windows. Water gushed from the pump through a length of PVC pipe, out to a gutter in the street.

Across the yard I spotted Roy McCall in urgent conference with two women wearing headsets and holding clipboards. As they strode away, McCall caught sight of me and headed toward us.

Ellie elbowed me. "There he is," she said. Near the house Harry stood with a girl in full makeup, leotard, and leg warmers. They appeared to be arguing.

"Hey," Roy McCall panted, reaching us. "Listen, I'd love to let you two watch, but we've really got our hands full here . . ."

Another efficient-looking young woman in a black satin Top Cat jacket rushed up to Roy. "Hey, we've got to do this ASAP. Power's off in the basement and the batteries are charged." She waved at a trailer pulled up alongside the house. From inside the trailer, the rumble of a diesel engine cut off abruptly.

"Why're they turning it off?" Roy demanded. "We need–"

A thick, black power cable snaked to the house foundation. It was like the setup that ran electrical systems on boats.

"I explained this before," the woman interrupted steadily. "The diesel makes current, stores it in the battery banks. *Lots,*" she emphasized, "of battery storage. So we don't trip circuits in the house," she added, seeing the question on my face. "Our lights draw way more power than household appliances. And that way you don't need the diesel to be running when–"

"Yeah, yeah," Roy cut her off, "so it's noise-free. Fine."

"But the batteries aren't the problem," she went on. "Water is the problem. The guys are having some trouble controlling the leak, and the cellar's starting to fill up," she finished.

Frustration filled Roy's face. "I told them, run it in slow. I want water in the background, on the floor, not over our heads. Is that so difficult to comprehend?"

"Not to comprehend," she replied matter-of-factly. "But you wanted a broken pipe in the background too, so they broke one and now the pressure is–" She waved her hands expressively.

"Rupturing it," I translated her gesture. "Making the leak worse. Leaks always make themselves worse. It's a leak rule."

She smiled briefly at me. "Yeah. So shake it, Royster, we've gotta roll, or you'll be filming an underwater disaster epic, not a music video." She sprinted away.

McCall's cherub face pinched worriedly. I got the sense that all this was more than he'd bargained for.

"Positions!" he shouted. More slim, leotard-wearing girls assembled, shedding leg warmers and trooping into the Danvers' house.

"We just want to talk to Harry," I told Roy, then spotted a van across the street and touched Ellie's arm. "Don't turn around now but when you can, grab a peek at what the cat dragged in."

Wyatt Evert sat hunched behind the wheel of his van, wearing a wide-brimmed safari hat from beneath which he kept sneaking glances, as if he thought he could keep from being recognized by this thin subterfuge.

"What's he doing here?" I wondered aloud.

"He was snooping around inside," Roy said. "And making noise about how I'd better not let any diesel fuel soak into the ground. I told him to shove off. Guess he didn't get the message."

"Roy! Let's go or we'll drown!" the efficient woman shouted.

"Talk to anyone you want," Roy called back as he hurried away across the lawn, "but not while we're rolling. You ruin this shoot and I swear, I'll be forced to shoot *you*."

He grinned to take the sting out of the threat, but I could see he wasn't far from meaning it. Meanwhile the argument between Harry and the girl had grown heated.

Fists clenched, she shouted something and spun away toward the house. I lost track of Harry for a few minutes in the crush around the door, caught up to him as he was going in.

"I need to talk to you about last night," I said, putting a hand on the sleeve of his leather jacket.

"Not now." He shook me off.

"Let's go, ladies and gentlemen!" Roy McCall's voice, taut with controlled tension, came from within the house.

I followed Harry inside. The house smelled of fresh paint and featured new wallpaper, the original wide-board floors newly finished with high-gloss poly, and pressed-tin ceilings. Also it featured a sound I knew well: a gushing leak in the cellar.

"I'm not leaving Samantha alone here," Harry said when, turning, he spotted me again. Samantha was the dancer Harry had been arguing with, I realized, remembering what Bob Arnold had told me about Harry having a girlfriend. "This is dangerous," Harry went on. "But she won't listen."

It didn't look dangerous. Most of the year the house stood vacant with sheeted furniture and lowered shades. Its owners used it as a vacation home, rented it or let it stand empty the rest of the time, and wouldn't even be here until August. It struck me again that Harry's mental train might be missing a few boxcars; the man seemed to see peril everywhere.

"Quiet, everyone!" McCall's voice came from the cellar amid a confusion of other voices both upstairs and down.

Harry descended the cellar steps, stationing himself on the bottom one; in his greying crew cut and battered leather jacket, his jaw thrust out and his hands clamped on his blue-jeaned hips, he resembled some 1950s-style avenging angel.

I peered past him. Now *this* looked dangerous. In the cellar, the dancers perched like bizarre living statues on the washer and dryer, on sawhorses and stepladders, and on every other raised surface, limbs frozen expectantly in exotic-looking positions.

But it wasn't their collection of precarious poses that gave me such pause. "We'll go straight through it," McCall told them.

A trapeze-seat slung by lines from a ceiling beam supported a camera operator. Lights blazed white; unnervingly so. With the water pouring down the old stone-and-mortar wall by the fuse box, having the power turned on down here would've been like licking a finger and sticking it into an electrical outlet.

But a battery wasn't really safer. It was one of the things Wade always hammered into new tugboat deckhands: You don't have to plug into a wall outlet to get electricity. A diesel and an alternator could turn deckhands into crispy critters in the blink of a careless eye. And here was juice enough to run all these big lights.

Thinking this, I noted distractedly a new, freshly mortared section of foundation, now getting soaked by water gushing down the wall. At the foot of it a few stones had already come out and some larger ones above were loosening, falling together of their own weight.

Seeing them I remembered again how very young Roy was and wondered anew if he was in over his head here, not only with the leak. The whole project was a lot to keep under control.

"First we'll roll cameras," he announced. "Count of four and the click starts." He glanced at a woman in a jumpsuit, holding what I guessed must be a metronome. Pushing a button on it, she demonstrated that it did click, a hollow-sounding *pop-pop-pop*.

"On the count of eight," Roy waved at the rafters, "the wire comes down. Samantha, you take it, just like we rehearsed. Don't worry," he added with a smile. "That wire's not really connected to any power."

"Oh, sure," Harry muttered amidst nervous laughter from the assembled company. "Trust your life to Mr. Fancy Pants, there."

"You all know the drill. We just need the action on film, that's all. You do your stunt, Samantha. The rest of you follow with each of yours, and . . . we'll cut. Got it?"

Nods from the dancers. "Let's do it," Roy commanded.

Samantha was pretty in a peas-in-a-pod way: gelled hair, big eyes, tiny nub of nose, small mouth. Generic-looking, like a successful, interchangeable product of a dance-school cloning experiment.

"Ready," the metronome woman announced. The cellar smelled of makeup, hot lights, and wet concrete. The water had now risen to the stairway footings. Somewhere outside a siren sounded distantly.

"What's going to happen?" I whispered.

Harry whispered back: "They dance. No sound—the music gets put in later. If you want to call it music," he added scathingly.

"Some choreographer's brilliant idea of drama, what's coming now," he went on, as the technicians took their places. "It's an electrocution scene. That's what the whole fake live-wire thing is about." His voice dripped disgust.

Roy McCall's, by contrast, was rich with manufactured confidence; he had a lot riding on this. And at first it was okay: metronome clicking slowly, but the dancers performing moves that if I hadn't seen, I wouldn't have believed could be done so fast.

A sort of peace began spreading on McCall's face: This was gonna work. But on the metronome's fifth click, I noticed Harry's gaze was locked on the rafter from which the fake live wire was set to fall.

I spotted the dangling end of it, fastened I imagined by a nail in the darkness where I couldn't see. The lights, clamped to cross beams, had been positioned well away from any possible contact with the water.

But Harry's eyes widened as the metronome clicked on. *Six, seven:* he turned in slow motion, his mouth opening.

Eight: Samantha's hand reaching gracefully, wire pulled by a technician yanking a length of invisible filament tied to it, the wire swinging down on cue.

"No!" Bellowing, Harry launched himself as Samantha's head jerked back, her body convulsing. McCall got there first, slammed into her, carrying her away with her hand still hard on the wire. There was a *snap!* and the hot sizzling smell of a short circuit.

From outside: the sound of an engine starting, roaring away as Samantha toppled. She landed with a splash and the sort of sick thump I knew meant she hadn't tried to break her fall, Roy on top of her. The metronome kept clicking.

"Turn it off!" Roy shouted, shoving Harry aside. They were struggling, almost as if to gain possession of her, amidst cries for an ambulance and for someone who knew CPR, shoving, and shouts to make sure all the power was *disconnected,* damn it!

The lights were off but the water was still rising; when I saw none of the people in it were being electrocuted, I waded in, too, found the main valve on the cellar wall, and cranked it shut. I'd done it at home enough times to know how; the gush of rushing water slowed to a trickle, stopped. Then I peered up at the place where the wire had been fastened, looking for a nail or hook.

I found it, too, screwed into a cross beam. But no wire hung from it. Instead a tiny, fresh-looking hole pierced the old wooden ceiling. It was unnoticeable unless you looked hard. Then I followed Ellie upstairs.

Outside, the dancers were all crying. The metronome woman had her arms around some of them, murmuring and scolding. Harry and

Roy had Samantha out, too, depositing her on the lawn. She was breathing, her thin little bird-ribs moving jerkily under the leotard top. "Where's the ambulance?" McCall implored.

My heart sank. The siren we'd heard earlier meant that the nearest ambulance was out on another emergency. Backup would kick in and the second would get here in a couple of minutes, cold comfort if you were the one waiting. But this wasn't the big city with safety nets under you twenty-four-seven. Here, it was what we had.

I wanted to head back in and find where that hole led to in the cellar ceiling. But just then Bob Arnold pulled up in the squad car, grim-faced. "Jake," he said, "you and Ellie better go home to your house. I'll be there soon. There's been an accident."

"No accident. It was—"

"No," he interrupted. "Listen to me, Jake. I mean at your house."

"But Bob, no one's home except . . ."

That siren.

". . . Wade."

"What the *hell* have you gotten stirred up?" Victor demanded. Tearing off his surgical gloves and tossing them, he stomped down the hospital corridor straight at me, full of sound and fury.

At the house I'd found only the frightened animals and the reek, unmistakable, of burnt gunpowder.

"You *always* do this." Tearing off his surgical gown, ripping the paper OR shoes from his feet.

"You *stick* your nose in, you can't let things *alone,* like it's *any* of your business . . ."

He'd heard already about our presence at the Danvers' house, of course. Victor was good at hearing of anything that had to do with me, in case he could use it against me.

He turned, pulling his white coat from a hook. His name was

embroidered in red script across the breast pocket, like a swirl of bright blood.

"You *always* . . ." he repeated, and then I was on him, spinning him, pinning him to the wall.

"Damn it, Victor, you *tell* me right now if Wade is okay."

"Jesus," he gasped. "Of course he is." He shook himself from my grasp, his face creased with distaste for my loss of control.

Relief ambushed me; I sank into one of the chairs lining the corridor outside the surgical area.

Nurses stared. "Jake," Victor grated. "You're making a scene."

Inside my ex somewhere I suppose there's some vestige of human beingness. But it's so well defended you practically have to hold a gun to his head to get a glimpse of it. Or if you have a tumor as big as a rutabaga, he'll be kind to you.

Otherwise he won't. "Wade's in recovery. He'll wake up soon. He had a close call but he's okay. And Sam's fine," he added thinly, letting me know how derelict it was of me not to have asked. Then he stalked away.

"Don't worry about it," Ellie comforted me when he was gone. "It's just his way of blowing off steam."

Right. But even after years of being divorced he still only blew it off at me, partly I guessed because mine were the buttons he knew how to push. Ellie sat beside me, handed me a tissue.

"Watch out for the contact lenses," she said automatically.

"Thanks. Did you get to talk to Harry?"

On an end table the day's issue of the Bangor paper lay open to the Downeast section. A photo of Sam's demolished car featured prominently.

"No," Ellie said. "Harry went in the ambulance with Samantha straight to Bangor. From there, they're airlifting her down to Portland. We can talk to Harry later."

"Okay." I blew my nose hard. "Ellie. I'm not crazy, right? This really *isn't* just a string of . . ."

"Coincidences?" she finished for me. "I don't think so."

The hall smelled of new paint, not quite covering the odors of fear and pain that no amount of disinfectant could ever eradicate. Victor dealt well with fear and pain as long as they belonged to other people, and as long as they were generated by a discernable physical cause that he could do something about.

It was the emotional stuff he had such trouble with. For approximately the millionth time, I put Victor away in the mental compartment I reserve for his psychopathology.

"This," Ellie said, "goes beyond coincidence. And we should start assuming Sam's car *was* tampered with, too."

A nurse appeared. "You can see him now."

In the recovery room Wade raised a hand weakly, let it fall. "How're you doing?" he asked me.

Tears spilled through my lashes although I tried not to let them; partly for his sake, partly on account of the darn lenses.

"No crying in baseball," he admonished me mock severely. He was half-drunk with anesthetic; a burn reddened his jaw.

The bad part, though, was the bandage on his neck. Clearly, something had just missed some very important anatomy. And Ellie was right: this all went way beyond coincidence.

"Wade, what happened?"

The good humor left his eyes, which were blessedly unharmed. "Shell. I brought the lever down—"

To compress the powder inside one of the shotgun shells he'd been reloading. *"Ka-boom,"* he finished simply.

The nurse came back in, suggested it was time for us to let him rest. "Wait. What's going on?" Wade demanded.

He'd seen our expressions even through a haze of painkiller: Ellie's especially, her gaze so penetrating they could have substituted it for one of the X-ray machines.

But now he was nodding, sandbagged by the drugs they'd given him. "Whoever did it," he muttered blurrily. "Rigged a reloading press. Righ' un'er my nose."

So he thought so, too: that this was no accident. His eyes drifted shut. "Guy's a real cowboy," he murmured.

Then he was asleep. Ellie led me back out to the corridor. "A cowboy," she repeated, her green eyes glinting. "Cowboys are daring, determined, imaginative—"

These were not qualities I wanted to find in my opponents. But Ellie seemed to relish the notion.

"Whoever this cowboy is," she declared . . . *Whoevah.*

". . . he just messed with the wrong Indians."

We spent part of the afternoon in the hospital with Sam and Maggie, who at her insistence were improving his time with the crossword puzzle from the *Quoddy Tides*. As the day waned we checked a sleeping Wade once more before going home, leaving George again in charge of guard duty; later, after feeding the animals and walking Monday, we confronted Harry Markle at his house.

Or we tried. But Harry had other ideas. He was packing, throwing clothes into a duffel bag and toiletries into a kit. "I'll have to give the dog back, Jake. I don't know where I'm going. You should take her tonight."

Her stubby tail twitching uncertainly, Prill looked back and forth between me and Harry. She'd stationed herself between us as soon as I entered, as if protecting him.

"Harry, you can't leave. What about Samantha? Don't you want to be here when she gets out of the hospital?"

"Samantha's not coming back. It's touch-and-go, they had to resuscitate her on the trip, and they aren't sure she'll make it. If she does, they doubt she'll dance again."

He tugged on his leather jacket. "That's what she gets for hanging around me. That's what everyone gets. Wade, Sam . . . I'm leaving now, before anyone else gets hurt."

He zipped the jacket. "Samantha was targeted because she was my friend. No other reason. I'm not going to stick around here so I can watch someone get killed."

He'd hauled out Harriet's old newspapers, stacking the bundles in the yard to await pickup. The chicken bones were gone, too. But there the effort ended, and now it seemed his nerves were getting to him, to judge by the cup lying on its side atop his formerly pristine table, coffee staining the book he'd been reading: *Practical Homicide Investigation* by Vernon J. Geberth.

A classic: Harry saw me looking at it, gave a bitter laugh. "Too bad old Vernon J. isn't here, give me some pointers. Because I don't know what to do anymore. I don't know."

"Harry," Ellie protested. "You can't just run."

I wasn't so sure. If he did go, trouble would go with him. But then my better angel kicked in. After all, Harry had pulled me out of some pretty bad wreckage, once.

"I don't deserve this," Harry said bitterly with a wave at the window. "This . . . peace."

Outside, the pointed firs were purple cutouts on the orange sunset. The first stars poked through the deepening azure sky in the east. But dark streamers from the south pushed threateningly toward us; by tomorrow, we'd have thunderheads.

"People here don't deserve my problems," Harry added.

"But," I said, still struggling with myself, "they'd want to help you, not send you away."

You don't dump people when they're in trouble, said the good angel. You just don't. "If they knew what happened to you, and what you did about it," I persisted.

That he hadn't got his man by shooting an innocent woman, I meant. If he had, he'd have ended up a hero instead of a scapegoat. It wasn't the story that had been printed in all the newspapers, probably even in some of the ones Harriet had read, that he'd stacked outside. But it was, I thought, the real story.

"They won't care that I didn't shoot her," he insisted. "No one here's going to feel a bond, no one'll identify with a sick, crack-smoking hooker."

I didn't contradict him; he hadn't been here long enough to know otherwise. Beautiful, remote downeast Maine did seem immune to city woes. But it had pockets of poverty, deep and ineradicable as bone infections, and all the agony that went with them. The kid, for example, that I'd read about in the *Examiner:* he'd been muling Oxycontin, a painkiller with more abuse potential than heroin.

"Maybe not," I temporized. "But people here do know about having trouble, and having nowhere to turn except to friends."

And, I reminded myself firmly, so did I. "But Harry, we need to know more about why you're so sure someone's . . ."

"I just know," he declared. "I know, and now you do, too. Or *do* you believe Wade screwed up with the shotgun-shell reloader?"

I'd already told him I didn't. "Excuse me," a voice cut in. It was Bob Arnold, looking severe as he walked in unannounced. "Harry, I'm very sorry. I just got word. Your friend didn't make it. She passed away a little while ago."

A silence, lengthening sadly. I broke it. "Harry," I said impulsively, "come to our house. You shouldn't be alone."

He turned away, the black squares of windowpanes reflecting his stony face. "If I do stay, and we catch this guy," he began, and I saw Bob Arnold open his mouth to put the kibosh on that idea.

But Harry saw it, too, catching sight of Bob's reflection in the glass. "Yeah," he gave in too quickly. "I'm not on the job, I should let the cops take care of cop business."

He faced Bob, stuck his hand out. "Thanks for coming to tell me. Let me know if there's anything I can do to help."

Bob didn't swallow it, of course. But he couldn't very well order Harry not to interfere when Harry had just told him he wouldn't. He did have one other thing to say, though:

"You'll hear it later, you might as well hear it now."

The dog stepped between me and Harry. "It's okay, Prill," I murmured to her, although of course it wasn't.

"In the Danvers' house," Bob began. "Somebody rigged that hot wire so it looked like the dummy one. Strung it into that length of filament so it fell right on cue. Trouble was, it was run up through a little hole somebody drilled in the floor and covered with carpet. Plugged into the household current."

So the circuit breakers for the basement had been off, but not the whole house. The power had still been on upstairs. "Somebody had to get in, in advance," I said. "Substitute the hot wire for the dummy, get everything all ready so plugging it in would be the only thing left to do."

In the confusion in and around the Danvers' house just before the filming began, that would've been fairly easy without the culprit being noticed. Everyone there had been focused on a task, not worrying about what someone else was doing.

Ellie and I, for instance, had walked right in. "And that's not all." Bob spoke very slowly, which meant he was furious; the madder he was, the slower he got.

Slower and more thorough. "After everyone else was gone, that cellar wall collapsed, all the water leaked in there, soaked that new mortar through, it let go. Any ideas about what we found behind the wall?"

I took a wild, awful guess. "Harriet Hollingsworth."

"Yup. Her and a couple bags of lime. And in her hand . . ."

He held up a plastic bag. Inside, the torn-off front page of an old *New York Post* with a blaring headline: TOP COP FLOPS!

"Oh, Christ," Harry muttered. Two photos: one a long shot of a city rooftop, black arrows where the action occurred. The other was a mug shot of a scowling, disreputable-looking woman with a nose ring, tattoos, and a missing tooth: Harry's murdered hostage.

"So if you *were* thinking of leaving," Bob said, "put it off. I'm going to want to talk with you. State cops, too."

I turned away for only an instant; when I turned back, Bob was on his way out the door and the cup lying atop Harry's book wasn't there anymore. Which told me that Bob was planning to run Harry's fingerprints. Like I said: thorough. But Harry didn't seem to notice the cup was gone.

"Any thoughts?" Ellie asked him when Bob had departed. " 'Cause if you are going to stay around, now'd be a good time to share."

"Someone's got a line on me," he answered bleakly. "Knows what I'm doing almost before I decide to do it."

I could think of another explanation. Harry seemed to see it in my face, and faced me frankly.

"The bank owned the house, not Harriet. They'd already had the redemption period."

Before the foreclosure auction, he meant. Once that period had been advertised in the papers and was ended you couldn't just make your back payments and get your house back. That ball game was over.

"They weren't going to let her stay in it again. Alive or not, she couldn't have stopped me from buying it. And even if that weren't so, why would I kill an old woman for a house, then hide a body with the equivalent of a big red arrow pointing straight at me?"

Good questions. "You met her, though? Harriet, before she vanished?"

He shook his head. "Few minutes, out on the porch. Next time I came back, a day later, she was gone." He wasn't sure when that had been, but: "It was when the tourist drowned." From Wyatt Evert's group, he meant. "Down at the diner everyone was talking about it, and it was in the *Tides*. Roy McCall was here then, too, scouting the location. I met him, and Wyatt Evert as well."

He took a step. Prill got up protectively. "So what if I do stay, try to corner this guy myself?" Harry asked.

My turn to object. But: "Not get in Bob Arnold's way," Harry hastened to add, "just keep my own eyes peeled. And maybe you two could, too? I know this creep's thinking pattern. I ate, breathed, and slept it."

Yeah, maybe too much. Harry looked from one to the other of us. "And you both know what's normal here, you'd spot anything out of the ordinary."

"Or *someone* out of the ordinary," Ellie agreed.

"Now, wait just a minute—" I began.

Harry didn't know our reputations. Only local people did. We didn't advertise that we were known around town as the Snoop Sisters; like the Shingle Belles, but with longer noses. Or that Ellie and I had spotted some things so emphatically not-normal they'd have curled even Harry's close-clipped grey hair.

All he wanted was two harmless Eastport busybodies to be his eyes and ears, ones with a growing personal stake in helping him finish an unfinished mission: catching the bad guy. Turning the tables, righting an old wrong.

"But if I catch him," Harry added, "whoever it is, he's mine. Not Bob's or the state cops'. I get an hour with him. That's all I need. Agreed?"

I opened my mouth again but Ellie spoke first: "Agreed."

It all sounded pretty crackpot; in particular I was doubtful about the idea of keeping secrets from Bob Arnold: the wisdom, or the possibility.

But Harry had saved me out of some bad wreckage, years ago. The least I could do was try returning a favor, especially since this particular wreckage wasn't even flaming.

Yet.

In the chilly darkness Ellie and I turned toward downtown and La Sardina, Eastport's Mexican restaurant. Its cheery lights and music plus a funky decor of huge potted plants, hanging pinatas, and candles jammed into Kahlúa bottles were just what I needed.

Something else I needed was there, too: information, in the prodigious brain of *Quoddy Tides* reporter Timothy Rutherford. Not that it came free, mind you. But I was prepared to trade.

"Drinking alone again, I see." I slid onto a stool at the bar beside the one Tim regularly occupied right up till closing.

He glanced at me in the mirror behind the bar, taking in my fading bruises. "Hey, just the woman I wanted to see. Hi, Ellie."

"Hi, Tim." Ellie ordered beer for both of us, and another orange soda for Tim. An Eastport native, word had it that in the early '90s he'd drunk himself off one big-city news desk after another, boom-boom-boom like falling downstairs. Then about a year ago he'd come home to Eastport, sober but with his tail between his legs.

"Little excitement around the old town, hey?" he observed with a nod of thanks as I paid for the drinks. Nowadays Tim could've had any of his old jobs back. His memory alone—the closest to being truly photographic that I'd ever seen—was a treasure.

But as he said, if it ain't broke, don't fix it. Five feet tall, maybe a hundred pounds soaking wet, he lived in an apartment over the dime store, belonged to every social and civic group in Eastport, and spent most evenings here at La Sardina gathering information, storing it for future use in that amazingly absorbent brain of his.

"Seems like you two are right in the thick of it as usual." Tim stroked his small ginger beard thoughtfully. "I see you've been up on a ladder again. But is Wade okay? And Sam?"

Tim's number was one of those on my caller ID at home; he wanted details. But now that he had me in his sights he knew better than to push hard immediately. In Eastport, pushing for a story was an almost guaranteed method of not getting it.

Or not getting it right. "Yeah," I said. "Wade's good. Sam, too. And I'll tell you all about it . . ." I drank some of my beer. "Later. If you'll tell me a couple things right now."

Tim nodded agreeably. Behind him the jukebox blared into a cover of "Here Comes the Sun," rendered by someone who should've let that number alone. I saw Tim's lips move. "Shoot."

"Harriet Hollingsworth." The music was convenient. I didn't want what I was about to say all over town in the morning.

"Those letters she wrote to the *Tides*," I went on.

Tim nodded. "Any of 'em interesting?" I asked. By now what *would* be all over town was the news that her body had been found.

Tim made the connection, shook his head in regret. "C'mere." I bent my head nearer to his.

"I thought of that myself," he shouted into my ear. "Went to the office, see if anyone kept 'em. Like for a joke, anything. I didn't find any, not that I really needed to."

Because he would remember. Word for word, probably. I looked a question at him. "Nah," he answered, "we didn't keep 'em around routinely. Had a Harriet Hollingsworth ceremonial ashtray."

Darn. "Burned them?"

He nodded.

"Well, but do you *remember* anything that . . ."

Because I was already pretty sure, now: Harriet's letters didn't have anything to do with her death. But I needed to be *sure* sure.

"Nope," Tim confirmed. "I know what you're thinking. Could be, someone wanted to stop that little leak at its source."

My turn to nod. The noise in here was astonishing, clatter of plates and din of conversation competing with the jukebox.

"But I read her letters when they came," Tim said. "People talked at first like they were full of hot secrets." It was a notion that Harriet herself had made sure got all over town. "Adultery!" he said. "Thieving out of the church collection!"

He sipped orange soda. The jukebox went off. Timmy modulated his volume to an unoverhearable murmur without missing a beat.

"But they were all about who didn't rake leaves off a lawn, whose garbage cans sat on the curb till the next day," he said.

Tame stuff. "And this became common knowledge, did it?"

Ellie looked vindicated. She'd said all along no one took Harriet seriously. But that was before her corpse was found sealed up in a wall.

"Yeah," Tim confirmed sadly. "Too bad. I'd've loved finding a story there. But as a motive for murder, they're just not on." Then he brightened. "You mentioned a trade?"

"Just a minute." Most of the beer had vanished from my tall glass and the unaccustomed sudden rush of alcohol had relaxed the trapdoors on my brain cells, letting another question escape.

"Lian Ash," I said slowly.

Tim grinned. "Keep free-associating like that, I'll have to switch you over to orange soda, too. But okay, what about Ash?"

Ellie checked her wristwatch. "Listen, I'd better go home. George said he'd call. He's not bringing Sam until they kick him out of Maggie's room. But if I'm not there to answer, he's going to be worried."

I looked down; my beer was gone and I definitely didn't want another one. But I didn't want to go home to that big, empty house, either. Meanwhile, Tim sat there waiting for two things:

First, to find out what I would tell him about the recent run of accidents around my place. I had offered to trade, after all, and I could see he intended to hold me to the promise.

And second, to learn why I was curious about the old mason who was working on my house, in case there was a story in it. I followed Ellie outside and Tim followed me. His newshound's nose was practically twitching.

"I'll be over later, after I talk to George," she called to me over her shoulder.

"Okay." I turned back to Tim.

All I wanted was to confirm what Mr. Ash had said: that he was a fairly recent arrival to the area, one with no interesting history that Tim in his chronically curious way might've learned and remembered. Because . . .

The question floated up startlingly: How *had* Mr. Ash known I hated heights? Probably there was a perfectly simple, harmless answer. But until I knew it, and *knew* it to be the truth, I couldn't have him in the house anymore.

Not with all that was going on around here. Then Tim startled me again, recalling even more than I had expected. "Yeah, I roomed with him in Machias," he said. "Two years back."

Surprise must have shown on my face; Tim misinterpreted it. "Well, not in the *same* room," he added. "Same house, though."

"Go on in if I'm not home," I called to Ellie. She shot me a look but made no comment as she strode away.

"So you knew him?" I questioned Tim. This didn't jibe with what Mr. Ash had told me.

"Nope. Not really. But I recognized him when he showed up here. Knew his face, he knew mine."

"Tim," I said, waving at his car parked at the curb, a tiny, shiny-new red Volkswagen bug. The twinkling strings of Christmas lights that La Sardina kept on in its windows all year reflected on its grille. "Do you feel like taking a ride?"

Tim looked at me, at the car, and at my face again. My own tumble from the ladder was no big news; as I may have mentioned, I'm not the surest-footed person on the planet. But he badly wanted the inside story on Wade and Sam. And if there was anything interesting to learn about Lian Ash, or anyone else in town, he wanted that too.

And Sam wouldn't be home for at least another couple of hours. Tim stepped to the VW and opened the passenger door with a flourish.

"Madam, your chariot awaits."

Probably it was a goose chase. Probably I had no earthly business heading forty miles away to Machias with the express purpose of hauling some poor landlady from a well-earned evening of TV and knitting, to quiz her about an old tenant. But something about Lian Ash just wasn't sitting right with me.

"I was still pretty shaky," Tim said about his own time at the rooming house. "Wanted to get my legs solidly under me, so I stayed away a little while longer. Like circling the airport a few times before landing, you know? If I was going to crash again I didn't want to do it in Eastport," he explained. "Then, when people assumed I'd come home straight from New York, I let them. No harm, no foul."

Maybe Lian Ash had done much the same. But if so, why? He hadn't just let me assume something, either; he had flat out said he'd come to Eastport from Portland, not from Machias. And—how *had* he known anything about me?

Tim downshifted smoothly into the speed zone at Pleasant Point, keeping the speedometer carefully under thirty-five until the houses thinned to trees and fields again.

"So, do you want to unburden yourself in return?" he asked. "Put me in the picture a little? Or am I supposed to put the cab fare on your tab, too?"

I gave myself a hard mental shake. That beer had been a bad idea. "Okay, the thing is this. I don't know what's going on, and if I tell you all I *don't* understand, it'll take a year."

He waited as an eighteen-wheeler highballed past us at the intersection of Route 1, then turned left onto the highway.

"So I'll fill you in later, when I do. Meanwhile, why don't you tell *me:* What *do* you know about Lian Ash?"

"Okay." Tim passed the eighteen-wheeler expertly on the last straightaway before the road narrowed and curved into the trees, leaving the big rig's headlights fading into the darkness behind us. "Like I said, I lived in the same house as him."

He drove the little car fast and well, accelerating out of the curves but with no flashy, dangerous-feeling fanfare. "I said good morning to him a few times, that was about the extent of it. Year or so ago, I moved up to Eastport. Not long after that, he did, too," Tim added.

"But not because *you* moved here, surely." A truck blew by us in a rush of wind and a billow of road dust.

"Oh, no. Guys get on their feet, they go out on their own," Tim replied. "Get their own place in Machias or come to Eastport or Calais. You stay in the area, there's not many other choices."

True. After Machias, the next biggish place was Ellsworth, another sixty miles south. "So it was like graduating. From the rooming house, I mean."

He nodded. "I started seeing him in La Sardina. Not often. He shows up, has a coffee or soda, pays and leaves. He isn't," Tim added dryly, "a big socializer."

So I'd gathered. "He told me he moved here just last winter." Which was a few months ago, not a year: another small discrepancy.

Tim shrugged. "Yeah, well, I'm just reporting what I know. Although since we're talking about him now I guess maybe you know more. Or think you do, you're all anxious to check it out." He glanced at me. "Or are you luring me somewhere for immoral purposes?"

From anyone else the comment might've made me nervous. I was not used to driving around at night with men other than Wade. But Tim's Jimmy Olson grin took the worry out of being close.

"I realize this sounds nuts," I answered. "But with all that's happened . . . it's small stuff, probably meaningless. Still, I want to check out the rooming house and talk to the landlady."

Tim made *Twilight Zone* theme-song noises. He was a sarcastic little bugger, another reason I liked him.

"Yeah, yeah," I conceded. "Bush-league snooping. And I really hope I *don't* find out anything bad about him. He seems so decent."

"But you asked him the equivalent of a straight question and he gave you a crooked answer and that makes you think maybe there's more to the story, so you want to go after it."

He braked smoothly. Deer stood in the road, unfazed by our appearance, a female and two fawns, mild-eyed.

"Come on, Mom, get 'em off the freeway," Tim said. And when they'd moseyed calmly into the brush:

"People lie for all kinds of reasons, Jake. Doesn't mean they're bad, just that they think what they're being asked is nobody else's business."

"Yeah. That's possible, too. But in the context . . ." My ears were ringing hard from the too-fast beer and suddenly I realized just how ridiculous this idea was.

"Or maybe I'm just drunk," I finished.

Tim didn't comment, taking the turns south of Whiting as if we were on a track on the NASCAR circuit. Chilly darkness whizzed past, broken by glittering tidal inlets, pointed outlines of firs pasted on them as if cut from black paper with sharp scissors.

Then, just as I thought he'd decided he was humoring me but nothing more, he spoke again.

"The context being that Sam crashed the car, Wade nearly got his head blown off, that dancer's dead, and a well-known missing Eastport crackpot has just been found walled up in a cellar."

I let a breath out gratefully. Coming out of the hills, the road curved sharply across the long, low bridge leading into the county seat of Machias.

"Yeah," I told Tim. "Thanks. That's exactly it. And it's making me nervous."

Tim just nodded. His career rise had been meteoric, his fall just as fast, so the story went. Nowadays it seemed he wasn't in a hurry about much of anything but this road. But he was quick on the uptake, and the fact that he wasn't laughing at an eighty-mile round-trip spurred on by little more than a beer-fueled impulse made me feel a little better.

"So you'll tell me about this once you've got it all worked out?" he asked.

He slowed over the causeway that spanned the Machias River, took the right-hand fork in the road past Helen's Restaurant in Machias. Visions of Helen's famous pie danced in my head but I was on a mission.

"If I get it all worked out," I promised. We climbed a hill, shot past the county courthouse and the lockup adjacent. Lights glowed behind the barred windows. The hapless drug smuggler I'd read about in the *Examiner* was in there somewhere. "You're sure it's not too late?"

Maine people, especially the older ones, were early risers. Eight in the evening to them was like midnight to me.

"Yup. And I've kept in touch with the landlady." Tim grinned briefly sideways at me. "Wait till you meet her, she's a sketch." We turned onto a side street. "Almost there."

"I hope she's still up." Now that we were here, I was even less certain than before that this was a good idea.

Tim barked a laugh. "Oh, she's up, all right."

We pulled over. "Listen, if you're not ready to talk about your thing, maybe you can help me on something else," he said as we got out of the car. "Wyatt Evert."

The street was silent, dead-ending a block away. Beyond lay two hundred or so dark miles of fields, trees, and rivers before any other street began; in Maine, when you're on the edge of town you are also on the edge of real wilderness.

"What about him?" We were going up a narrow walk leading to the steps of a glassed-in porch. The house was smaller than I had expected, with a grassy little rut of a side driveway and a one-car garage.

"I asked him what else he does besides the tour groups," Tim replied as we mounted the steps. "For a feature we might run on the different jobs people do to string a living together around here." He knocked and after a moment the porch light went on.

"Crooked answer?" I said as a face appeared at a window.

"Says he runs a nonprofit, it benefits endangered species," Tim said as the inside door opened. A woman in slippers and fuzzy robe, her hair in a towel and cream all over her face, came onto the porch.

"Just a sec!" she called fretfully through the glass.

Tim's absence of scorn aside, I was even sorrier that I had given in to what was obviously a truly dumb notion.

"Thing is," Tim went on as the woman fussed, muttering, with the balky door lock, "I looked up the organization Evert mentioned, in the lists of nonprofits registered in any of the fifty states or with the federal folks, the IRS."

The lock popped. A greasy face peered out doubtfully at us.

"No such outfit," I guessed. You register nonprofits to get tax-exempt status, among other things. I'd done lots of them.

"Bingo," he confirmed. Then: "Mrs. Sprague? It's me."

The woman frowned, still squinting. Just as I'd feared, she'd been getting ready for bed. And we hadn't even called first; I wanted to sink through the sidewalk and disappear.

"Tim, let's just go—" I began.

But then a huge grin, its toothlessness rendered irrelevant by its happiness, broke through the face cream.

"Thimmy!" the woman shouted joyfully, and ushered us in.

Chapter 5

M r. Ash was a lovely man," Sheila Sprague told us fifteen minutes later. She'd put her dentures in, abolishing
her lisp without diminishing her cracked, radiant charm.

"He was working for the road crew where they were blasting for
the new bridge, down at Cherryfield." Still wearing the face cream,
she'd brought us into the parlor where she served us iced root beer and
Ritz crackers with slices of processed cheese.

To my surprise, I was thirsty and starving. Mrs. Sprague beamed
approval as I devoured crackers and slugged down the root beer, meanwhile taking in my surroundings.

Brown shag carpet covered the floor. The heavy furniture's thick,
sturdy upholstery was a hideous orange plaid, above it on the walls a collection of heavily framed paint-by-numbers scenes. *Reader's Digest* con-
densed books lined up on a low shelf; a black china planter in the shape
of a crouching panther, a philodendron straggling gamely from its back,

stood on the TV below a wooden cuckoo clock whose strike of each quarter hour was prefaced by a cataclysmic whirring of internal machinery.

In short, it was crowded, crammed full of bric-a-brac, and so utterly, undemandingly comfortable I wanted to move right in. And I gathered I wasn't the only one; a half dozen empty chairs crowded in a semicircle in front of the TV.

"All six of my gentlemen go to bed early," Sheila explained to me. She was a sketch, all right.

A *sharp* sketch. If Ellie's eyes were X-ray, this lady had CAT-scanners installed in her forehead. "They're all working men, and need their rest. So I have the evenings to myself. For," she touched a fingertip to her face while batting her skimpy lashes self-parodyingly at me, "my beauty routine."

The house didn't seem big enough to accept one tenant, much less six. "Mrs. Sprague keeps the rent down by boarding two to a room," Tim told me. "Fellows here, mostly just getting going again."

"Like you," she agreed, beaming through the face cream. Her affectionate regard for him was obvious. "And just as I predicted, haven't you done lovely for yourself? I knew that you would."

She jumped up, her slippers padding away swiftly. "If you'd like to see Mr. Ash's room, you're welcome to. It's just now come vacant again. Though I don't know what you could find. He didn't leave much, and it was quite a long time ago."

Tim followed me as I followed her to a back stair. The kitchen smelled of Ajax, the floor's linoleum covered with brightly woven rag rugs, the appliances quaint relics from five decades ago. A round-shouldered Frigidaire wheezed beside a Formica table, its six red leatherette-and-chrome chairs neatly pulled up to it.

Upstairs, she put a finger to her lips. The carpeted hall was dark except for the glow of the night-light in the bathroom, whose door stood ajar. "Let's be mice, now," she cautioned sweetly, opening a hallway door. "Everyone's asleep."

The cell she showed us was barely large enough to walk into. It featured a narrow bed, a dresser, and a tiny closet containing a few wire hangers. Another braided rug lay on the floor. She pulled a string to switch the bedside lamp on.

"This is a single room," she said unnecessarily as I blinked at its small size. If she'd turned all her spare rooms into rentals, this one must've been the linen closet.

"I've rented it several times since Mr. Ash was in it," she whispered. "But it's just the same as when he left. He took all his things with him, of course, not that he had much. Not a man for a lot of possessions, Mr. Ash."

She gestured at a shelf under the bedside table. "Except a few books. They're still here. That was one funny thing. He asked me when he left if anyone ever came looking for him, to give them his books."

I knelt to peer at them: Kessel's *Handbook of Explosives*, a biography of Frederick the Great, and a grammar text: *Synonyms, Homonyms, and Antonyms*.

"I thought it was odd," she added. "But harmless. Why don't you take them along with you, dear?" she whispered.

I gathered them up. The handbook and the biography had the soft, handled feeling of books well read; the grammar felt crisp; the smell of a new, unopened binding rose poignantly from it.

Back downstairs, she had little more to tell us about Lian Ash. Quiet, hardworking. A gentleman; it was the term I'd have used about him, too. As for his past:

Mrs. Sprague put a gentle hand on my arm. "I don't ask any of my tenants about that, dear," she said. "For so many of them the past is what they're trying to get over. You understand."

She'd taken in the damage to my face without comment as if to demonstrate the wisdom of this policy. She was not, perhaps, as simple a woman as her decorating style suggested; the opposite, possibly. The moment passed; she was disappointed we couldn't stay longer. She planned a snack of tomato soup and crackers, and wouldn't Tim and I like to join her in it?

The soup sounded good, safe and normal like the rest of her kitsch-filled but oddly appealing little refuge. Still, I wanted to get home, call the hospital to check on Wade, and see Sam, who was probably home, too, by now. Ellie would be with him and both of them were certainly wondering where in the world I'd gotten to.

"After her soup she'll make bag lunches for the boarders to take to work tomorrow," Tim told me as we drove back down toward the center of Machias.

He'd hugged her warmly, heedless of the face cream. It was late, everything hushed and surreal-looking in the lights from gas station and convenience store lots, mostly empty.

"She helped you a lot, didn't she? Mrs. Sprague."

"Saved my life," he agreed bluntly. "She started taking boarders after her husband died, get enough income so she wouldn't lose the house. But now I think taking care of guys who forgot how to take care of themselves, guys on the skids, is what keeps her going."

"Do they all turn out to be gentlemen, like she said?"

"Yep. Mrs. Sprague's a sweetie, but she's shrewd, knows how to pick 'em. In fact it was Lian Ash who said something to her once about getting her a gun, just in case. But nothing ever came of it."

"Was Mr. Ash on the skids?"

He shook his head. "Worked all the overtime he could get and never spent a dime he didn't have to. But it seemed he had what he needed."

"So that's how."

Tim glanced a sideways question.

"The house he bought on the shore road," I explained. "He was saving up for it, probably."

"Oh. The down payment. Yeah." A silence. Then:

"Doesn't it bother you, Tim? Sitting in a bar every night?"

"No," he replied easily. "I was never much of a bar drinker. I only drink alone. Drank," he corrected himself, "alone."

But then he changed the subject. "So was it a goose chase?"

"This trip? I don't know. Probably it was." There was another reason Tim had been willing to make it, I realized. A way not to be alone. "I didn't get any questions answered, but I didn't find out anything bad, either. Probably there's a perfectly simple reason for what Lian Ash told me. And if Mrs. Sprague thinks he's okay . . ."

"Yeah. She's a good judge of character." *I hope*, his tone added wistfully, on his own behalf.

He slowed for the S-curves just outside East Machias, then accelerated for the long run up the coast. We drove in silence a while longer, Tim lost in his thoughts and me in mine.

It was a Frederick the Great story that Mr. Ash had told me when I asked about his past. The Kessel handbook was an annual, a new one published every year; Sam had one for the demolition seminar he was going to, and a blasting handbook made perfectly good sense for a man with a job on a road crew, handling explosives.

The grammar book didn't fit. But I'd spent half an hour in his presence, tops; not nearly enough, surely, to explain all his choices in reading material. "Some people aren't good at recalling how long ago things happened," I said.

"Sure," Tim agreed. "And maybe he thought mentioning a stay in a boardinghouse that caters to recovering drunks wouldn't boost your confidence in him."

"That, too. But he asked me if falling off the ladder meant I would dislike heights even more than before. I just wish I knew how he knew *that*."

Tim glanced over incredulously. "That's what you're worried about?"

"Well, mostly, I guess. Because the rest I can rationalize, but . . ."

"Hey, Jake? Seen yourself in a mirror lately? Anyone asked you how it happened?" Tim sounded amused.

"Well, no. Not around Eastport. Because . . ."

Because they already knew. The whole town knew. Bob Arnold hadn't given it a second thought; Purlie Wadsworth hadn't even commented. As Sam would've said: *Doink.*

"Oh," I said embarrassedly. "So I guess that explains it."

"Yeah. Believe me, no one who falls off as much as you . . ."

". . . enjoys going up," I completed Tim's sentence. And of course it was well known; in Eastport, what wasn't? "So let's say he walks into Wadsworth's, mentions who he's working for . . ."

"Purlie fills him in," Tim agreed. " 'Geez, don't let her go up any ladders.' That, or he figured it out for himself. It's not," Tim finished, "exactly a stretch that if you're not vastly skilled at something, maybe you don't enjoy it."

"Right. I guess not, huh? Okay, then," I said unhappily.

I felt like an idiot; another simple explanation, and likely the truth. This trip had been a fool's errand and while I was gone, anything could have happened. Suddenly I wanted to be home even more than before.

"Are Sam and Maggie serious?"

I blinked, jolted from my musings. "Serious about what?"

We were in Whiting already, passing between the general store and the white two-room schoolhouse that served this area to grade eight. Tim lifted one finger in a minuscule wave to the state cop idling in a squad car in the darkened lot beside the store.

"About each other," he replied mildly, turning uphill into the last long stretch of wilderness before the turnoff to Eastport.

I glanced at him in surprise. "Maggie just joined the Quoddy Choristers," he explained. "Singing group. Nice alto she's got. I belong, too. I just wondered, that's all."

"I don't know. You'd have to ask her." The notion of Maggie taking up with someone else gave me a pang. But it would happen sooner or later if Sam turned out to be foolish enough to let it.

Maggie was no beauty queen, any more than Mrs. Sprague; you had to look hard to notice loveliness that didn't come out of a cosmetics ad. I sensed Tim had that kind of vision, though, that he'd tried the other kind of beauty and found it wanting.

But if not Tim, then someone else would come along to steal Maggie away from word pairs that sounded the same and Scrabble contests that went on for hours. After another long silence I said:

"About Wyatt Evert. You think he's got some racket going?"

Tim frowned, taking the turn off Route 1 onto 190. It was the last leg of our journey. "Dunno. I think there's more to his story, though. All that ecology crap he spouts, I think that's a smoke screen. Don't get me wrong, I'm not against the environment."

"Right," I replied evenly. "And I'm not against banks. Just against bank robbery."

He laughed, taking my point. The first thing any con artist working a charity racket said was, "How can you be against . . . ?"

Starving children, vanishing forests, the ozone layer. Fill in the blank: there was a racket to exploit it.

"Anyway," Tim said as we crossed the causeway. Across the bay the lights of the Canadian cargo terminal shone whitely like airport beacons in the surrounding blackness of maritimes night. "I'm in no hurry. Want to be sure I've done my homework before I confront him."

"You're getting ready for a move," I guessed. Tim's usual beat included Eastport shipping news, school personnel changes, navigation-chart corrections, and minutes of the marine terminal business meetings.

"Thinking about girls, thinking about big stories. In spring a young man's fancy turns?" To love and money, I meant.

And wider horizons, jobs he could keep now that he was sober again. That would explain why he wasn't hopping on to the Harriet story with both feet. A body in a basement was major news around here; elsewhere, it would barely be a blip on the radar.

"Maybe. Gotta get back on that big horse someday, or Mrs. Sprague'll be disappointed in me." We came into town, past the Bay City Mobil. "She thinks I'm gonna be another Sinclair Lewis someday."

He laughed to show he didn't take this ambition seriously. "But it's a biggish story if Wyatt's what I think he might be. I could take it down to the *Boston Herald* . . ."

Maggie loved Boston, the bookstores and music clubs where she sat in on jam sessions with her banjo or fiddle whenever she could. It wasn't often; instead she hung around where Sam was, waiting.

"Listen, about Sam's accident," Tim ventured. "I mean, was he . . ."

When Sam was a young teenager he'd had a substance abuse problem. Now Tim and Sam attended the same AA meeting when Sam was home. "No, he wasn't drinking. He hasn't done that or anything else for a long time. They think the accident was mechanical failure."

He nodded, looking relieved as we came into town. Sam had told me someone else's slip always scared him, too, made him see how easy it was. "Good," Tim replied. "I like Sam. I don't want to mess him up, especially if he and Maggie are . . ."

We pulled up in front of my house. "An item? Like I told you, I don't think I'm your source on that story." I gathered Mr. Ash's books. "And as far as tonight's adventure goes . . ." The porch light went on as I opened the car door. "We *have* had a lot of trouble all at once. First Sam, then Wade. And now with Harriet's body, and the dancer, Samantha . . ." I took a deep breath. "Well, it was like you said at first. Me feeling nervous, wanting to cover all my bases, that's all."

Bob Arnold hadn't told Tim about the newspaper in Harriet's hand, or Tim would've mentioned it. So I didn't, either.

"Which I have," I added. "Covered them." But not with glory; in the clear night air my earlier suspicions seemed trivial, even paranoid.

A few little white lies didn't put Lian Ash on the FBI's most wanted list. And if Ash had been a bad dude in the past, he wasn't anymore or Mrs. Sprague wouldn't have had him in her house.

As for his books, whatever that was all about it had nothing to do with me. I hadn't known Mr. Ash until recently, wouldn't've known him now if I hadn't put an ad up looking for a stonemason.

"So thanks a lot," I told Tim. "If I find out anything new about Wyatt Evert, I'll let you know. Wade and Sam's accidents, too," I added, "if anything interesting comes up about them."

He drove off with a good-humored but skeptical wave. News guys heard similar promises ten times a day, the gesture told me.

And I felt a little guilty about it; I already knew plenty that Tim would've found interesting. But it all seemed connected to Harry Markle one way or another. And when it came to promises, in my book it was still first come, first served:

Ellie and I had told Harry we'd help him, not broadcast his troubles to the media. And I didn't want Tim's interest piqued by my *off*-the-record comments, either. It was one thing that do-it-yourself home repair and homicide-snooping had in common:

If anyone was going to upset any applecarts, I wanted first crack at them.

So when I went in I felt at peace with my decision, which boiled down to doing what I'd said I would do, the way I'd said I would do it. But by the next morning I was having second thoughts about my home-repair *and* homicide-snooping philosophies.

Third thoughts, too.

"We shouldn't have told Harry that," I groused to Ellie. "We let him set the terms as if we were working for *him*." I was in a foul mood. My field trip of the evening before felt even more like a humiliatingly silly stunt.

And me like a harebrain who needed better impulse control. "Riding around with a beer buzz on, with a guy from my son's AA group, of all things," I said. "It's embarrassing."

"Yes, well, they don't cancel your membership in the human race for that. Just," she added tartly, "the opposite."

"Meaning I like life to be at least a little under control?" Shoving aside the tins of varnish remover in the hall, I yanked two respirator masks from the utility closet.

"Under control. That's putting it mildly, Jake. You're allowed to do something unusual now and then, is all I'm saying." If I were an axe-murderer, my pal Ellie would put the kindest possible face on it.

"Unusual," I repeated scathingly. "It was *nuts.*"

"You were upset. You needed to do something useful about the situation, but there wasn't anything, so you tried to do something about something else. Big deal. Quit beating yourself up."

But I wasn't ready to let myself off the hook just yet. "Why should I?"

"Because the ability to do something stupid," she replied serenely, "is a necessary component of the ability to do anything at all."

"Oh. Well, in that case." Trust Ellie to boil it down for you.

"And," she added, "since when is finding out that there's really nothing to find out a useless errand? Nothing you need to worry about, I mean."

She was right. Mrs. Sprague was an excellent litmus test; with her recommendation I'd probably be safe in trusting the old mason with my checkbook, never mind just the stones in my cellar. "You have a way of making the most annoyingly correct points, Ellie, did you know that?"

"My, we are in a great mood." She grimaced at me. "Anyway, Harry wouldn't have stayed otherwise. Unless we agreed to doing it all his way."

"No big tragedy, either," I retorted, hauling on my canvas apron. Another thing that I'd decided overnight: my better angel was a fool, too. "And his way means acting like vigilantes."

Meanwhile I mentally marked off a section of the front hall floor, presently coated with a dozen or so layers of old varnish. Eight feet by eight was ambitious without being reckless.

Unlike our bargain with Harry. "Jake," Ellie said, "we only agreed that he gets to deal with whoever's behind all the mayhem if *he* catches someone."

Not, she meant, if someone else did, like maybe Bob Arnold. Or if the culprit didn't get caught at all. It was an idea that did not provide me with any further cheer whatsoever.

"I guess," I grumbled. Ellie's mind, obviously, was already made up. "And at least it's quiet here, now."

Too quiet, actually; to my surprise and initial alarm, Sam hadn't been home when I got there. He'd stayed at the hospital, refusing to leave while Maggie was still there even though *she* refused to abandon the homonym list, so Victor had finagled another night for him.

George had stayed too since if Sam wasn't going he wasn't; George would carve Sam's enemies up with a plastic knife from the hospital cafeteria, if he had to. And Wade, though improved, was still doped up; Ellie said George had set a chair in view of all three patients' rooms and was eagle-eyed when she spoke with him.

Finally, Roy McCall was in Portland, his music video on hold while he talked to state cops and his insurance people, arranged for Samantha's body to be transported home, and—this had been on late-night TV when I got home—was interviewed about the tragedy for the E! Entertainment Network and MTV, who were all over the story.

"Which," Ellie said briskly, "doesn't guarantee that we *are* going to. Do it Harry's way, I mean."

"Uh-huh." A foghorn hooted distantly. My windows were opaque in a fog as thick as, Sam would've said, sea poop. From the closet I pulled some yellow crime-scene tape I'd gotten from Bob Arnold, so no one would walk into the mess that we were about to make.

"Are you sure you wouldn't rather let George put the sanding machine on this when he gets home?" Ellie asked.

"Absolutely. If we don't get the top layers off first, you won't like the result." Stripping an old floor with only a sander is like trying to get gum out of a kid's hair by heating the gum.

I opened the front door: salt air, tinctured with woodsmoke. "It turns the varnish to warm goo," I continued as I got out two long-handled sponge mops, and put them with the rest of the items by which we would avoid (I hoped) asphyxiating or otherwise injuring ourselves.

These included safety glasses, the chemical respirators, and surgical caps for our hair. Two pairs of thick, blue rubber gauntlet-length gloves completed our outfits. Once we were suited—the animals having been locked in the ell away from the fumes that would rise—I opened the first tin of chemical stripper.

Outside, Mr. Ash's truck rumbled in with a rattletrap roar. A note on the door let him know to use the cellar entrance. I'd taken the three books from Mrs. Sprague's house up to my own room, and left them there.

"Well, here goes nothing," I said, my voice muffled by the rubber mask of the respirator, and began to pour stripper onto the thick, dark varnish.

"*Mmphglbmphgl,*" Ellie said through her respirator. Stripper blooped from the can in orangey globs.

"Darn right," I said; it came out *"dmrphgl."* We took up the sponge mops for the spreading portion of the operation. But then:

"Glmph." That the mops would absorb some of the stripper on the floor instead of spreading it had not occurred to me. But it was happening and as a result the varnished surface of the floor was being transformed into the La Brea tar pits.

"Hglrhyh!" Ellie said.

Hurry. I grabbed two more cans of stripper and walked into the gooey mess the floor was becoming, hoping I could get the new cans opened before the contents of the old ones had dissolved my shoes. Working fast we spread stripper goo with the sodden mops, now also beginning to dissolve.

Finally at the edge of the coated section I stepped out of my shoes onto the clean floor, which I'd covered with old issues of *National Fisherman* and *Gun Times* from Wade's used newspaper stack.

Then I picked up my shoes. Or rather, I tried picking them up. *"Hrph,"* Ellie said, watching. *"Mphlucnsrphmph?"*

Maybe you can scrape them off. I took the paint scraper she offered me, pried at the edge of a sneaker. Its sole seemed to be flowing, bubbling as it dissolved.

"There." The sneakers popped up from the clean floor with a wet, sucking sound, leaving distinct outlines like the footprints of an Arthur Murray dance lesson from hell.

"Hey! What the Sam Hill're you two doin' up there?" It was Mr. Ash's voice. I tore off the respirator; fumes hit me. Those footprints were smoking, little wisps rising up from them.

"Mr. Ash, go out the cellar door, don't come up here!" The fumes were *intense;* the skin on my face began stinging.

"Sheesh." I hotfooted it onto the porch and leaned against it gasping while Ellie hurried to let the animals out of the ell. Monday gamboled on the grass as Cat Dancing turned her crossed eyes balefully toward the bird feeder.

"Key-riminy," Mr. Ash expostulated, emerging from the Bilco door of the cellar into the backyard, "what're you women up to, mustard gas production? A fella could have his lungs burned out in that house."

Apologetically I explained the mishap. "We ended up needing to use much more of the stuff than we planned," I finished. "I'm so sorry. Did you breathe much of it in? Are you all right?"

"I b'lieve I'll survive. Substance got the better of you, did it? I c'n understand that. Why, I remember one time I . . ."

Suddenly he stopped, seeming to think better of telling this story.

"Anyway. Everything all right inside? Don't have any birds in cages going to suffercate, no burners left on, or any pilot lights?"

"I don't think so." A school bus rumbled up Key Street. A sweeper truck motored the other direction, its brushes whisking up the last tan swathes of sand that had been spread when the streets were icy-slick, during the previous winter. A boy on a bike blithely hurled rolled newspapers, pedaling dreamily.

Mr. Ash raised a bushy white eyebrow. "Could'a been worse, then. You could've decided to skip the stripper and use blowtorches."

I decided not to tell him that had been my fallback plan. A few birds twittered sleepily in the bushes edging the lawn, mist drifting among them like smoke. In the fog they couldn't even find the bird feeder; tail twitching, Cat Dancing stalked up the steps with a mutter of bird-deprived frustration.

"Fumes from that stuff sinks, y'know. Flows downhill. But it'll clear quick," Mr. Ash told me. "I turned off the furnace and yanked the cellar windows before I vamoosed. Kill any varmints're down there, for sure."

Including any spiders Wade might have missed capturing. Good, I thought, but it was the only good thing I could think of.

"Do you want to take the rest of the morning off?" I asked. "I won't mind if you do, after we nearly gassed you to death."

Now that he was here, the night before felt even goofier. I wondered again what that grammar textbook was about. But all he'd really done was say he'd come from Portland instead of Machias, and that he'd arrived a little more recently than he really had.

Was he embarrassed about needing a boardinghouse room, and Mrs. Sprague's help to get on his feet again? Maybe the jail time was more recent than he'd let on, or he'd had a booze slip he was ashamed of. There could be lots of reasons, all harmless. And as Tim had gently suggested, none of them were even a little bit any of my business.

"You two go on down to the diner for coffee or some such while you wait for the house to air out," he instructed us.

He looked around. "I'll stay, keep an eye on the critters." As if to second this motion Monday pranced up; he leaned to pat her glossy head. "Shake, girl."

Monday gazed at Mr. Ash for a long moment, then lifted her paw and deposited it in his hand as I stared in astonishment. She was a wonderful dog but she could no more do tricks, even simple ones, than I could jump off a building and fly.

Until now. Abruptly, I came to my final decision: not to confront Lian Ash about the books or anything else. He was working on my cellar, not marrying into my family; whatever questions his past might've held, the answers could remain there, too.

"We'll stay," Mr. Ash amended as Ellie came up behind us. "Me and the critters'll hold down the fort." I had the odd feeling that if he'd known about my snooping he might not have minded, that he'd have understood my reason and sympathized.

Still, I hoped he wouldn't find out. "Got work to do," Lian Ash said peaceably. "I like work. Always have."

He looked at Ellie and me, his mild, utterly benevolent gaze as unreadable as the drifting fog.

"And," he added, "I like it here."

Five minutes later Ellie and I slid into a booth at the Waco Diner: smells of coffee, hash, bacon, and eggs, amplified by heat from the energetically hissing radiators. Red leather stools at the counter were occupied by burly men in coveralls, sweatshirts, and rubber boots, devouring their morning meals.

Chilled by the fog, I shivered gratefully in the warmth of the booth. Ellie looked refreshed, her eyes glowing with renewed energy. But Ellie grew up here, where people wear T-shirts on the first day of spring no matter how hard it is snowing.

And *there* was a bad thought: What if the storm didn't come as rain? What if it came as . . .

"Snow," Edna Barclay predicted dourly, setting mugs in front of us. "I've seen snow in Eastport in every month but August."

Eastpawt. Edna's hair this week was a particularly vivid electric blue-white, her bracelets jangling, her eyes ringed with mascara, and her lipstick vivid.

"Nah," one of the men at the counter contradicted her. "Wind out of the south, gonna swing around. You wait, that sucker hits outta the northeast? Man, she's gonna *blow.*"

"We'll see," Edna muttered darkly. After thirty years at the Waco she still believed she might be discovered and wafted off to her rightful place in Hollywood, in the pantheon of the stars.

But not today. "Video's done for," she announced gloomily. "Boys over to the boat school heard McCall's lost his financing," she added, and went back behind the counter.

"There goes my paying guest," I moaned to Ellie. Roy McCall's presence had taken some of the sting out of the need for the new clapboards. But Ellie wasn't listening.

"That's why," she murmured.

"That's why *what?*" I swallowed hot coffee. Fog off the water applies itself from the outside but chills from within.

"Why we *can't* let Harry Markle leave."

"Ellie, *what* are you talking about?"

Edna glanced over curiously at me.

"Look," I went on more quietly, "I do owe Harry and I am going to try to help him, or I won't be able to look at myself in the mirror. The thing is . . ."

Behind the counter, Edna raised her hand casually to one of the tight, blue-white curls just above her left ear, which I knew was the location of her hearing aid.

111

I hastily dropped my voice to a whisper. "I'm convinced, okay? Harry *is* the reason Sam got hurt. Wade, too, and probably Samantha. I don't understand how, but I do know one thing. If Harry changed his mind again and decided to leave town, all this—whatever *this* is—would be over just as quick as it started. And things would go back to normal. Safe. End of story."

There, I'd said it. But Ellie was shaking her head. "No, Jake. That's not what would happen at all. Remember what Mr. Ash said?"

"What's he got to do with anything?" She always did this: picked up some little detail, then drew out a string of reasoning as if she were pulling a loose thread.

Even more annoying was the fact that, usually, she was right. "Okay, it's been a year now since Harry left New York," she said.

"Correct. He moved around the Northeast a little, made one brief visit back to the city, ended up here." Our Internet research confirmed it via his credit cards; I may not be a hot-shot money person anymore but I can still get in the back doors of some nifty databases.

"And as far as we know, nothing's happened since then," she persisted. "Since he left New York the first time. Until now, here in Eastport."

Right again. "But maybe Harry didn't stay anywhere long enough to get it all going again until now."

"But he hasn't stayed very long here, either, has he?"

Like I said; annoying. And persistent:

"What *I* think is, Harry was right. Someone *knew* he'd stay in town. After all, if Harriet's involved, the trouble began weeks ago," Ellie said.

"And she is involved. Otherwise why that newspaper in her hand, with the story about Harry? But how would someone know . . . ?"

"That Harry was staying? Maybe because if you buy a house in a place, it's a pretty good bet you're planning to stick around?" Ellie replied.

Another thought hit her. "Jake, we don't even know for sure the nature guy isn't part of it, too. The one who drowned, from Wyatt Evert's group."

"Oh, Ellie, that's really . . ."

Pushing it, I'd been about to say. But then George Valentine came in and spotted us, and came over to our booth.

"What are you doing here?" I asked, alarmed. "I thought you were with Sam and Maggie, at the hospital. And who's watching out for Wade?"

George put a hand on my shoulder, slapped a copy of the *Bargain News* against his leg with the other. He was always on the prowl for old engine parts and tools. "Took Sam home, Maggie over to her house. Set a fan up in the hall, paint thinner stink's nearly out. And Wade gets *really* mean when he's in pain, did you know that?"

Wade wouldn't get mean if his leg was in a bear trap. "Just kidding," George added. "But he said he's coming home, don't need a baby-sitter, and did I want my nose punched? So I took off."

I gathered Wade was getting his gumption back. "And I didn't walk in your varnish-stripping project or let the animals in, and Mr. Ash is with Sam," George finished.

He bent to kiss the top of Ellie's head. "Hey."

"Hey yourself." She preened unconsciously; Ellie in love was like roses in bloom, or Paris in springtime. She'd resisted George's courtship for longer than was good for either of them but now his mere presence made everything hunky-dory for her.

"I was just about to tell Jake about the nature guy's boots. Is it okay?" she asked.

Over behind the counter Edna Barclay fiddled madly with the hearing aid, not even bothering to hide it. The guys eating their pie were listening, too, their talk of boats, the forecast storm, and the fishing regulations newly publicized in the Maine *Record* ominously silenced.

And by the look on George's face, Ellie's question had hit a nerve. "Funny you should mention that," he said. "Come on."

We followed him out past Edna's thwarted scowl into the fog. In the few minutes we'd been inside, the weather boom had lowered. You couldn't even see the end of the fishing pier except for the dim glow of the beacons on the tugboats lurking massively in the gloom, headlights on passing cars blurry smears in the murk and foghorns bow-*whonk!*'ing lustily.

"I've been thinking about that all night," George began as soon as we'd lost our audience. "Because at the time we didn't want to get stories started. And Bob Arnold agreed there was nothing solid, nothing to follow up on. But . . ."

"George," I demanded, "*what* are you talking about?"

"That tourist's boots," Ellie replied. "George happened to see them, thought there was something funny about them, back when it happened. After the man drowned."

"The tourist from Wyatt's group?"

"Ayuh. But Arnold said if he tried getting the state cops in on it, they'd just laugh," George continued.

"So you talked to Wyatt?" Of course he had. George would hop over and have a word with Satan, if he felt the situation called for it. And by the look he wore now, the conversation with Wyatt had come out just about the same way.

"I told him, Wyatt, those boots that guy was wearing looked kind of fiddled with. And Wyatt, he near to had a stroke. He said if I ever said anything like that to anybody else, it'd hurt his tourist business and he would sue me, make me pay big-time."

"To which I said, so what if he sues?" Ellie put in stoutly.

"But Ellie," he reminded her, "we talked about it. I don't know what's true. And if it came to a lawsuit over it, you got to defend against those things, y'know, or the other guy wins."

"He does if it's not a frivolous lawsuit," I agreed, "and it could cost thousands to defend. And you could lose, especially if Bob had to testify that there wasn't evidence enough for him to pursue it. If

Wyatt could prove he had real material losses, you might have to pay. But . . ."

Wyatt Evert's tourist-herding business had never made much sense to me; he didn't like people enough to be around them so much. But if it was a way to line rich suckers up for donations to some phony non-profit, as Tim Rutherford had begun suggesting the night before, it made more sense.

In that case he certainly wouldn't want a client's death investigated as a murder. But his business records wouldn't take the examination that bringing a lawsuit would require, either. So . . .

"He was probably just blowing smoke," I concluded. "Worst case, you'd end up settling out of court."

George nodded miserably. "We'd be ruined before it even got that far. So we thought, nothing we can do about it, we'll keep our mouths shut. Not tell anyone. Three of us," he said, glancing at Ellie. "Us and Bob Arnold. Just go on like nothing happened."

Which maybe nothing had, though Ellie's face said it had about half-killed her not to try finding out. But she was like the grave with secrets, and keeping shut of a Wyatt Evert lawsuit was a motive I could definitely get on board with.

It didn't surprise me, either, that George and Ellie had decided to tell me about it at practically the same moment. Some couples seem to be joined at the hip; with these two, it was more like the frontal lobe.

"So what was it about the boots that looked strange to you?" I asked as an eighteen-wheeler rumbled past, headed for the quonsets at the freight dock.

"They were all chewed. Shredded like some chemical had been eating at the bottoms," George answered when the noise had faded.

"Corrosive chemicals? Like paint stripper, or . . ."

"Ayuh." He nodded seriously. "What made me think of it was, my old man had a shoe repair shop. Back in that alley," he aimed a finger up Water Street, "behind the furniture store."

A fading arrow painted on the red bricks still pointed up the alley. "Last few years the old man'd lost his concentration," George said. "Still tried to work, but he mixed up things."

He put an arm around Ellie's shoulders. "Story about the Moosehorn accident was, guy just had a lousy pair of boots. The public story. But Wyatt's nature folks don't buy lousy gear."

He frowned some more. "Only other time I ever saw boots half as wrecked, my old man tried resoling a pair, used triple-strong solvent, 'stead o' glue."

"You mean maybe somebody could've sabotaged the boots?"

It was a fairly uncertain method. Unlike, say, rigging a hot wire to be touched by a person standing in water. But if you were to time it right, I supposed it could be effective.

"Yep. Deep marsh, loss of footing, boots filling up with water. It would be easy to drown," George replied. "Bob Arnold said so, too. But where the hell is any motive?"

We crossed the street together. "That's what we decided to think at the time, anyway," George went on. "And they *were* old boots. Good an' broken in, the kind a guy likes to wear. Even a quality pair, sooner or later they *will* come apart, you wear 'em long enough."

"Sure." Like George's truck; the wheel hadn't just come off. It had rolled off, despite his regular maintenance, while he was driving the thing. He could have been killed.

And if pulled on an inexperienced person, the boot trick could be deadly, too. The thought came again: The simplest answer is usually correct. But at the moment no explanations I could think of for any of this were simple.

We started home, past the old clapboard houses like white faces peering at us through the fog. "Where are the boots now?"

George shook his head regretfully. "Tossed out, I guess. No reason to keep them. Like I say, nothing else suspicious. Far as I know, the guy didn't even know any other group members, 'fore he arrived. Or Wyatt, either. From New York, the guy was."

And of course it was unlikely that a casual tourist had made a mortal enemy, in town or among the other members of his group, in only a few days. "So the state sent an investigator . . ."

They always did, for an unexplained death. "Stayed an hour. Wrote it up as an accident just like Bob said he would," George replied.

"Wouldn't the guy notice when he put them on? The boots?"

He shook his head. "They went out before dawn. You put your shoes on in the dark, do you stop to check the undersides?"

"No. No, I don't."

"Prob'ly didn't really come apart till the water hit them," George said. Ahead an old truck materialized from the mist in my driveway, reminding me of another thing.

"Ellie, what were you saying about Mr. Ash?"

"That he said he liked it here," she replied slowly.

"So?" My house came into view: green shutters, red chimneys. A pane in one of the dining room windows needed replacing.

"So *when* he said it, I was wondering *why* all Harry's trouble is starting again just now," Ellie continued. "After so long."

"Maybe it took a year for someone to find him?"

But Ellie rejected that idea, too. From the cellar came the regular *clang-thud* of stones being pried out with a crowbar.

"Jake, you're not the only one who can follow a credit card trail. Harry shouldn't have been that hard to find. I think it's more like what Mr. Ash told us. Maybe some real motive got it all started in the first place. But now something's changed."

Inside, the chemical smell was just a faint acrid presence, not the throat-closing poison cloud it had been earlier. George's fan whirred efficiently in the open front door. "Sam?" I called, and his reply came promptly from the parlor.

117

By contrast, the silence from Wade's workshop was deafening. I closed my ears to it, telling myself it was no worse than if he were out on a boat. Through the kitchen windows I spotted Monday outside with George, Mr. Ash joining them after a moment.

"Harry's leaving wouldn't stop it," Ellie went on. "Mr. Ash made me see it; what he said about enjoying his work. And—"

She turned to me. "Somebody likes all this, Jake."

Harriet, Samantha, and now the nature tourist, maybe. All dead, Sam and Wade lucky not to be. I was lucky, too.

So far.

"The fear, the confusion."

Her tone sent a renewed chill through me.

"And," she finished somberly, "somebody likes it *here.*"

Chapter 6

W hen Ellie and George had gone I found Sam in the parlor. His chest was sore, his arm in a sling to keep his collarbone from moving, but he was cheerful.

Almost *too* cheerful: "Mom," he enthused from in front of the TV. "Mr. Ash is cool. He knows about dynamite!"

Right. I already knew that. "Great," I replied, but my lack of enthusiasm had little to do with Mr. Ash.

Now that Sam was home, I would have to start trying not to think about the seminar he had lined up for that weekend, the one on the theory and practice of safe, effective underwater demolition.

"Because sometimes you need to get rid of something in the water," he'd explained. "A wreck, a ruined wharf. So . . . bang!"

Wonderful. I'd never told him much past the bare facts about my own personal history in the bang! department. I hadn't wanted him to develop phobias. And now look what I'd done:

"Mr. Ash says if you know how to do it, you can blow one bad brick out of a chimney and replace it without having to take the whole chimney down," Sam reported.

"Terrific," I responded.

The seminar was four days off; clearly, Sam would be well enough to go. Ruffling his hair, I walked away from him; he hated being fussed over and at the moment, his weekend plans were even less cheering to me than they'd been.

Besides, I had a chore to perform: reluctantly, I hoped even foolishly. But after checking that Mr. Ash was still out with the dog, I left Sam flipping the TV remote and went to the cellar.

The steps, steep and narrow, curved down to a dirt-floored chamber. Large and low-ceilinged, with massive adze-marked beams crisscrossing overhead, it stretched away to cobwebby corners, shadowy stone niches, and rooms full of shelves loaded with old canning jars, their glass gone bluish over the years.

Piles of rubble marked where Mr. Ash had been working, floor jacks set up to stand in for the missing foundation section. Big stones lay on the floor, chunks of ancient mortar still clinging to them; in the earth where they had been, thick white tree roots coiled forlornly like the fingers of a long-buried corpse.

Chill damp air blew in through the hole in the stone wall under the ell, another long section removed there since I'd found the break in it. Mr. Ash hadn't wasted any time opening it up, I thought distractedly. And the hole was huge; any bigger and the mason could drive his truck down here, to haul the old stones out. But that wasn't my problem right now:

In a rafter at the opposite end of the cellar hung the lockbox where I kept a handgun and the ammunition for it. The Bisley .45 was a six-shot revolver, an Italian-made reproduction of the weapon the lawmen used to bring order to the Old West. Unlocking the box, I removed the ammunition box and the weapon itself; in a pinch I could use it to establish some order around here, too.

Soon after I met Wade, he taught me to put six shots in a six-inch target circle, so I had little fear and no ignorance of the handgun's power. What I did fear was what I was admitting by getting the gun out at all. There in the quiet cellar it was easy to believe that my growing sense of the other shoe getting ready to drop was an illusion.

But Ellie's comment had spooked me more than I wanted to admit, even to myself. In the next instant a new sound from upstairs made me claw open the ammunition box, pop the cylinder, drop the projectiles into the slots with cold, unnaturally steady hands.

"Jake? You down there?" The cellar door creaked open. I fingered the trigger.

It was Bob Arnold. Breath rushed out past my pounding heart. "You scared the wits out of me."

"Yeah, yeah. Come on up here, will you?"

I locked the rest of the ammunition up, mounted the stairs.

"I saw no reason to pass this on earlier," Bob began. "But with what happened to Wade, and finding Harriet with that paper . . ." He sighed. "Well, it's made me think again."

"About?" The Bisley's weight felt reassuring. When your pocket contains enough stopping power to drop an elk it eases your mind somewhat about the possibility of the elk showing up.

"What happened in New York City," Bob said. "When the guy killed Harry Markle's wife and girlfriend. You knew about that?"

The girlfriend part, he meant. "I knew."

He swallowed some coffee he'd poured for himself, set the cup on the old red-checked tablecloth. Out the window past him I saw Monday duck into a play posture, then sprint to chase something that Mr. Ash had thrown for her.

"Story I got," Bob said, "Harry was in a bad spot. Wife an invalid, had been for years. Bedridden in a nursing home. Harry stuck by her. Living alone and doing for himself. Pretty much all he did was visit her, and work."

Work on trying to find my father, for instance. And on not turning innocent bystanders into collateral damage.

"But then," Bob said, "something happened. Harry met a gal who was on the job, like he was. Someone he could talk to. And—"

"Yeah. And. So she was the girlfriend?"

In the parlor, Sam had discovered *Night of the Living Dead* on Turner Classics. From the sound of it, a passel of zombies had just broken down a door.

"Bob, what are you getting at? What difference does it make if Harry had a girlfriend?"

I had a long day ahead. And then there would be the evening; for an instant I wished I had the big Doberman back from Harry. Prill was a cream puff, but just the sight of her would turn back zombies.

"The difference is," Bob answered, "it was worse than whatever Harry told you. Whoever the guy is who was doing this stuff, he didn't just want to *kill* people. He wanted to *hurt* them. So what he did was, over a period of weeks he photographed Harry with his girlfriend, on the sly. Then he killed the girlfriend."

"Right, I know that part. But what does that have to do with what he— Oh." Screams from the television. "Photographs."

Bob nodded somberly. "The wife was a physical wreck, but she could see and hear. She could understand. And until then, she did not know there was anybody else. So this son of a bitch"—his voice hardened at the thought—"he sneaks into the nursing home."

A sick feeling invaded my stomach. "You're kidding. He shows her pictures of Harry and another woman, before he kills her?"

Bob looked at the floor. "Ayuh. Left the photos, so that's what they figured."

It was so fiendish, neither of us could speak for a minute after that. Then:

"Jake?" Bob stared pointedly at my sweater pocket. The sag didn't look like anything but what it was: a cannon.

And Bob disapproved of my going around with it. As he said, it doesn't matter what targets you shoot. If you've never faced down a person with your weapon, you can't know what you'll do.

"Yeah," I confirmed, bracing for the lecture. But it didn't come; I got the feeling I could have set up rocket launchers in the windows and he wouldn't have made a peep.

Which meant Bob was convinced too, now, that Harry's paranoia wasn't mere smoke and moonbeams. But:

"Told the state cops all this," he said. "But they're not exactly speed demons, you know. Their job is finding things they can prove in court."

Meaning it could be some while before they had answers: on Harriet's death, or Samantha's murder. The state police worked on lab results and sworn testimony, evidentiary links that took time and legwork to assemble. And time was a thing I was starting to worry we might not have.

"I guess you'll be around here the rest of the day?" Bob said, gesturing at the hall.

The stripper on the varnish had bubbled up loathsomely. All it needed were demons scampering over it with pitchforks to make it resemble one of the more disgusting departments of hell.

"Yep." I moved with him toward the door. Outside, his squad idled, so I knew better than to detain him with more questions.

And I didn't want to bring Wyatt Evert into it just yet. His threats of a lawsuit were still viable and I was reluctant to put George and Ellie at even the slightest risk.

"Got to talk to some reporters," Bob said. Roy's interviews had alerted the other major media to our trouble, I guessed. "And to the coroner."

The one handling Samantha's death and Harriet's. Bob hustled down the steps as I went back in, musing over his visit. He was in a rush, but he had stopped by anyway to give me a message, the only bulletin he thought I needed.

If I hadn't already gotten the Bisley out, he'd have suggested it.

Unwilling to leave Sam, I spent the afternoon on my hands and knees, scraping up chemical goo and the varnish the goo had lifted. And as usual, old-house fix-up freed my brain to go off on its own, to ruminate.

Chewing over the details of recent events didn't nourish any brilliant ideas, though. I slid the scraper under another glob of stripper and lifted it up, wiping it on a rag. The exposed wood beneath, smeared with remnants of varnish, resembled a face, but I couldn't make out whose.

All I did know was that three other strangers had come to town when Harry had: Wyatt Evert, who perhaps didn't qualify as a complete stranger but was still plenty strange; his assistant, Fran Hanson, whose smart city looks didn't jibe with her silent passivity; and my guest Roy McCall, whose sweet, youthful buddy act I was beginning to think had a couple of cracks in it.

On TV the night before he'd actually shed tears, but he couldn't quite hide his gratification at being in the spotlight. *Me,* his eyes had shone legibly. They're looking at *me!*

But what link had any of them had to Harriet Hollingsworth *or* Harry Markle? And what might some tourist's boots have to do with it? Maybe someone else also belonged on my list of interesting people. Or maybe . . .

But that second "maybe" I shoved savagely to the back of my mind, just as I'd been doing since Harry Markle first brought it up, the night of Sam's crash. *I know about your father . . .*

Pushing the scraper under a stubborn lump of gunk, I went on scraping the smelly stuff messily off the floor. Physical labor, the more mindless the better, was a refuge I'd learned to escape into deliberately since moving to an old house. And I'm not sure if it was the hard work or the faintly dizzying effect of fume remnants rising off the floor, but by about three-thirty when the telephone rang, my mood had improved.

In the next moment it improved even more. "Your ex-husband," Wade announced cheerfully, "is a power-mad weasel with a Napoleon complex."

I laughed aloud. It felt wonderful, and so did hearing Wade's voice without a sedative blur in it; my own pains had gone down to minor-annoyance status, only the purpling around my eye reminding me that I'd been injured. I attributed the persistent ringing in my ears to the aftereffects of the floor chemicals.

"So you're not coming home today?" I'd been putting off the trip until I knew; if Wade was going to be here, there was no reason to go there.

"A power-mad, *vindictive* little weasel," he emphasized.

A load of worry slid off my shoulders. "I feel fine," Wade confirmed. "But Victor says I need to stay here a little longer. He says he needs to *observe* me."

Personally I thought another night in the hospital was wise, much as I wished the opposite. That neck wound had looked wicked.

"But what's he going to observe?" Wade complained. "Suppose he's still trying to figure out how to be a human being?"

"If he is," I replied warmly, "he couldn't have any better role model. But one more night isn't so terrible."

Wade spent lots of nights away, harbor-piloting. So we were used to it. "Yeah. Too foggy to drive anyway," he conceded.

Route 1 in a fog is so bad that you don't dare go too fast because you can't see, and you don't dare go too slow because the eighteen-wheeler roaring up behind can't see either, and he might put his hood ornament up your tailpipe.

"Right." For his trip home tomorrow, Wade asked for clean clothes, his own razor, and his belt with the big silver anchor buckle on it, all of which reassured me even more; when he feels well, he is particular about his dress and grooming.

Then we hung up and I finished the floor, a job that took me right up until it was time to take a shower and make supper. Sam and I ate on trays in front of the TV, and after I'd stacked the dishes we sat together watching *The Blair Witch Project.*

"Mom," my son said quietly after a while. "I am still going, you know. To the demolition seminar."

He pretended to be watching the screen. I suppose he thought if he confronted me too hard, I might confront back. "I know."

But I'd been thinking about this, too. "I imagined you would. And if you think it's important, you *should* go."

It was the one thing Victor ever told me that turned out to be worthwhile: I'd been dithering about the training wheels on Sam's bike, insisting they should stay on. And I can still feel Victor's hands on my shoulders as Sam pedaled wobblingly away.

"Let him go, Jake. You've got to *let him go.*"

Besides, setting bombs off underwater was starting to look safer than hanging around here. Now, with a possible contretemps averted, Sam settled into his nest of pillows on the sofa. His new wristwatch said it was 2030 hours.

After a while: "Sam," I ventured. "About Maggie."

I wanted to tell him to look over his shoulder, that someone was gaining on him; if not Tim Rutherford, then someone else. But if things turned out wrong, I didn't want it to be on account of my meddling. So all I said was, "She's not going to be happy playing word games forever, you know."

"Yeah." Eyes on screen, avoiding mine. He knew the gist of my thought if not the details; we'd talked about this before. "I know, Mom. And it's not that I don't love her."

126

On the TV, a crew of youngsters sallied forth into a haunted woods. "But every time I get close, it's like it's too close, and then I've got to push her away, sort of."

The youngsters had video cameras, their generation's method of keeping things under control. That the control was illusory they had yet to learn; thus the plot of *The Blair Witch Project.*

"Or?" I probed. On the TV screen, a girl told the rest that she knew the way through the forest. Famous last words.

"Dad says don't give yourself away," Sam responded. "You might want yourself back."

Sudden fury at my ex-husband threatened to consume me, turn me to ash right there in my chair. But I controlled it; Victor is Sam's father and Sam has worked to keep, as Sam puts it, a decent scene going with him.

"I see," I replied carefully. Back when I was married to Victor, I used to believe there was a magic word, and if I could only think of it and say it, everything would be all right. I guess in the end the other thing Victor taught me is that there is no magic word.

And I guess I have never forgiven him for it. "Sam. I'm not trying to rush you. Maybe Maggie just isn't the one for you. And you're young, you don't need to—"

His eyes glazed; I was turning into Lecture-Mom. On the TV, tiny stick figures dangled hideously from haunted tree branches, and looking at Sam's face I knew just how the stick figures felt: dry and vaguely threatening. Still, I had to say it.

"But if when you're ready, you make your choice wisely," I finished, "then not being able to get yourself back is what you want to have happen." Like George and Ellie. Or Wade and me, as different from one another as floor varnish is from floors, and in all the important ways as near-inseparable.

A beat, while Sam absorbed this. "Yeah, huh?" Then:

"Mom? Do you hate him? I mean, after everything that happened between you and Dad, do you, like, wish he was dead?"

"Sometimes," I replied jokingly. But then I stopped, because the answer to his question was no joke. Not to me:

When Sam was a toddler, he fell and smashed his forehead on the corner of a coffee table. Blood was everywhere and he was howling as if his eye had been put out. And of course I couldn't *see* that his eye hadn't been put out, because blood was . . .

Well, you get the idea. Victor scooped him up, thrust his head under running water, snapped out a diagnosis—scalp wound, superficial— and had Sam's head shaved, the split closed with butterfly bandages, and a big smile back on the kid's face before I could even finish having my acute nervous breakdown.

The next night, Victor took a surgical nurse to a ball game at Yankee Stadium. Bottom of the fifth, two on and two out, I was watching it on TV when I saw them sitting behind home plate. I threw the coffee table off our balcony. Fortunately, I didn't kill anyone in the courtyard of our apartment building.

"No, Sam," I answered now. "I don't hate your dad. And I don't wish him dead, either. That's in the past."

"And the past is provolone," he murmured drowsily.

He meant prologue. It's the dyslexia-thing; when he's tired, sick, or stressed, it pops out in his speech.

On the TV an ancient curse came back to life, wanting new victims. "Provolone," I agreed softly. It was better than the alternative and anyway, he was asleep.

Outside fog billowed morosely, mounds of it lumbering like huge animals in the dark, empty streets. Ellie called to see that I was all right, and Wade called again.

But finally I was alone, Monday snoring while the TV showed *Mars Attacks!* I turned the sound down, oddly comforted by the special-effects TV aliens with their jerky, aggressive movements and ridiculously exaggerated facial features. At least on TV, you could see right away who the villains were.

But when you've seen one alien's day-glo head explode you've seen them all. So at length I went to the back parlor and sat at Sam's computer. There in the bluish glimmer of the screen, with the Bisley in my sweater pocket, I fired up the e-mail software and tried to think of what to say to my old friend, Jemmy Wechsler.

I had no notion of Jemmy's location, nor did anyone else; it was why somewhere he sat at his computer tonight, too, instead of reposing in an oil drum at the bottom of the East River. To me he was just a collection of pixels, now, my memories of him—

—snatching me off the street when the numbers-running gig turned into a death trap due to a feud between two hard guys with me as the stalking goat; getting me into the dormitory, safe and quiet, of a Dominican girls' school, and later into the school itself—

—by turns funny and sad. Jemmy made those killers look like a collection of B-movie extras; he was the real thing, which was how he had survived. Even I couldn't have found him, which was well-known and why no one showed up to put bull's-eyes on my kneecaps about it.

But I had an e-mail drop for him. Now I waited for high-tech relays to bounce my message to him via the equivalent of some mad scientist's Rube Goldberg apparatus, so the message and his reply couldn't be traced. The latter arrived quickly.

Although when I read it there was a moment when I profoundly wished it hadn't arrived. Short and sweet, it made no specific reference to the names I'd listed: Harry Markle, Roy McCall, Fran Hanson, and Wyatt Evert. Instead, it said:

"If you think there's a target on your back there probably is."

Outside, the foghorns' honking grew louder as the wee hours approached. I read the message again, my thoughts wandering to the scrapbook I'd kept for a while on my parents' deaths: tabloid newspaper clips, mostly. Among the many details about my father, my mother seemed to disappear. But he was the one who had vanished: blown to bits, his body consumed by the fire.

Or so the investigators said when I'd tried to learn exactly what happened. Over the years, though: a few unsigned cards, each mailed from a different city. A hundred bucks in an envelope once when I was living on ketchup soup.

Nothing more. But now I knew the investigators had been lying in case I was in touch with him and might tip him off.

Are you alive? I wondered again as I pondered Jemmy's note. *Are you?* But to that message, there came no reply at all.

I got up to check again that the house doors were locked. Trust Jemmy to come out swinging the big anxiety stick. He used to say nerves were God's way of putting eyes in the back of your head. Maybe that was why I saw it. *Something . . .*

Gripping the Bisley, I rushed to the kitchen in time to catch another glimpse of someone's hasty departure. The screen door slammed behind it as Monday scrambled in, barking. A shape darted past the window, vanished in the fog as I snapped the light on.

Sam appeared, puffy-eyed, Cat Dancing twining around his ankles. "What happened?" He squinted owlishly at the clock. "It's two in the morning."

On the table lay a knife clotted with red. Under it was a sheet of paper. Two words were scrawled crimsonly on it: HA HA.

When the sound came from the porch I was in firing stance in a heartbeat: feet braced, body relaxed, my head full of the clear unshakable notion that this had better not be a midnight-riding contingent of religious persons bent on converting me. I was about to convert something too: to smithereens. "Sam, back away."

When you opened that porch door from inside, as the intruder had in order to exit, the lock stayed open until it was locked deliberately again. So it was open now. And in about two seconds, I was going to turn whatever came through it into so many pieces that even Victor wouldn't be able to reassemble them.

But I didn't, because it was Harry Markle.

I lowered the gun, let my breath out as he spread his hands help-lessly. I had to give him credit; at the sight of the Bisley he hadn't even flinched.

"Harry, what the *hell* are you doing here?"

"Couldn't sleep. Thinking. Decided to take a walk, clear my head," he said.

"And?" Even in Eastport, people out on walks don't generally just stroll in my back door at two A.M.

"I saw someone. From the corner I saw someone come out and run around behind your house. It looked suspicious. So I ran too, trying to head them off."

Monday sniffed him interestedly. Harry said, "Whoever it was got away in the fog. Chased 'em to the corner but after that, it was no good. You can't see ten feet."

I sighed and dropped the Bisley back in my sweater pocket. Like Harry, Sam hadn't turned a hair at the sight of the weapon, which made me think my thumbs weren't the only ones prickling tonight.

"That stuff." I waved at the knife and the red-smeared missive on the table. "If we slide it into a plastic bag we can preserve whatever might be on it, give it to Bob Arnold in the morning."

Harry scowled. "You mean you're not going to call him now?"

"No," I retorted in exasperation. "What's Bob going to do, drive around in this pea soup looking for somebody when we don't even have a description?" I opened a plastic bag, sliding the bag's edge under the knife before lifting it and sealing it. If Harry had tried to give in-structions, I'd probably have smacked him.

But he didn't. I put the bag in the vegetable crisper next to a white carton marked in Wade's handwriting: *Fishing Worms! Do Not Open!!!* Then I slammed the refrigerator door, to give feeble emphasis to the notion that I was the one giving the instructions tonight.

"Right now," I went on, "*you* should go to bed." I pointed to Sam, who, for a wonder, turned away obediently.

"And *you* should go home before some other nervous housewife really does blow your head off," I told Harry.

Tomorrow when it was light, we would talk all this over with Bob. But at present I was battening down the hatches; don't let the aft one hit you in the backside on your way out.

"All right," Harry said, with unconcealed reluctance. "But I'm going to look around some more. Maybe it *is* a waste of time, but maybe it's not."

He looked so troubled that I relented: "Okay. Thanks, Harry. We'll see you tomorrow, then."

"Yeah." Brief, sad grin. Outside, his shape blurred, vanished into the streaming darkness.

After that there was silence, way too much of it after Sam had gone to bed; when the animals followed me upstairs I was glad for their company. As Ellie always says, It's not the ghosts in the house that'll get you, it's the ghosts in your head. And that night my head was full of apparitions shaped like question marks.

I laid the Bisley on the bedside table by the phone with the caller ID box perched atop it. The box had originally been Wade's idea; he liked to know who was calling, especially at night when it might be somebody from down at the freighter terminal. He said it helped him work on a fast answer if he knew in advance who was going to be at the other end, asking the question.

Now I closed my eyes to the ready-light on the box. I needed sleep. My face ached and my ears rang in the silence. But with the light off I kept seeing Jemmy's message, and the note:

HA HA. Which was probably why, lying there in the dark, I remembered one of the first things Jemmy ever taught me, back in the days when I still thought Jemmy pretty much walked on water.

He'd been teaching me to play poker, the kind with big-money stakes that other people conspire at, ganging up on an unwary new player to raise their own haul. The victim in that game, or in any con, actually, is called the pigeon. And what Jemmy said was that if you're sitting at a poker table wondering who the pigeon is, the pigeon is you.

Ordinarily I wouldn't have found this realization the least bit pleasant. But it helped me keep my head a little later, when the phone rang and a voice told me that Wade Sorenson had just died unexpectedly in Calais Hospital.

The numerals on the caller ID were glowing redly at me and I was still thinking of what Jemmy had said: *Don't be a pigeon.* Which was how it came to me so fast, that the dialing exchange on the ID box didn't belong to Calais Hospital at all.

In fact I happened to know, having had a teenaged son for what felt like all of my own life plus several other similarly eventful lives, that the number belonged to the pay phone on the breakwater across from Rosie's hot dog stand. Sam used to call me from there if he wanted to stay out later than we'd agreed.

Now, if the fog weren't socked in so thickly I could look out the window and almost see . . .

"Who is this?" I demanded.

But the merry prankster had hung up.

Some of the things Wade does for me are obvious, like those gutters. And others aren't. For instance:

Immediately after the prank call, I phoned Calais Hospital to make sure Wade really was okay, and he was. But that wasn't enough; I wanted him *home*. So the next morning, I hotfooted it out to Wade's truck as soon as Mr. Ash had arrived, and headed for the hospital. On Route 1 the fog had begun clearing as the wind shifted, branches overhanging the road shaking droplets onto the windshield.

George, who despite Wade's impatience had returned to guard duty, looked up from his coffee and *Bangor Daily News* as I hurried down the hospital corridor toward him.

"Ayuh," he agreed when I told him I needed him at home, and that Wade and I would be there soon. In his room, Wade took one look at my face and swung his legs out of bed. Gangway, his own look said.

"You realize," Victor intoned lugubriously as a nurse gave instructions on how to care for Wade's surgical dressing, "that this is against my advice."

But he'd already had the "one more night" he'd insisted on. Besides, if I'd spent my life worrying about Victor's advice, I would be a rich, bitter New York fashionista by now, wielding my smile like a straight razor across a table at the Russian Tea Room, drinking vodka stingers and commiserating with the other ex-wives on the affront of having been replaced by a trophy wife.

Fortunately I'd tumbled early on to the fact that Victor's ideal trophy wife is, among other things, inflatable.

"Shut up, Victor," I said pleasantly. "We're leaving."

The next time somebody called to say Wade was dead, I wanted to look confidently over at the next pillow, not check with a crew of nurses. In my previous life, I'd had enough of finding my husband by calling nurses.

"Oh, all right," Victor gave in petulantly. He'd been up all night himself with another patient, but his hair was combed, his jaw was shaven, and his long white coat seemed to have about a pound of laundry starch in it; Victor always looks as if he just popped out of a box marked: "Contents: One Surgeon."

"But don't blame me if the stitches let go and he bleeds out all over you," Victor fussed impotently.

I rounded on him. "Oh, yeah? Well get this, buddy: I'm going to blame you if he gets so much as a ragged hangnail. You just better hope those stitches you put in him are made of titanium." I zipped the duffel. "I blame you for everything, Victor. You know that. You made that bed and now you're sleeping in it."

Wade just buckled his anchor belt. Any other man would have cringed at the sound of his wife and her ex-husband still feuding like the Hatfields and the McCoys. But Wade goes through life so serenely you would think his nervous system was made of titanium, too.

"Do not," Victor snarled, "let him get the incision wet. And he should come in next week, get the stitches removed."

"Yes, sir. Anything you say, sir." I salaamed backwards away from him down the corridor. "Will there be anything else, sir?"

Yeah, it was childish. So sue me. But then I stopped, took a deep breath, and went back. "Victor."

He was at the nurses' station reading a chart. "I apologize," I said. "Thank you for everything you've done for Wade."

He put the chart down before replying. "You're welcome, Jacobia." Then, to my astonishment: "There's a job on that new medical boat. They want a trauma guy with general medical experience like mine."

"Really?" Victor on a big vessel was like me on a ladder but worse. "It sounds . . . exciting."

Actually, it sounded lethal. He liked small, fast boats, the kind that skim thrillingly over the wave tops but you can't tell that you're really on the water. The only other boat Victor ever went on was the Circle Line around Manhattan, and on that he got so seasick they had to re-hydrate him with IVs.

"Now that the Eastport clinic's up and running," he said, "they can get another doctor for it easily. And I need a change."

Right. Replacing all his DNA might do it, I thought meanly, then caught myself. "Well, they'd be lucky to get you. Let me know what you decide. Wade's outside." Waiting for me, I meant.

Victor nodded, looking as usual as distant and unreachable as the stars, and went back to the chart.

"So how's it going otherwise?" Wade asked a little later.

I laughed, but only to cover my renewed fury. He had already taken the dressing off and the wound was scary looking.

I wanted to put my hands on the throat of whoever had done this to him and squeeze. "The blood on the knife and the note was fake," I reported instead. I'd already told him about the prank call that had informed me of his death.

"That was obvious as soon as I examined them more closely," I went on tightly. After I'd called Calais Hospital, I'd called Bob Arnold, and he had been at my house minutes later.

I'd given Bob the note and knife, too, and he'd promised to hand them over to the state cops. But he didn't hold out much hope of them turning out to be useful. Or even of the staties believing they were linked to the murders at all. I'd only summoned Bob because I was so unnerved, not because I'd thought he could actually do anything.

"The note, the knife, *and* the call were only on the level of pranks," I added. "Mean ones, but not like what happened to you and Sam." Pranks, but they'd frightened me, as Wade could tell by the quaver in my voice. So I shut up and we rode along silently a while.

The sun climbed to our left over the hills of New Brunswick. The slopes were a hazy, ethereal greenish-gold. I accelerated up the curve by the St. Croix River, past the scenic turnout with its ornate sign directing attention to the island where in 1604, the French settlers tried spending the winter. There, they thought they'd be safe from attack by Native Americans, whom they dreaded.

They were safe, too, but not for the reason they believed: the Native Americans must have thought those French people hardly worth attacking, since very soon they would perish on their own. No one wintered on St. Croix Island.

By the following spring all the settlers were dead or dying, having underestimated the awful bitterness of Maine winters. A few remaining stragglers had staggered ashore and departed as fast as they could, the luckiest missing only their toes.

"Hey," Wade said suddenly, breaking my grim reverie. Twenty

miles to go: fields, old farmhouses, vast stretches of woodlot, bluffs, and steep drops on the left overlooking the river where it widened into the bay. All I wanted was to get back home and lock all the doors again. But Wade didn't.

"I feel too good to go home," he answered my look of query.

He was taking nearly having his head blown off very calmly. But then, Wade was boarding an oil freighter once when the ship had nearly its whole superstructure blown off; something about an embargo, some contraband arms shipments (that being why he'd been getting onto the freighter; it was during the Gulf War), and a missile that had (or perhaps had not) missed its intended target.

By all reports he'd been calm then, too. Now he gazed happily across the bay at the red-tiled roof of the hotel at St. Andrews, over in New Brunswick. Nearer by, the net-draped tall sticks of a herring weir stuck up from a cove, its reflection like a mirage on the placid water.

Next came hairpin turns flanked by big old gnarly spruces in Red Beach. Wade's look of appeal as we passed between them was as loud as a shout, and impractical. On the other hand, he *had* just escaped death by inches.

"Oh, all right," I gave in, and he grinned at me.

I checked the rearview, slowed for the turn: a few hundred yards of frost-heaved pavement, then a dirt surface so bumpy, you could use it to test how fast vital parts might be made to fall off cars. Luckily I was driving the truck, so all we tested was how fast the vital parts could fall off me; despite the frequent jolting, Wade seemed not to mind the rough ride in the slightest.

The lane narrowed, its washboard gravel devolving to a rough bulldozed track edged with rucked-up stones. About a mile in we descended a hill, then crossed a culvert where the track bisected a beaver pond. "Look at that," he marveled.

Across the marsh a heron lifted from the cattails, its body the same bluish-white as the clouds above. "Wade, we're just visiting, right? I mean, I know you feel pretty well, now."

But later he might be miserable. And being in serious pain at the wrong end of five miles of rough road is bad strategy.

Also, much as I hated to admit it, (a) no, Victor wouldn't approve, and (b) yes, I cared. The fact that in his private life my ex-husband is a sociopathic doofus doesn't keep him from being a more-than-adequate clinician, whose advice I trust. Or anyway I trust it when he is not trying to apply it to *me*.

"You look a little tired," Wade said mildly, not answering my question.

What I looked like was hell. "Yeah, I'm losing it," I admitted. "The way I went off on Victor in there . . . my nerves are shot."

"Sure," he said sympathetically. "It's no wonder."

We bumped slowly on. The trees were a canopy of pale green freckled by crab-apple blossoms. Quail ran herky-jerky into the huckleberry shrub where snow lay in lingering triangular patches at the bases of boulders and in the north shade of evergreens. The perfume pouring through the truck window was of pine sap and clean, cold water.

"Beautiful day," Wade said casually, glorying in it. Which was when I realized he knew how close a call he'd had. It could have been fatal and as usual he was making little of it. Except:

"The sun's shining, birds are singing, and the ice is out of the lake," he exulted as we jounced, jolted, and juddered down the primitive old road. He turned to me.

"Honey, we're going to camp."

In Maine, your camp is your summer place: anything from a patch of rented land and a ten-dollar tent to a palace of cedar and glass. Wade's was a shingled, gambrel-roofed cottage with a sleeping loft and an air-tight woodstove, surrounded by birches, firs, and pin oaks, on the edge of Balsam Lake.

"So," he said as we sat on the deck overlooking the water at the end of that day. The sun had set and the surface of the lake was mirror-calm; an evening chill crept out of its depths as the light faded. "What's really up? What're you not telling me?"

Because he knew, of course, that there was something. I'd told him about the trip to Machias and he'd teased me about it. "Riding in cars with boys," he'd commented, shaking his head. But he was fully aware how out of character it was.

How unhinged. No blackflies here yet, I noticed with relief. To most people the insects were only an annoyance but to me, their bite spelled a week of misery. Behind us in the cabin, gas lamps glowed yellow—no electricity here, either, and no phones—and the fire behind the wood-stove window flickered orange.

Appealed to via the cell phone in Wade's truck, George had showed up with supplies and the dog. Still damp from swimming, Monday now sprawled by the stove, exhausted and happy.

A loon laughed, out on the lake. I took a breath, said the words I'd been working hard not even to think. But I had to, now; think it, *and* say it.

"I'm very worried about what Harry told me the other night. I'm afraid my dad really is still alive, even after all this time. Alive, and out there somewhere."

The words hung in the air like the wisps of mist rising over the water. "I see," Wade replied gravely.

Not: *Don't be silly,* or *That's ridiculous.* If it worried me, Wade never thought it was silly. Fifty feet away the weathered dock was the color of a bar of pewter in the fading light.

"What would that mean?" he asked. "If it's true?"

"It would mean I could find him. Find out if the worst thing of all is true, too," I said softly.

"*Someone* drove off that day after the explosion," I continued. "I can hear it as clearly in my head as I can hear you now." The sound, after a blast so powerful it demolished a house, of someone starting a car out in the Greenwich Village street, and roaring away.

And who—*who?*—would be driving away after such an event?

Wade changed the subject. He will do this: give me a little breathing room. "You okay having Sam alone in town?"

Wade hadn't taken any more of the pain pills Victor gave him. When I asked, he said it hurt but it was a good hurt.

"As long as George and Ellie are there," I said, "Sam's fine." If I knew George, he'd be out on the porch with a shotgun in his lap all night.

More silence. Then: "Jake, if the worst *is* true."

If my father killed my mother on purpose and tried to kill me: was it that far-fetched? A radical whose ways had included armed bank robbery, he would set a timed charge for diversion, then pick off a bank that he knew had just gotten a big cash delivery. He was little more than a kid himself at the time, but he was a criminal, my old man, and he knew his bombs. And his body had never been found.

The underbrush rustled. Deer, probably. Or a moose. "Harry hunted for him for over thirty years, first on the task force, then on his own time. Those cops who pursued him for so long didn't believe he was dead."

We'd spent most of the day doing nothing, on the lake in the canoe. Now that I'd learned a decent J-stroke I could paddle and steer too, so Wade had just sat soaking it in: water and sky, the liquid *plop!* of a trout leaping openmouthed into the air, through the clouds of hovering hatchflies.

"Sure. But that was then, and this is now. Look," he said into the darkness, now complete. "One thing's fairly certain: somebody's got it in for Harry but now that he's here it's spreading onto us. An old grudge, or whatever it is. Probably that's it." He was smoking a cigar; its end moved like a red eye. "You don't know why, so your feelings are supplying you with all kinds of reasons, making all kinds of connections. Some may be valid ones," he added. "But if I know you it's not the facts that're bothering you, not even the facts you don't know yet. It's your feelings that are blowing your doors off."

Right. Carrying a gun around, racing to Machias to check on a little fib, embarrassing Wade by needlessly losing my temper with Victor; it was nuts, all of it.

Or most of it. "Say you're out in a boat in a storm," Wade went on. "What you feel like is heading for shore."

I waited. For dinner we'd had two of those trout on the gas grill. With it: wine, new potatoes, a salad of fiddlehead ferns and baby dandelions in olive oil and balsamic vinegar. George had brought us some of Ellie's double chocolate cake for dessert.

"Straight for shore," Wade said. "Waves'll hit you broadside, swamp you, then you're *really* in trouble."

He sipped his wine, took a reflective puff of the Dunhill Cabinetta '86 that arrived in a box of fifty, no return address, soon after I'd let Jemmy know Wade and I were married.

"And this," he said, "whatever it ends up being, it's the same kind of bad. Like a storm. Starts out slow and sneaky, fools you. Gets worse, maybe." Which was what I was so afraid of.

"But when the waves're coming one way," he went on, "rain's coming another, and the wind's right out straight from hell—"

Like now: Harriet, Sam's car, Wade, my father, prank calls, Samantha, the intruder . . . but all one storm, Wade was saying, and if you stuck to the facts instead of going on your feelings, kept your wits about you and didn't panic, you wouldn't be swamped.

Wouldn't drown. I'd known that. Really, I had.

But it still helped to hear it. He curved his arm around me. "Not quite summer yet," he observed.

Stars glittered like tiny ice chips over the lake. I pulled a wool blanket onto our laps, propped my feet on the deck rail.

But Wade wasn't finished. "So, what if you find out your dad *is* still alive? I'll tell you what," he answered himself firmly. "First, it's a real long shot. The best were looking, no luck, probably he's dead."

That word again: *probably*. "But even if it happened, and you found him, and . . . Jake, nothing would change. We would handle it, you and me. I'd still be here, and so would Sam. Our house, the life you've made here, your friends."

Monday shoved her head under my hand as if sensing all my worry, gazed up adoringly. *And me. I'd be here.*

"It's the sneakiest damn trick," Wade said, "when the bad-old-days baggage tries making you think it still owns you." His arm tightened around me. "But it doesn't. You're allowed, Jake."

"Allowed?" I was thinking of the cold: that there must have been a time on St. Croix when the settlers knew they should give up, try something else while there was still time.

But they didn't until it was too late; even if they'd made it to the mainland there was no way out of a Maine winter. They had set their hearts for so long on St. Croix that in the end, it had little choice but to claim them.

"You are allowed," Wade repeated, "to put the old baggage down."

"Wade, could you have—"

His grim chuckle cut me off. "Used the wrong primer? Or too much wadding? Cranked down the reloader handle too fast? Mistaken a can of black powder for a can of Pyrodex? What do you think?"

"Yeah." In other words: No. His workshop explosion had not been an accident. None of it was, however much I kept wishing it would be. "That's what I thought."

He finished his wine. Across the lake the smoke from another cabin's chimney twisted in the moonlight. Nothing else moved.

"Sometimes the old baggage takes off by itself. Then again," Wade allowed, "could be it'll need a shove." Which meant, he didn't believe my carrying the Bisley around with me was nuts.

"Do you have all the shooting stuff in the truck?" I asked. In Wade's lockbox, I meant, bolted to the truck bed: ammunition, targets, gun-cleaning supplies. The Bisley was in my own bag, of course.

"Uh-huh. I surely do." A pause. Then:

"Jake?"

"Yeah."

"Could you have done it? Pulled the trigger, if it hadn't been Harry Markle in our kitchen?"

"I don't know. I knew so fast that I wasn't going to, I didn't have time to ask the question."

Soon after that we went inside, turned the lights down, and climbed into the big bed up in the sleeping loft.

"Ouch," Wade said, not very convincingly.

Then: "Ouch?" Not convincingly at all.

"Like this," I said. He shifted carefully, whereupon I took advantage of my situation.

"Oh," he murmured. And later:

"Huh," he said dazedly. "I didn't know you could do that."

I hadn't known I could do that, either. Pulling the quilts up around us, I relaxed against him, felt his breathing slow. But later still when the silence was total, Wade sleeping quietly and the darkness in the loft around us complete . . .

. . . even then I could still hear that loon laughing out on the lake.

The next morning Balsam Lake was a bowl of dawn-tinged mist, pierced by the distant honking of Canada geese headed north for the summer. I stoked the woodstove and fired up the percolator; when it was done I took my coffee to the end of the dock and sat with Monday beside me, watching a water snake cutting a speedy S-curve on the lake's silvery surface.

Wade was up and about too, and as I'd predicted his neck was as sore as a boil. I set him up in an armchair with the coffee thermos and a bottle of brandy, by the stove which I'd encouraged to a proper blaze.

He grinned wanly at me. "I'm fine," he insisted. He was still refusing to take pills.

"Right. And I'm Howdy Doody. You're sure about this?"

"Do it. If your nervous system could hold on to those skills forever there wouldn't be any such thing as firing ranges. No one would need 'em."

What with the varnish-stripping, the cellar foundation, and the ell floor, not to mention those dratted downspouts and the fallen siding, I hadn't been on the firing range for weeks. And if it turned out that some sort of unpleasant baggage did need a shove, it would be nice to know that I still had the marksmanship chops to give it one.

Also, there was a twin to the Bisley under a floorboard in the cottage where Wade could get at it, if required. So I left him, maneuvering the truck over the ruts to the Charlotte Road.

The hard blue sky of winter had softened to pastel; dark clouds mounded ominously on the horizon. Along the road, maples linked by plastic tubing flowed with sap; in the Moosehorn Refuge, acres of flat water lay prickly with cattails and studded with nesting boxes. A bald eagle soared overhead, its huge wings flapping flexibly in slow motion.

Ten minutes later I arrived at the firing range and pulled up the drive to the low, red-painted wooden hut. Under the sign posting the safety rules I opened the lockbox in the bed of the truck, took out a pad of bull's-eye-printed paper targets.

I carried a dozen of these and a small soft-cardboard box of ammunition to the firing table. There was no one around when I pressed the first target onto the notches of the firing backdrop.

But then I heard it: something—or someone—moving in the brush at the end of the range. At first I put it down to nerves. But then I heard it again and the Bisley didn't seem big enough.

What I wanted was a Hannibal rifle loaded with one of the cartridges Wade had gotten into his shop the winter before. The Tyrannosaur was named for its muzzle energy: 13,700 joules, three times that of a standard .308 high-powered rifle cartridge.

According to Wade, the cartridge had a kick like the animal it was named for. I'd never fired one; a broken shoulder hadn't been on my list of must-haves. But I'd have risked that fracture and a dozen more as I stood frozen on the firing range, wondering who was out there.

The ten-point buck that stepped out of the sumac sixty seconds later answered my question. His liquid eyes held mine, his great yellowish antlers a thicket of sharp tips: not Bambi. Then the frightened breath I let out in a rush sent him crashing back into the safety of cover with a harsh bleat of alarm.

All of which reminded me of how exposed I was at the moment. So in the end I disobeyed rule #7 on the safety poster. I didn't put on the hearing protectors that were a standard element of target-shooting costume. If someone came up behind me here—or anywhere—I wanted to know about it.

After that for a while it was load, post, and shoot: six paper targets and six groups of six shots, all but one series placed tight. By the second series I'd gone ahead and put on the earmuffs, by the fourth, my arms ached. On the final round, I started missing the center circle.

But if you don't start missing until the thirtieth shot, it's a decent bet you've already hit whatever you were shooting at. So I felt okay; back in the city I'd thought guns were for hard guys or in an emergency for guys like Jemmy: in other words, for *guys*. Now I put the Bisley away and got out the little .32 semiauto I like to finish up with.

The .32's kick is less jarring and its *crack!* less deafening than the Bisley's. You don't feel it in your chest, a short sharp thump from inside, your heart bumping against your breastbone as if a good-sized fish were jumping in there.

Soon, though, I'd used up my second wind and my ears were ringing with the insult I'd given them before I put the earmuffs on. I cleaned shell casings off the table, policed for strays, and wadded used targets, leaving the area tidy for the next shooter. Driving back to camp with the truck windows down and the radio on I felt my mind clearing as if a fog bank had moved out to sea.

At the cabin, Monday danced to meet me. Wade sat on the deck. "Time to head home?" He looked better, too, shaved and all packed up, ready to go.

Inside, the dishes were washed, the canoe paddles and life rings stowed, and the floorboard with the Bisley beneath it was undisturbed. Humming, I walked down to the dock for a last gaze at the lake.

The water was high, nearly up to the planking nailed to the tree trunks that formed the dock's underpinnings. I lay flat and peered down into it, at first seeing nothing.

But then the flicker of a translucent gill caught my eye and held it. Instantly a big fish whose mottled stillness had hidden it materialized in the water.

With a fin-flick it was gone; I blinked, seeing it again for a vivid, illusory moment against my retina.

And knew, suddenly, what I'd been missing.

Chapter 7

The Eastport breakwater is an L-shaped concrete structure perched massively atop forty-foot pilings. Metal gangways lead to the wooden finger piers of the boat basin; on one of them I found Ellie deep in conversation with Eastport native Forrest Pryne.

". . . last to see Harriet alive?" I heard Ellie ask as I made my way down the metal gang.

Until that moment I'd been feeling pretty proud of myself. But her question made me wonder why I was always last to get the brainstorm: that when Harriet died, Harry's plan to stay here in Eastport hadn't been known to anyone, maybe not even Harry.

While I was gone Ellie had wised up to the obvious just as I had: that somehow Harriet Hollingsworth was the start of all this.

It had been there in front of my nose all along. Harriet was a part of it somehow, and so was Harry; he'd bought her house, and the newspaper page clutched in her dead hand pointed even more certainly to

147

some link with him. But her disappearance hadn't harmed Harry at all, nor could it have been expected to.

So had there been another reason? Had Harry's arrival been a convenient distraction used by someone who knew or learned of his past? Were later deeds meant to further the notion of his involvement?

And to hide the real motive, perhaps unconnected to him or to anyone he'd ever pursued . . . ?

But that way led into a thicket of speculation. And unlike the youngsters of *The Blair Witch Project*, I had no confidence in my ability to find my way out again.

Just the facts, ma'am, I told myself firmly. *For now.*

"If you saw anything or heard anything, Forrest, I'd like to know," Ellie was saying as I joined them on the pier. Her red hair was pulled back in a purple scrunchy, her heavy sweater was a riot of primary colors, and the daisy shoes were bright on her feet.

Forrest's big hand dwarfed a rag full of metal polish. He was a heavyset man, moon-faced with high shiny forehead, wearing a denim coverall, red long-underwear shirt, and yellow rubber boots.

"Whoever killed her, I guess," he replied at last, the hand with the rag in it moving on the brightwork of a 36-foot cruiser.

Whoevah. Ellie shot an exasperated glance at me. "I mean who *before* that?"

Forrest went on polishing imperturbably. Around him bobbed Eastport's working fleet: draggers, lobster boats, small utility vessels freelancing for salmon farmers, hauling feed and so on to the offshore underwater pens where the fish were raised.

But Forrest's job was with summer people soon to arrive in town, wanting their pleasure boats ready and waiting for them when they got here. And from his vantage point Forrest could see all the goings-on downtown while he dipped regularly from his tin of Bright-All.

Which vantage point I gathered was what had brought Ellie to question him, me wagging behind like the tail on a friendly but slow-witted dog. "Before," he repeated. "Hmm."

Forrest's laconic nature was one reason he was popular with the summer folk; things he might find while cleaning up after a party cruise, for instance, he kept mum about.

But Forrest saw all. He put down the rag. "Guess that'd be me. Saw Harriet with Wyatt Evert, evening 'fore she went AWOL. And no one has said *they* saw her, any time later'n that."

Ellie stared. "Forrest, did you tell the police?"

Forrest plucked a crumpled pack of smokes from his coverall pocket, cupped his hand to light one.

"Nope. They didn't ask me."

Of course not. And getting him to volunteer information was like trying to pry a clamshell open with your thumbnail.

"Speak of the devil," Ellie murmured as Wyatt Evert himself appeared suddenly on the breakwater above us, glaring down.

"Hey!" he yelled, gesturing curtly. "I want to talk to you."

Ditto; in light of what Forrest had just told us, and Tim Rutherford's suspicions, I was even more curious about Wyatt's presence outside the Danvers' house just before the deadly live-wire incident.

But Wyatt had other ideas. "You've got pull around here," he said as soon as I reached him.

"I want you to tell that fool he's got to print my article," he went on, stabbing a finger at the office of the *Quoddy Tides* a few hundred feet distant.

The office, a tiny blue-and-white wooden structure with its entry on Water Street, perched on the rocks over the boat basin as if readying itself to leap. By "that fool," I assumed Wyatt meant the *Tides'* editor, whose only connection to fools was his ability to see one coming; thus Wyatt's inability to get anywhere with him.

"I don't have any pull," I retorted, "with—"

"Don't give me that," Wyatt snapped. "I'm not stupid, I see how things work around here."

He jerked his head to where Forrest was confiding something to Ellie. "You and her," Wyatt sneered. "Nothing but a couple of busybodies, but people here listen to you. So I want you to *tell* that idiot . . ."

Apparently he thought bad temper would help get his message across. "Jake," Ellie said urgently, coming up the gangway.

". . . my article explaining why *all this area* ought to be set aside," Wyatt declaimed angrily, waving his arms to include Water Street, the boat basin, and apparently the whole known world.

Or all of Maine, anyway. "It's a precious environment, you people are ruining it with logging and lumber mills and scallop dragging and fish farms," he fulminated. "It's got to be stopped."

Men getting out of their pickup trucks on the breakwater had turned to look at him. They carried toolboxes, boat parts, lunch bags, and plenty of warm clothing for the work which would go on all day and into the evening.

"Hey!" Wyatt yelled, but they only stared at him, eyes haggard. Men getting to the pier this late in the day always looked exhausted, but around here they were regarded as lucky: besides their boats, they also had work somewhere else.

"It belongs to everyone!" Wyatt yelled. Funny, you could have fooled the families who'd lived here for decades, getting along on salt fish and potatoes to stake their claim. Or the native tribes before that.

"It should all be a national park," Wyatt shouted. He was on a roll now. "This whole town, it should be for the *people* . . ."

What did he think these guys on the dock were, hand puppets? But he was getting to that.

"It can't all just be left to all you . . ."

Forrest Pryne mounted the gang behind Ellie, his pale hair sticking out from beneath a ragged watch cap he'd pulled on.

"... rednecks!" A pearl of spittle formed at the corner of Wyatt Evert's angrily flapping lip.

Wordlessly Forrest grabbed Wyatt by the shoulders, marched him down the ramp and out the finger pier.

"*Listen to me!*" Wyatt expostulated as they reached the end of it.

"Sure," Forrest replied mildly, and pushed him off.

Wyatt Evert's thin arms pinwheeled. Then came a splash, his shouts muffled by cheers from the men on the breakwater.

"Yikes," Ellie said. "We'd better go get him, Jake. I don't think Wyatt's love of nature extends quite that far."

No one's did; in that icy water, he'd be lucky if his heart didn't seize like an old engine, his blood turned to instant sludge.

But one of the men working on a lobster boat was ahead of us, tossing Wyatt an orange life ring. Shrieking and sputtering, Wyatt flailed for the boat hook the guy extended to him.

"Freakin' idjut," was Forrest's comment as he came back up the gang. "Nature's our daily bread too, not just his." He pulled out another cigarette. Wyatt was now safely aboard the lobster boat.

"Guy shows up here," Forrest said, "from the city where they *use* all the paper, build stuff with the wood, eat the fish. Spend more money in a month than most a' those guys see in a year. But Wyatt looks at the way some guys are livin' here, barely gettin' along, doin' their best. And you know what he thinks? I'll tell you what he thinks. He thinks it ain't *photo-genic.*" He gave the word a sardonic twist. "Some of 'em got their hearts in the right place, I know that. Want to save things, that's fine. But not Wyatt. He's just mad 'cause it ain't all been set aside for *him.*"

And because, I was beginning to suspect, a reputation for being a hothead environmental savior fattened his pocketbook.

Forrest turned to us. "Anyway, so happens I *was* here, night b'fore Harriet went missing. Guy owns this boat called me, would I come down, check 'er over."

He blew a plume of smoke. "And you c'n spy the window of her house from here, y'know," he added reluctantly. "Not always, but back then you could."

Actually I hadn't known that. The pleasure of shoving Wyatt Evert off the finger pier had apparently loosened Forrest's lips: good luck for us.

"And," I guessed, "Harriet wasn't the only one with binoculars?" It was the only answer that fit, especially given Forrest's clear embarrassment about what he was telling us.

He looked shamefaced. "Yeah, there was a pair on the boat. Took a peek through 'em. Just that once. I don't make no habit of it like she did."

"And saw . . . ?"

"Wyatt," he confirmed. "And Harriet. Fussin' at each other. That's all. Put them spyglasses away, haven't touched 'em again. Don't want to get no reputation like *she* had."

"But it's *not* all," Ellie put in excitedly to me. "Her window! If Forrest could see it from here, then *she* could see . . ."

I got it: not now, with leaves on the trees, as Forrest said. But the sky wasn't the only thing that had changed since Harriet vanished; back then, the branches had been bare. "So Harriet," I theorized, "could've seen all the way downtown."

"Yup. She'd 'a seen a lot, too. Roy McCall was stayin' at the Motel East," Forrest said. "Scoutin' out the territory 'fore he moved up t'your place so's his crew could have them rooms. Evert was there," he added as if mentally ticking on his fingers, "with that little girl he runs with, one who looks like Peter Pan with makeup."

Fran Hanson. "And so was that drowned fella," Forrest went on. "Such an outdoorsman, he accidentally inhaled half the water in the Moosehorn Refuge. Happened the very next day after I saw Evert with Harriet. Come to think about it . . ."

He turned his mild, impassive gaze slowly on me. "I saw that old mason o' your'n that evening, too. What's his name, again? Somethin' like mine, seems to me. Let's see, now; forest, tree . . ."

"Uh-oh." Ellie looked stricken. "Jake, I'm so sorry. That reminds me. Lian Ash is up at the house waiting for you. Not working. I was so excited about what Forrest's been saying that I forgot to tell you."

I'd dropped Wade off but hadn't gone inside; George had been out on the porch and said Ellie wasn't there.

That she was here. "Not working at *all*?"

"No. He told me he needed to talk with you, first."

"Let me guess, he found buried treasure in the cellar foundation." After all, it *could* be good news, couldn't it?

Wrong.

I found Lian Ash in my kitchen with some notes in his hand. The foundation work was definitely halted.

"This here," he pointed at a diagram of my cellar, "is the section I thought I'd have to bring down."

He pointed to another spot on it. "But the break you found under the ell, when I got the stones out I found a second section ready to fall in, all along here."

Of course he had. That's another thing about old houses: each part is inextricably connected to the next part, which itself is only slightly less ready to collapse than the part you were working on in the first place. In my house, you can start out by changing a lightbulb and end up replacing the plumbing.

"Show me," I told Ash, and when he did I wanted to weep: half of the old mortar in the old foundation was turning to sand. You could crumble it out with your fingernail, years of water damage from a time when the house didn't even have any gutters. "It's a wonder the kitchen isn't *in* the cellar already," I moaned.

"Well," Mr. Ash said. "It's not as bad as that. Not," he added optimistically, "the *whole* kitchen."

We went back upstairs. "Thing is," he continued, "I *was* going to replace the old stones, original to the house, just like the craftsmen first built it."

All that time ago: hauling them. Setting them. Even without water damage, most mortar won't last more than a couple of centuries.

"Now," he broke the news gently, "this much reconstruction, it'd be cheaper to use concrete block. More materials, but less in labor. Your choice."

"It'll look," Ellie remarked tartly from the hall where she was hand-sanding some remaining varnish off the floor, "like a little old lady with tin wheels where house slippers should be."

Mr. Ash nodded. "Unless you put a foundation planting in front of it. Nice little row of bushes? Maybe box hedge?"

Box hedge is beautiful when it's a hundred years old. Newly planted, it resembles a row of Chia Pets.

"Right," I retorted, "and I'll put up aluminum siding so the clapboards can rot faster, plastic shutters in place of wood, and hey, how about a satellite dish on a corner pillar? Make it look like I'm tracking flying objects for NORAD."

I swallowed coffee grumpily. The choice was between new and hideously unauthentic concrete blocks, versus a zillion bucks for the original stones that had been there in the first place.

"I can work with you on the labor cost," he said, "but it'll still be more expensive. Practical choice is concrete block, but it all depends on how much you want to stay hooked to the past. For that you pay a price. For cost efficiency, you gotta let the old stuff go."

He paused, then added the kicker. "Don't try stayin' betwixt an' between, though," he warned. "That won't work."

Exactly what I'd been innocently contemplating; original stones now, in the parts that were desperately crumbling. More work later on a gradual schedule, maybe? But Mr. Ash put paid to that thought.

"Halfway measures won't take the weight," he admonished. He sounded like Moses delivering the Eleventh Commandment.

Just once, I'd like to hear about a job that costs more to do wrong than right, I thought as he returned to the cellar.

"You want to maintain the house's character, keep it looking hooked to its history. But doing it that way feels so extravagant," Ellie summed up.

"Uh-huh." I knelt beside her. The old wood coming out from under her sandpaper was white maple, grain tight as granite and as beautifully figured as the long-ago day when it was milled.

Ellie kept sanding; it was time for the machine sanding but she wanted to see more of the wood. Fragile-looking as a sprig of lavender, that woman had the stubborn stamina of your average pack mule.

"Maybe we should've only taken half this varnish off," she said. "The top half."

"Ellie, what in the *world* are you—oh."

I knew what she meant: halfway measures didn't work. She sat up and folded her arms. "Jake, how long have we known each other? Almost five years," she answered herself, "so I know *you*."

My fingers worried a scrap of sandpaper. Ellie never pried but she was awesomely effective at winkling the secrets out of a dour downeast native like Forrest Pryne.

Or out of me. "Dancing around the past, the damage that was done. It's not your fault but you're still stuck with it, aren't you? And you don't want to face it for fear of what it might cost. But it isn't going to cost *less* later, is it? And sure, concrete block will work."

Right. If you kept your eyes closed. "The question is," she persisted, "what do you really want holding things up? Something you can't stand to look at, or the right stuff? And if I know you, I know the answer," she finished.

I got up. A patch of the old hardwood was nearly clean now. And it was beautiful. "Mr. Ash," I called down the cellar steps.

His face, clean-shaven with his blue eyes shining alertly in it, appeared in the gloom.

"Don't order any concrete block for the foundation, please," I said. "I want you to rebuild it with the old, original stones."

Ellie was smiling up at me. I said, "Because around here . . ."

I paused. How would I ever pay for the work? My old house wasn't a money pit; it was a crevasse. "Around here," I repeated firmly, "we hang on to all the past we can stand."

Mr. Ash nodded. "Yes, ma'am," he replied, looking pleased; more so when Sam appeared in the hall asking if he could help.

"You come on down here, young feller," Mr. Ash said, "but no heavy lifting. Even your young bones don't heal that quick."

He waved at a crate. "Set yourself here," he instructed Sam. "We'll list you on the work roster as supervisor. That," he added with a wink at me, "means all you exercise is your gift of gab."

"They get along well," Ellie observed as we cleared out the hall to ready it for the sanding machine.

"Mmm," I replied distantly. I was thinking about Wyatt Evert, the drowned eco-tourist, Harry Markle, and Roy McCall all being in Eastport when Harriet Hollingsworth vanished. About Harriet seeing so much from her window, and about the newspaper page in her dead hand.

"Ellie, Harriet knew something. Or saw something."

"Uh-huh. And she was *first.*"

"That, too. Almost the same time as Wyatt's tourist."

I was thinking about the fish I'd seen hiding in plain sight and about the look on Wyatt's face as he'd sat in his van outside the Danvers' house: angry, expectant.

All that, and the sound of his van speeding away, like the sound I'd heard years ago: of someone *going* when almost anyone's impulse would've been *stay.* It was a pretty good bet Wyatt wasn't going to explain it, especially after his recent saltwater swim.

But the more I thought about his rudeness, drunkenness, and general ill-temper, the misery it must be having to work for him, the more I thought somebody else might explain Wyatt Evert to me.

His assistant, Fran Hanson.

"Odd," **Ellie said** in surprise, putting down the phone a few minutes later. "I can't find her."

Fran wasn't at any of the bed-and-breakfasts; she wasn't in a cabin at Sunrise Camp Grounds, or at the Motel East. A pang of unease struck me. "You don't suppose he makes her sleep in the van, do you?"

Ellie shook her head. "I doubt even she'd put up with that. I'm going downtown to ask around. Maybe I'll get lucky and I can ask Wyatt himself."

She leashed Monday; when they'd gone I checked the e-mail on Sam's computer and found the follow-up I'd been waiting for from Jemmy Wechsler. As before, no personal remarks were in Jemmy's message, only info-bits.

"Samantha Greer, born Yonkers, NY 1976, hired by Roy McCall personally for Shake It Till You Break It, *her first professional appearance and McCall's first project for music video company Top Cat Productions."*

He went on about the dancer: blah blah. Jemmy's own survival depended on his knowing many odd details, so not surprisingly his write-up was full of them. But the final part was fascinating.

"She will be replaced in the production by Tonya Hemming, rumored associate of . . ."

Here Jemmy named a guy so terrifying, I'm not even going to identify him. Suffice it to say that when anybody big vanishes west of the Mississippi, this guy did it.

Or had it done. If he was hiring for Top Cat Productions, it was a revelation that put an entirely new spin on Roy McCall's situation. Next paragraph, new subject:

"Wyatt Evert aka Walter Evers, wants and warrants numerous, scam specialty charitable nonprofits, travels w/ female Frances Marie Hargreave aka Fran Hilyard, Fran Hannaford, probation state of Florida rsp, no other record."

And aka Fran Hanson, I was willing to bet. Fran was turning up like a bad penny all of a sudden; rsp was short for "receiving stolen property."

Jemmy's scam info was always superb; before he got into the money game he'd been a scam guy himself, moving VIN numbers off totaled wrecks and onto stolen cars of the same model and year. Last on his list was a single line.

"HM: Bronx H.S. > NYPD > detective 1st grade > retired."

Harry Markle; the brevity of the entry meant nothing notable between high school graduation and retirement from the cop shop.

Finally, two comments: *"Longer a guy's memory, more he will have a sense of humor, my experience."*

And: *"Look at McCall. Show business: no such thing as bad buzz."*

Jemmy was noting the prank aspect. As grisly as they'd been, there was a ghoulish humor about the deaths. Drowning because your boots leak, being walled up, even grabbing a live wire were things that could have happened in an animated cartoon.

And with the memory comment he was suggesting a possible Mob connection. No one knew better than Jemmy Wechsler how long those guys' memories were.

I closed the e-mail program and shut down the computer as footsteps came up the back porch. Wade had gone down to the fish pier to see if any freighters were scheduled imminently; if so, he'd said he would get the other harbor pilot to work them.

Which meant that despite the reassurances he'd given me, he was worried, too. Wade went to work with a bad case of flu, once, ate sleet for a week when a nor'easter blew up unexpectedly and came home with double pneumonia. But he'd had his paycheck, and forgoing one now was a storm signal clearer than the red pennant flying down at the Coast Guard Station.

"Wade," I began, "how about some . . ."

But when the door opened it wasn't Wade. It was Roy McCall, looking every inch the successful music-video producer: manicured hair, black Top Cat Productions T-shirt, jacket and slacks.

Jemmy's e-mail revelations washed over me like an icy wave. Roy might be charming but his production company was hooked up with crooks. Bad ones.

". . . coffee," I finished flatly.

Roy glanced warily at me, headed for the stairs up to his room. "Oh, no, you don't. Right this way." I steered him back to the kitchen.

"Sit," I said as Ellie came back in, too.

"No sign of Fran," she reported. "Or Wyatt. But I did learn a very interesting new—"

Then she saw Roy, and her tone chilled noticeably to match the atmosphere in the room. "Oh, hello." She hadn't liked Roy's grandstanding on MTV. *Dancing on a grave,* she'd called it.

"What's going on?" Roy wanted to know, so I told him that I knew his financial angel was a devil so dark even I wouldn't have had him as a client, not that the guy hired people like me.

He killed people like me, and anyone else who got in his way or had anything he wanted.

Like Samantha. "I didn't have a choice," Roy protested half an hour later. It had taken that long to get him to admit Jemmy's report on him was true.

Then he caved, telling us more. "I was coming off a flop. It wasn't my fault. It was that misbegotten girl group whose leader suddenly came out with news that she's really a boy. Can you imagine how that would've played in Paducah?"

Nope. And I didn't much care, either. But as Roy went on it hit me that Jemmy was right: *publicity.* For his maiden effort, Roy McCall desperately needed all the prerelease ink he could get, even if—maybe even *especially* if—the ink was mixed with blood.

"Okay, so my backers aren't Boy Scouts. But they wouldn't kill the talent just to get rid of it," Roy went on. "Or to get rid of me. We'll be back in production again, soon. What you are thinking is ridiculous," he finished indignantly.

Actually, it wasn't. Not that Roy would necessarily be to blame, personally; he might not even have known about it until it happened. But his buffed, sunshiny pizzazz wasn't so charming anymore. I noticed he hadn't once called Samantha by her name. She was dead, but this was all about *him.*

"Anyway, it's not like you go there, Los Angeles, everyone wants to hire you," he said sulkily. "It's not about *talent.*"

Some guys hit a little adversity, they go from being the cat's pajamas to the cat's litter box in no time flat.

"You need connections," he said, trying to explain. "And you can't do it all your own way, either. There's no such thing as creative freedom, and no one cares about your artistic vision."

In L.A., he meant, as if it might be different anywhere else. Personally I've always liked coloring inside the lines. You watch who you sign up with but when someone hires you, you do what they want or you walk away from it, end of story.

But it sounded as if it had come as a bad surprise to Roy that the world wasn't a fairy tale, that it was run by guys who would slit your throat as soon as look at you. Or someone else's throat, as a demonstration of what might happen to yours if you crossed them again.

"So you hired Samantha even though your backers wanted Tonya Hemming, their own talent. Who's a known associate of someone you knew didn't like being contradicted. What're you, stupid?"

Across from him Ellie sat listening silently, connecting the dots. She connects dots the way a herring weir collects herring, gobs at a time.

McCall's shoulders sagged. "I'd done everything else they asked. I hired their musicians, their hair and makeup people."

"But you liked Samantha. You thought she was good. So you went ahead and hired *her*. Figuring maybe they wouldn't notice."

"Or wouldn't care. Tonya's one of their girls, she works all the time."

He looked up at me, hurt confusion in his eyes. "What's *she* need me for? I don't get it. They're taking her off a toothpaste commercial, reshoot the whole thing with other talent so they can send Tonya here? Why?"

I knew, even if Roy was telling the truth and he didn't. But I didn't have the heart to enlighten him. He needed to learn a lesson about the guys he'd partnered with. When they say jump you don't tell them you want artistic vision, or creative freedom. You say *how high, sir?*

And when you say it, you're already in the air, if you know what's good for you. Maybe someone was trying to teach Roy that lesson. On the other hand . . .

"I don't know. It doesn't seem efficient," Ellie said when Roy had gone upstairs. With most of his crew already out of town for the production hiatus, the Motel East had vacant rooms again and he was moving to one. It was the insurance people, he said, not his backers, who'd shut him down.

But only temporarily. If Roy had it right, and I believed he did, a new girl would still be dancing in *Shake It Till You Break It,* and Roy sounded as if he, at least, believed that his backers hadn't been angry enough over Samantha to get rid of her permanently.

"I see how an 'accident' would send a message to Roy," Ellie mused.

"Sure. You want me to get the message, forget Western Union. Chop someone's head off with a helicopter blade, or shoot them with a slug that was supposed to be the harmless *pop!* of a fake pistol. I'll catch the drift."

"But Roy *didn't* sound frightened enough for that to have happened, did he?" Ellie asked thoughtfully. "And it's not just Samantha," she went on. "A lot of people are dead, or nearly."

And professional killers don't do extras to cover their tracks. Pros don't leave tracks. "Where was Roy before?" Ellie asked.

"New York. Getting his crew together. Lights, craftspeople, all that." Because while we had plenty of painters and carpenters here in Eastport, we were short on costumers and choreographers.

"Like Harry," Ellie mused. "First in the city, now both of them here. He'd have had access to the wire Samantha grabbed. He was here in the house, too. He could have gotten into Wade's shop and at Sam's car. He had a house key?"

I nodded. Supposedly Roy had been in Portland the night of the intruder and the prank call. But Portland was just a charter flight away, and if he'd asked to have it kept confidential, it would be. If he'd wanted to badly enough, he could've gotten here and back with no one the wiser. "Forrest Pryne said Roy was here in town when Harriet went missing, as well," Ellie reminded me.

"If Roy had heard of Harry's New York history . . . but I don't know," I said doubtfully. "Kill Samantha himself to get publicity for the video, try blaming it on Harry, somehow? But if Harriet getting killed was to set *that* connection up in advance, with the newspaper page . . . then why *hide* her body?"

"And why the other stuff?" she agreed, backing off the idea. "Speaking of which, remember how flustered he got just trying to hold a video shoot together, at the Danvers' house?"

"Right. It's got to be someone who can handle something as *complicated* as this is turning out to be."

"Roy doesn't have it, does he?" Ellie concluded unhappily. "The daring, or whatever it is that it would take."

"No. I could be wrong, but I don't think he does. Scratch one suspect, maybe." The part about it being complicated still bothered me, though; somehow I thought it *wasn't* complicated, that we were missing something.

Something . . . *simple.* "Speaking of Harriet," Ellie told me, "I saw Bob Arnold on my way back here."

I turned from the window. No sign of Wade on the street, and I could see the tugboat's blue stack over the roofs of the houses downhill. So he hadn't gone out on it.

"He says the autopsy was inconclusive. The lime in the wall didn't help the coroner's people, of course."

I could imagine. And neither had the weeks Harriet had spent *in* the wall *with* the lime. Luckily, the weather had been cold.

"Lots of general bruising," she went on, "but so much time's gone by it's hard to tell from when. No head traumas or hits on the tox screens." From this summary I knew Harriet hadn't been shot, stabbed, skull-clubbed, or poisoned. "So they're doing more tests," Ellie said.

"Good. She didn't wall her*self* up in that cellar." I glanced out the window again. Sam was coming up Key Street, pushing Maggie in a wheelchair. One-handed, he spun her around under the spring-green trees, both of them laughing.

"But the other thing Bob Arnold said *really* opened my eyes," Ellie continued. "I thought I knew everything about everyone in this town, but it just goes to show . . ."

". . . that in Eastport there's always more to learn," I finished as I turned from the window. "What did Bob say?"

"I asked him about Fran Hanson, where she might be." She was peeling an apple, its skin unfurling like a red ribbon. I like to fix things when I'm thinking; Ellie cooks.

"Harriet *was* disliked," Ellie said in apparent non sequitur. But with Ellie, it was never a non sequitur. I waited.

"Harriet," she said, "had all the enemies she needed, right here in Eastport. Maybe we've been ignoring things we shouldn't."

I got two eggs from the refrigerator, lined them up with the other in-gredients Ellie needed as Maggie and Sam came in.

"Mmm, apple cake," he remarked. "You know, Mom, if you cooked more instead of spending all your time on house projects, we'd eat a lot better around here."

"If I cooked more, we'd be eating at the hot dog stand and the house would be falling down," I retorted.

I handed Ellie the baking soda as Sam and Maggie took the long way out to the parlor, avoiding the hall floor; they'd left the wheelchair out-side. "Plunge," Maggie said schoolmarmishly, to which he responded in obedient tones: "Fall, collapse, descend."

They were working on synonyms now. But moments later the TV went on, an old sitcom theme burbling cheerily.

"The simplest way of hiding in plain sight *is* to be here all along," I conceded as Ellie creamed sugar into the butter. "But who among the locals have you got in mind?"

She'd cut apples into slices so thin you could read through them and spread them in a buttered dish. I glanced out the window again, saw Wade, felt my shoulders sag in relief. But . . .

"Anyway, what Bob Arnold told me," Ellie said, "is that Fran Hanson *is* from here. I can't imagine how I missed knowing that. But it explains why she isn't at a motel. She doesn't need to be. She's staying with her sister, who happens to be . . ."

The penny dropped. "Wilma," I said, gazing in dismay out the win-dow. "Fran's sister is Wilma Bounce, isn't she?"

Floating beside Wade was a tentlike smock so bright it could put your eye out at twenty paces, inside it a woman I recognized only too well, talking a mile a minute: Wilma in the flesh.

"Yes. How did you know . . . oh." Ellie looked over my shoulder, spotted the woman in question.

"Wade was there while I was talking to Bob Arnold," she explained. "He heard Bob telling me Fran was at Wilma's."

So Wade had gone and gotten Wilma for us.

"I swear, Jake, if that husband of yours could follow a train of thought any better, he'd be a caboose."

From the parlor Sam and Maggie sang together with the TV's theme: *"They're creepy and they're kooky . . ."*

How appropriate. *". . . mysterious and ooky!"*

That, too. "Wilma *despised* Harriet," Ellie said. The TV's volume went down as Wade and Wilma mounted the back porch. "Wilma thought Harriet had something to do with Wilma's cat disappearing. Or so I heard."

"Right." I remembered, now; the story had gone around a couple of weeks before Harriet had vanished, herself.

"I hope it's not Wilma Bounce behind all this trouble." Ellie slid the cake pan into the oven. "I won't be able to stand it if the whole thing boils down to a dead cat."

Wilma came in, glanced around with a dismissive snort. The parrot smock seemed even brighter in close-up than it had been at a distance. "Huh. Can't say the place looks any different. I heard you were *workin'* on it. Guess I heard wrong."

Without the money I'd put into reinforcing that old floor, she'd have been in the cellar by now. But I bit my tongue and didn't say so as she looked around for refreshments.

Silent, I poured her a cup of coffee and put some oatmeal cookies on a plate. Wade winked, then vanished up to his workshop.

"Aww, 'oosa widdle puddy tat, hm?" Wilma crooned, catching sight of Cat Dancing.

"Yowrowl," Cat replied sensibly, and fled.

"We're so sorry about Munchkin," Ellie told Wilma.

Munchkin being Wilma's missing feline. Word around town was, Wilma screamed blue murder if a dog so much as looked at her yard, but felt her cats digging in others' gardens was natural.

"We were," I lied, "devastated." Harriet, the story went, had kept a

tin of rat poison on her window with the label facing out; thus her reputation for being a cat-killer.

But as I say, this was all just rumor; I hadn't confirmed it myself, any
more than I had witnessed any blood-pool on Harriet's porch. And Wilma
wasn't commenting, reaching instead for another cookie. The smock was
so bright I had to look away and when I did I kept seeing it anyway.

Wilma slurped coffee, clattered the cup down. Her thin brown hair
was slicked back into a rubber band, the top of her head gleaming as if
each strand had been pulled through a block of lard.

"Anyhow, your man said your boy might be lookin' for work." She
chewed energetically. "Ast me to come up here, pass along a few tips. M'
niece is doin' housework mornings over t' the motel, an' m' nephew, he's
workin' fer Terry Gibson, learnin' electric. Both places're hiring."

I glanced at Ellie; this wasn't just a train, it was a high-speed express. Wilma had just reported someone who could get into rooms at
the motel, and someone else who could rig a wire, and both were from
a family headed by the woman who in all of Eastport was the person
widely reported to despise Harriet most: Wilma, herself.

"So," I began very carefully when Wilma had devoured a few more
cookies. Ellie's face remained sphinxlike. "What do you think of the
new guy in town, Harry Markle?"

It was too much to hope for. But when Wilma's mouth popped
smackingly open again, more than crumbs flew out. "Oh, I know *all*
about *him*," she bragged.

Wow, Ellie's eyes said, and I'm sure mine did, too. Wilma scanned
the tablecloth, spotted a stray raisin, and consumed it. "*Knew* all about
him, anyway. Bank had the house up for sale an' he was goin' to buy
it," she added. "Ex-cop. Got a fat pension after he messed his own nest
down in the city."

As the matriarch of an extended Bounce family, Wilma had a spy
web so complex it should have belonged to the CIA. And it wasn't only
felines that Wilma let run wild in the streets of Eastport.

When one of Bob Arnold's sparrows fell, one of Wilma's kids had probably shot it; between her army of cats and her BB-gun-toting children, Wilma was responsible for more dead birds than the institution of Thanksgiving.

"Aunt o' mine works up at the bank," she went on, "they sent him a list of foreclosed properties before Markle ever got here. An' she thought she'd seen his name before, in the newspapers. So she looked 'im up on the computer, and found out his whole story."

And how, her triumphant look added, *did I like that?* "Fran was over here for dinner the other night," I said. A smooth segue would've been wasted on Wilma, or maybe missed altogether. "And I'd really like to talk with her again about . . ."

Criminy, what could I want to talk to Fran about? ". . . hair coloring," I improvised hastily. "Hers is so attractive and I've been thinking about doing my own."

A snort that might have been a smothered guffaw came from my pal Ellie, but Wilma didn't notice. You'd have to hit Wilma over the head with an anvil before she would notice.

But: *Never base your plans on the other guy's brains,* Jemmy Wechsler counseled suddenly in my head. *He don't have to be smart to shoot you in the back.*

Wilma's blank gaze was as empty-seeming as the eyeglasses in a Little Orphan Annie cartoon, but she had relatives with skills. And she was said to have a recent motive for harming Harriet, one that if true probably hadn't felt far-fetched to her.

"Fran's outta town," she replied curtly. "Back tomorrow, mebbe. Come over then, ya might find her and ya might not."

Stolidly, she applied herself to the task of chewing and swallowing, making no move to go.

"Well, thanks for stopping by," I said, hinting. But the aroma of apple cake kept the wretched woman glued to the chair until I had the bright idea of calling Monday out to keep us company.

Noticing a person who disliked dogs, Monday plopped her head immediately into Wilma's lap. Instantly Wilma heaved herself upright.

"Tell your boy about them jobs," she said. "He's old enough, quit wastin' time with silly book-learnin', do some real work."

Like I said: a spy network. "That guy sure did," she wheezed darkly on her way out, "want that old house."

"But banks don't need you to be dead before foreclosure on your property," I told Ellie when Wilma Bounce had at last thumped down the porch steps. "Harry had no motive, no matter what Wilma seems to want to suggest."

"So what if instead *she* killed Harriet, already knew about Harry's past, and used him to cover her own tracks? Make it seem as if *he's* the one people ought to focus on?"

"Niece steals the boots from the motel where she works and sabotages them, puts them back," I theorized.

The oven timer dingled and I took the cake out of the oven: dark-gold and bubbling, a rich glaze of butter and sugar crusting its edges. I put it on a wire rack to cool.

"Later the electrical-apprentice nephew rigs the wire in the Danvers' cellar, so it's hot when it shouldn't be." Every tradesperson in town including the local electricians had gotten work out of Top Cat Productions.

"Of course, it's not just motel rooms and booby traps. One of them would have to murder Harriet, and then hide her," Ellie said. "And get hold of the newspaper page somehow, too. But otherwise . . ."

"A weird sense of humor is a built-in Bounce accessory," I pointed out. "Remember when that girl-gang of Bounces found a drunk out cold on the fish pier, and stapled his clothes to the dock?" When the guy had woken up from his stupor and couldn't move, he'd thought he was paralyzed from the rotgut he'd been swilling. "And there are enough Bounces to pull a prank every hour of the day. Tampered brakes, rigged shotgun reloader, odd notes and calls. Even spiders, I imagine, if they put their minds to it."

"You can buy live spiders on the Internet. I checked."

Trust Ellie to sweat the details. "You couldn't find a clan likelier to do mayhem if you cloned the Addams Family," I said.

"True." Ellie was inspecting the cake. Then she opened the freezer and came out with the ice cream.

"See, this is what I meant about ignoring things that maybe we shouldn't," she told me a few minutes later when fresh coffee had finished brewing. "Not that we should rule anyone *else* out, at this point."

I hadn't; not even Roy. Not for sure. And we hadn't talked to Wyatt Evert yet, either. Still:

"We've been assuming it's some outsider who came here when Harry did." Ellie poured coffee for us both. "Mostly because that's what *he* thinks. But Wilma could've done it. Or at least planned and supervised it."

"Are we going to tell Harry any of this?"

"What, that maybe he's the one on the goose chase? That he should pay a little more attention to what actually happened, and a little less to how it might—or might not—be connected to him?"

Ellie ate some ice cream, then shook her head. "No. Let's not tell him anything yet. It keeps Harry out of our hair to have him concentrating on other angles."

"Big crimes for a little reason if it does turn out to be Wilma. But I guess it wouldn't be the first time that happened, would it?" I said, scraping crumbs from my plate. That apple cake *rocked.*

"No," Ellie said. "And it never seems like a little reason to the person who does the deed. That drowned tourist's still a question mark, though, if it turns out his death *was* murder. And we *still* don't understand the point of *hiding* Harriet's body. If the point was to, well, *point* at Harry, why put the newspaper in her hand but then keep anyone from seeing it?"

"Maybe somehow Wilma knew it would be found?" I suggested.

Meanwhile: good old Wade. He'd overheard enough two and two

to think that if Fran wasn't available, Ellie and I might want to try making four out of Wilma. So he'd fetched her. Or . . . had he? A new thought began occurring to me.

"Maybe," Ellie mused. "Or Wilma could've meant to make *sure* Harriet's body was found, eventually. But Wilma's not perfect, either," she cautioned.

As a suspect, she meant. "It's true she doesn't seem like a person who could hatch a complex scheme or follow it through," I agreed. But . . . "The thing is, she came over here so willingly."

Ellie caught my drift at once. "As if that was just what she'd wanted to do, all along. Wade had a story ready for her but she might not've needed it, to get her here."

Instead she could have fastened onto Wade like a barnacle when the opportunity arose: knowing via the ever-active Eastport grapevine that Ellie and I were poking around into Harriet's death. Eager to keep the focus on Harry Markle while braying out her triumph in a sly way so no one could call her on it.

"A missing pet's *not* much motive for murder," I said. "And those Bounces are pretty bad, but I've never heard of one of them actually killing anybody. Not in cold blood."

Still, if Wilma had murdered Harriet or had someone else do it, then drummed up enough violent confusion so her own interest in the matter would be obscured, then so far she—

—or somebody just like her, secretly smart and utterly ruthless—

—was getting away with it.

Chapter 8

People weren't quaint in 1823. Or at any rate they didn't seem quaint to themselves. They felt *fabulous,* darling:

The dogs of war had been shooed temporarily back into their kennels, Andrew Jackson was riding to the Presidency on the glory of having won the Battle of New Orleans, and Lewis and Clark had been back for some while with the news that if you thought New England was tasty, you should see what *they'd* found: California!

Which was why I felt no qualms at all about putting clear satin polyurethane finish on that hall floor instead of replacing the antique brown varnish with which it had been covered.

"You don't think it's a contradiction?" Ellie was eyeing the polyurethane cans doubtfully.

I shook my head firmly while readying the equipment for the next part of the floor job: her husband, George, plus an electric floor sander so heavy and powerful that if you didn't keep it moving while it was running, it would grind all the way to China.

"Nope." I'd had this argument with myself, and won it. "The poly's what they'd've used if they had it. More durable, better-looking, and *modern*. People were mad for modern in 1823."

"Especially," George agreed, clamping fresh sandpaper into the sanding machine, "plumbing. This house would've had a hot tub with hydromassage if they could've rigged one."

Which was probably true and a hot tub would've been fun. But George also wanted to replace all the plaster in the house with wallboard and the wavery-glassed old windows with thermopane, so I had to be careful about encouraging him on this topic.

Instead I sorted through my pile of tack cloths, wide sheets of cheesecloth impregnated with sticky stuff the consistency of softened beeswax, to make sure I had enough fresh ones. Because while George had the heavy work, which was sanding the floor—

—the sander outweighed me massively, which put my using it into the pulling-yourself-up-by-your-own-bootstraps department—

—there remained the little matter of cleanup. I'd hung plastic sheets in the doorways and draped tarps, but the dust George raised would need elimination with tack cloth before I could apply the poly.

"Ready," George announced, and we left him to it, closing the door behind us as the sander went on with a roar, sounding as if it were not just scouring the old floor, but devouring it.

"Whoa," Sam said, looking up from his apple cake as the huge sound erupted. "What's he doing in there, feeding the banisters through a wood chipper?"

Across from him sat Mr. Ash. Between them were yellow notebook pages scrawled with diagrams and mathematical equations. "Mr. Ash is helping with the theory problems for the seminar this weekend," Sam explained.

It was late afternoon—or as Sam would've put it, past 1600 hours—and the mason had finished his work down in the cellar for today.

"See," Sam added, "you don't just blow stuff up any old way, underwater. First you have to know where the force vectors'll go, what's going to impact what."

Personally I feel "impact" as a verb has a negative impact on the English language, but never mind: if Lian Ash could keep force vectors from impacting my son, I was all for it.

Just then Victor came in, as usual omitting to knock; Victor treats my house the way swallows treat Capistrano.

"Came to check on Sam," he explained, although he hadn't. He'd been passing, heard commotion, and decided to investigate in case there was anything going on that he could criticize.

"Little late for a demolition project, isn't it?" he said, helping himself to a slab of apple cake. Without being asked he added some ice cream, poured coffee, and sat down.

Mr. Ash slid papers aside, eyeing Victor as intently as if storing his features for a high-tech face-recognition program.

"If you do it at the end of the day, the dust settles by morning," I said, "so you can—"

The sander went off, leaving a hole in the air where the noise had been. ". . . wipe it up," I finished defensively, then caught myself. What did I care what Victor thought of my schedule?

On the other hand if you need somebody to poke holes in your theories, my ex is your perfect stiletto. Ellie started another pot of coffee while I tried mine on Victor: theories, I mean, on who was committing bloody murder.

"It wasn't bloody," he objected, spooning up ice cream.

"It's a figure of speech. Just listen for once, will you? We feel it's unlikely, but it *could* be Roy McCall, to get publicity for his video. Because it's got a scary theme, so scary things will be newsworthy."

"Assuming they don't halt the project," Victor said.

"Or," I agreed, "*that* could've been the whole point. Maybe someone who was angry with Roy wanted to end the work altogether and make Roy's career go," I glanced at Sam and Mr. Ash, "boom."

Wade came downstairs just then to wash the gun oil off his hands and join what was becoming a kitchen party; a few hours in the company of weapons always cheers him up, and he grabbed some coffee and cake like the others and put his oar in:

"Guys at the dock say Wilma'd kill you in a heartbeat, she didn't like you, thought she could get away with it," he commented. "Wilma's gonna be another Ma Barker, someday, have her own gang."

"Wyatt Evert's still in the picture too, and we're going to talk to Fran Hanson about him," I put in. "And of course there's still Harry's idea: that some unknown person is really after *him*."

"If that's so," Mr. Ash spoke up pensively, "strikes me somebody's slowin' down in his old age."

Victor frowned. He disapproved of a hired laborer sitting at the table at all, much less joining the conversation.

"Because," Mr. Ash went on, "if you go by what Markle says, this villain of his used to get everyone he tried for. All those people back in the city, you didn't hear of any of 'em getting away, did you?"

He sipped some coffee. "But now if this same mystery man of Markle's is behind it all, guy's only managing about fifty percent of his targets."

"I'll be damned," Wade said slowly. "He's right. I wondered why it was such a damn-fool botch job."

His "accident," he meant. And Sam's. "If you really want to hurt someone," Wade went on, "you don't mess with brakes or even rig up shotgun shells to explode."

"Or fool with any boots," George contributed, joining us. "You get yourself a high-powered rifle, and—"

But he didn't get to finish that thought because just then Cat Dancing leapt onto the table, spotted Victor, and put a paw firmly into his ice cream so she could shove her head purringly into his face.

Instantly Victor recoiled in fastidious horror, rushing to the sink. Mr. Ash watched with interest as Victor began sudsing his face with hot water and dish soap.

"Clean sort o' specimen, ain't you?" he said.

Groping for a towel, Victor scowled in reply. He felt that people who got covered in dust were inferior to ones who got bone chips spattered over themselves in their own daily work.

"Pthaw," he said feelingly. Then, his face brightening: "Say, Jacobia, what's for dinner?"

So that one way and another, we never did get back to the topic of murder. But later that night when everyone had finally gone home, I took Monday out for a walk.

The night air was thick as a damp cloak, the streetlights white with unnatural brilliance in the growing humidity. The storm was teasing us, wreaking havoc off Cape Cod. A few lamps still glowed behind drawn shades in the upstairs windows of the old houses. The first tentative trillings of frogs in distant ponds carried clearly in the silence.

The dog and I wandered past the old Shead mansion. Its windows were broken and its roof crumbled tragically, its eaves pigeon-infested. Monday's ears pricked at a sound from the shadowy yard, but it was only a skunk trundling fearlessly to cross our path.

Harry's lights were on. "Hi," he said when we'd mounted the shaky porch and knocked on the door. Prill appeared behind him in the hall, stubby tail wagging. "Come in." Harry led us into the dining room. "Has something happened?"

Over the mantel he'd hung a big corkboard: on it was tacked an Eastport map and a time line of the accidents and deaths. Colored pushpins showed the locations; the details of each event were noted on stickers, along with where each of us had been at the pertinent times.

"No," I answered. "Nothing's happened. We were out for our walk and I saw your lights on, that's all. This is impressive." I waved at the wall chart, crisply drawn and well organized. Looking at it, you expected your answers to jump right out of it. "Made any new connections?"

But Harry's face told me no answers had appeared. Instead he had something else to say, something I hadn't expected.

"Got a call from my old job this afternoon. Records guy at the NYPD. Seems our buddy Bob Arnold asked them to check my prints against a sample he'd sent them."

"Can they do that?" That cup Bob had taken; I'd forgotten about it.

Harry nodded, trying to seem matter-of-fact about it. "Sure. In case somebody makes an evidence-handling screwup, gloms a fat thumbprint onto something at a crime scene, lab'll know whose it is. You know the drill."

I didn't. But Bob did. "And?"

"And I was just wondering if that was his idea," Harry replied meaningfully. "Or if maybe it was yours."

"No. Not my idea. I didn't think of it. But I'd have suggested it, if I had. No offense, Harry, but this . . ."

I waved at the chart whose clarity was nothing like the chaos of what I was thinking. Or feeling. "It's all just so worrisome, is all. I'm sorry if that bothers you . . ."

"No," he cut in. "No, it's a good idea. I told the records guy, go ahead and tell Bob anything he asks. I'll ask them to call you, too, if you want." He laughed uncomfortably. "It feels weird to be on the other side of things, is all. I just wanted to clear the air."

"Yeah. Clearing the air is good." I kept my eyes on the chart but it told me nothing I hadn't already known.

"You from the city originally?" I asked. "Have family there?"

"Yeah. Brooklyn. But no family anymore. My parents died in a robbery when I was twelve."

He said it matter-of-factly. "Guy was never caught," he went on, "and I got raised in foster homes. I guess that's what got me wanting to catch bad guys, myself."

He opened a drawer in the table beside his makeshift bed, drew out a small black box, like a jeweler's box. He opened it.

"Here it is. All I've got left, now, of catching bad guys."

It was an NYPD gold shield. "Didn't wear this, of course. You put it in a safe-deposit box, or you hide it somewhere good if you keep it at your place. You wear a duplicate for everyday work, take this baby out on special occasions," he said.

"I can see why." The shield was more impressive than anything from Tiffany's, as much for what it meant as for its monetary value. Seeing it, I thought of richly garbed ceremonial warriors.

"Yeah, that was me. Badge 1905. Not anymore, though." He put it away again, slid the drawer shut.

"Harry. What do you think got it all started? I mean, if you're right and it began back in the city, all this . . ." I waved at his chart. "Whatever it is."

He shrugged. "Somebody was mad. Angry at cops. Angry with me for some reason, too. Very," he emphasized quietly, "angry."

"Yeah." I looked around at the clean, well-lighted place Harry had made for himself. "It must be harder," I ventured, "to lose your parents at that age. I mean, to know what you've lost. Mine were gone before I knew them, which made it easy in a way."

"No. Not easy. Just different. We all deal with it in different ways. But only people who've been through it can really understand, I think."

A silence, as we both did understand. Harry was right; the absence of my parents wasn't something I thought about much, but it was like a missing layer of sky: the cold stars at night were just that much nearer.

Too near. "I'll be glad to get my own things in here," he said. "Own furniture, books. I've had a lot sent up from my last place, put it at the U-Stor-It on the mainland."

"Yes," I said inadequately, "that'll make it more like home. I mean . . ."

"Yeah," he said, covering my gaffe; we both knew his last real home had been a horror show, at the end.

We made a little small talk. He'd gone to Calais and bought dress shirts, still stacked in clear plastic wrappers on his bed. He meant to fly to Pittsburgh for Samantha's memorial service.

"Funeral's private, but I can still pay my respects at the other thing. Hope one of the shirts fits. I got them at Wal-Mart. Been a while since I bought one. I wonder if they still have the little celluloid strips in the collars?"

"Wade buys shirts at Wal-Mart. I don't know about the strips but they run pretty true to size. Did you get those there, too?"

I indicated the boots he was wearing; nice, new ones, as I'd first noticed on the day we met. That seemed a long time ago now.

"What?" He looked perplexed for a moment. "Oh. No. Bought 'em at the L.L. Bean store on my way here, in Ellsworth."

And more in this trivial vein until he walked me to the door. After a rendevous with Monday, Prill had stationed herself as usual at his side. "Harry," I began, looking out into the chilly darkness of a spring night in Eastport.

I knew why I'd come here. I just hadn't let myself admit it until now. "Harry, *was* he alive, do you think? I mean, what do you think about it, when you look back on it?"

He understood. "No. I hate to say it but I think we were wasting our time. They were hot for him, you know? A big piece of a radical network." He sighed. "Jake, your dad would've been a real feather in someone's cap. But after all we did, all the tiny little leads we went chasing, we never had a whiff of anything that told *me* he was really out there. So I think it was good for my career, but that was all." He sighed again. "Not," he added, "that it made a big difference, in the end. Anything else you want to know?"

"Yeah." This was hard to say. "When you found me. Was there any sign that anybody had tried to protect me? Put me somewhere that I wouldn't get too hurt, or . . ."

Or what? A little crash helmet and a flame-resistant suit? Nothing less could have helped except dumb luck, which I'd had.

And I'd had Harry. "No. You were wearing pajamas. Everything covered with soot. All I saw at first were two big eyes looking out from under a piece of sheet metal."

Across the bay, the lights of Campobello twinkled innocently against a backdrop of velvet black. Things always looked innocent when viewed from a distance, I guessed.

"No," Harry repeated. "I'm sorry. But you'd had, as far as I could tell, no protection from anyone."

The next morning was a pastel wash of cool, pale tints and salt-tinctured sea air. A little white scallop-dragger tootled serenely on the blue water; gulls dipped and wheeled above it. A harbor seal's head surfaced, trailing a v-shaped wake.

Still no real sign of a storm but it was out there getting itself ready. "Wilma's nephew could've gotten into the house and walled Harriet's body up, too," I said, "not just rigged the wire. I saw fresh mortar but of course I didn't make anything of it then."

Ellie and I strode down Water Street past La Sardina. A whiff of chili spice hung in the damp air outside the restaurant, replaced by the smell of fresh doughnuts as we passed the bakery.

"The Danvers family won't be here for weeks, yet," I added. "A work truck or a van parked outside their house for a little while—"

Long enough, say, to lug in Harriet's body, perhaps rolled in a tarp of the kind workmen everywhere are always hauling–

"–wouldn't even have been noticed."

"They had been having a lot of work done before they got back from Florida," Ellie concurred. "Lots of painting and all. Probably the rent from Top Cat was helping to pay for it."

It was a strategy I approved, the more so since my check of the hall floor showed more dust than I–or anyone–could have bargained for, punctuated by cat footprints that had carried it efficiently all over the house. As far as I was concerned at the moment, the only good state to be in during home repair was the state of elsewhere, and if you could get someone else to pay for it, too, so much the better.

"Look," Ellie said, angling her head at the bakery window. Ahead of us, Monday pranced jauntily, pausing to nibble street-treats; old bubble gum was her favorite.

Fran Hanson stood at the bakery counter. Monday yanked the leash, scrambling at a crumb of dropped pastry. Inside, Wyatt Evert's assistant looked up at the sudden movement, caught my eye, and looked down again.

"Not feeling sociable," I observed as Ellie and I went on past the Eastport Art Gallery, the dime store, and Quoddy Crafts. Now that I knew Fran was in town again I was in no big hurry to quiz her; Wilma was my quarry this morning.

A few minutes later we climbed into the warren of streets lining the hillside below the Fort Sullivan ruins. Days after the British invaded it in 1814, Eastporters were billeting redcoats and signing loyalty oaths to King George, their fingers crossed behind their backs. Now, perhaps in memory of that humiliation, the fort was a nothingish pile of stones, unmarked.

"There." Ellie pointed past scrubby softwood trees whose new green leaves obscured a clear vantage point over the harbor. "That's Wilma's house."

"Ye gods." Tucked back into the brush and junky trees loomed a ramshackle dwelling with a shiny tin roof, brown asphalt siding punctuated irregularly by tar paper, a porch roof propped on two-by-fours perched on rusty paint cans, and a connecting maze of sheds in different stages of collapse that jutted at every angle.

Also, the house was positively bouncing to the bass-thump of music booming within, and so full of people that they seemed to be falling out of the windows.

"You insisted," Ellie reminded me sweetly, "that you wanted to visit Wilma, first."

"But . . ."

Undeterred, she led me up the steps toward what I had imagined might be an unpleasant but survivable sit-down with the formidable aforementioned. Now, however, it felt like imminent doom, as more small Bounces appeared.

A posse of them shinnied down a trellis, their avid eyes suggesting that behind their smeary lips, their teeth had been filed to carnivorous points. A squad of teenagers had already formed a blankly staring cordon behind us, blocking possible retreat. Even Monday blinked uncertainly as masses of diapered toddlers assembled, infant grins signaling the intent to grab her nose and see if they could make it go *oo-OO-gah!*

"Heel," I said firmly and she lined up like a shot, her tail tucked and her ears lowered unhappily. Which was what did it, finally. Most of the time you can menace me with impunity; on my own behalf I am a mild-mannered person. But threaten my dog and I'll cheerfully feed both your lungs to you for breakfast.

"Scram," I snapped, turning to stamp my foot at the advancing teenagers. They backed away, startled.

"Shoo," I told the toddlers, scattering them with brisk little waves of my hands. "Go on, *scat!*"

The children who'd been coming down the lattice at me halted in

181

mid-shinny and began making their way up again, scrambling in through the open window. One after another, little rumps tumbled over the ledge and were engulfed by the percussive thumps of a boom box so loud, it could've been used to divert the migration of whales in the North Atlantic.

But while I was repelling the Children's Army, Monday had taken advantage of my inattention; now she was in the sandbox, surrounded by plastic toys, slurping milky cereal from a bowl that had originally held Cool Whip.

Then I spotted the first cat, and the second and third, and understood what else that sandbox was surely full of. "Monday!" I bellowed. She ambled to me, which was when Wilma finally appeared in the thundering darkness of her own front doorway.

"Yeah?" She wore a bloody apron. A cigarette dangled from her lips. A big knife was clenched in her hand.

There were cats on the rooftop, cats on the walls, cats in the bassinet on the porch, which also had sleeping babies in it, apparently undisturbed by the decibel level. I could only conclude the boom box's blaring had already deafened them.

"Wilma," Ellie said quietly. "Please. We need your help."

I glanced sharply at her; this was not an approach I thought could work. But something in Ellie's attitude had changed while we stood there. "These aren't all Wilma's kids," she told me softly. "They can't be. Can they?"

Wilma squinted at us through the cigarette smoke spiraling into her dark eyes. She flicked the burning butt at the sandbox, then beckoned for us to follow her.

Some of the bigger children had returned to their morning routine, which I didn't want to think about too much; I kept imagining a neighbor child somewhere out in those scrub trees, being boiled in a pot.

"What's it matter," I told Ellie, "whose . . . ?" At least I didn't see any gun-toting infants. But I did spot a squirrel pelt nailed to a door frame; probably they were all out hunting.

"You want help? I'll help ya. Maybe then the stories goin' around'll quit bein' about me." When it reappeared from the shadows, Wilma's face was impassive but her tone now took on a distinctly querulous note.

"Come on," she said flatly and vanished once more into the din.

As I hesitated several things were occurring to me, one of them being that Wilma was no one's fool. At least, she apparently took care of all these children who, despite their wild air, didn't look abused or malnourished.

"Well, you comin' or ain't you?" Wilma called impatiently.

The children were beginning to close ranks around us again, eyes avid, sticky hands outstretched. Maybe they didn't look abused but they did remind me of another of Sam's favorite movies: *Night of the Living Dead.*

As if, if they touched me, I might start to like the ghastly music booming at heart-rupturing volume from upstairs.

We followed Wilma inside.

She led us to a room I identified with difficulty as the kitchen. A table peeped from under heaps of laundry and coloring books; toys and juice bottles mingled with dishes piled in the sink. A refrigerator wheezed in the corner, crayon drawings and finger paintings plastered to the front of it.

"Sit," Wilma commanded, sweeping old newspapers from a pair of wooden chairs. I obeyed; Ellie remained standing, the better to let her mild gaze rove over her surroundings.

Wilma returned to the task she'd been doing before we showed up: cleaning a big fish. With five swift whacks she relieved the fish of tail and fins, tossing them to the floor where they were instantly snatched by cruising felines.

"Now, you wanta tell me how the hell I'd even know if a cat was missing?" Wilma demanded without preamble.

In one blade-flash the fish was relieved of its interior, the result pounced upon by more cats. Wilma glanced dourly after a feral-looking feline, caught the expression on my face.

"Hell, you think you're the only ones figure I might've got rid a' the old snoop?" she asked, responding to my surprise.

Blade-flash; fish fillet. "Munchkin," she added with a loud, dismissive snort. "Who the hell thought that one up?" *Whack*. "I got enough tryin' ta remember kids' names, 'thout namin' cats."

"You mean you *didn't* name it that?"

Over in a corner behind a padded wooden rocking chair with a child asleep in it, a feline the size of a terrier was devouring something growlingly: the fish's head.

"No, I didn't," Wilma declared. "Eastport rumor mill dished out that little detail, not me. And I don't live nowheres near that skinny witch, Harriet Hollingsworth, either. Over in high muckety-muck-town, like you." So much for not speaking ill of the dead. Or for us being the ones asking the questions:

"Yeah, I heard you was stickin' your noses all around. So I followed your old man home, acted like I believed that fool story he was tellin', like that kid of yours needs anything, just so's I could find out what *you* two had cookin'."

She made a sound of disgust. "Shouldn'a wasted my time. Knew when you mentioned the cat what you were thinkin'. But why would any cat o' mine be all the way across town, anyhow?" she went on, lopping off more fillets. "Cats don't range that far."

Drat, she was right. Cat Dancing was an indoor animal, so I hadn't thought of it. "You mean you were just stringing us along?"

"Yeah. You deserved it, try'na play detective with me. My nephew, he fixes trucks for the electrician, don't do no wiring."

"Why'd you mention the motel?" Ellie asked. Because Wilma's story about wanting to know if we'd swallowed town gossip about her didn't *quite* wash; the death of Wyatt Evert's eco-tourist had not been linked to Harriet's by anyone but us.

"I just tossed that in for atmosphere. Niece does yard work there, is all. Why?" Wilma added curiously, "did I get lucky?"

"Yeah," I told her, discouraged. "You did."

Wilma scratched her scalp with the tip of the knife she was using to cut chowder pieces. I didn't see any fishing gear around but probably some of the larger children had caught the fish with their teeth. "Had ya goin', huh? So why'n't you two snoopy-doos spread *that* on a cracker, take it all over town?" she demanded. "I got enough trouble, this crew, 'thout the whole world thinkin' I'm a killer."

Seizing the fish skeleton she strode to a window, flung the remains into the teeming yard. "Although I guess the newspaper in the old bat's claw'll finish that idea, I give it enough time."

Which was just what *we'd* thought: that the newspaper could've been Wilma's attempt at misdirection. But now it seemed unlikely she could've planned it that way. She'd spun us, was all. Motive gone, the means and opportunity similarly vanished . . .

Slamming the window, Wilma wiped her stained hands on the front of her sweatshirt, which bore the legend "Don't Freak With Me—I Freak Back."

You sure do, I thought glumly. Two gory handprints streaked fishily through the legend as if to punctuate it. "All right," I said, crestfallen; what a letdown. "But what about . . ."

A series of thuds, crashes, and shrieks from above suggested that more murders were being committed that very minute. "Shut the hell up!" Wilma bellowed at the ceiling.

Silence fell briefly, followed by the sound of thundering feet down the stairs, out the door—*bang!*—and over the front porch.

". . . Fran," I finished weakly.

Wilma slapped the fish fillets onto a platter, thrust the plate into the refrigerator. "What about Fran? That damned Wyatt has got a mad on about somethin', laid her off. He don't get rid of it, we're gonna be *eatin'* cats, Fran don't have a paycheck."

Which answered the question of how Wilma had any house at all; despite battalions of swarming children, I saw no evidence of any Mr. Bounce, or anyone else who might earn income.

Curiouser and curiouser, I telegraphed to Ellie, who nodded minutely.

"Fran's the only moneymaker in the house," Wilma said, "or as ever was. We'd be down the tubes without her. Wouldn't we, Eldred?"

A child in diapers had wandered in sleepily; Wilma mussed its hair roughly but with affection, grabbed a pacifier from a clutter of cat toys, and popped it into the child's mouth before it could howl.

"Yes sir, Fran's our angel," Wilma Bounce declared. It was the first time I'd heard her utter a sentence that didn't have a swear word in it, or sound as if it ought to.

"Not here much but she comes home when she can," Wilma told us. "An' when she does, my little sister stays right here with me an' the young'uns, anytime she's in town."

"I don't see why you want to talk to me," Fran Hanson said crisply when we'd located her again. "Wyatt's not *my* problem. Or not anymore. He thinks he fired me? Well, the hell with him. I quit."

We'd found her at the end of the fish pier, gazing glumly at the water as if she might jump in.

I'd felt like jumping too, even though Ellie had said ruling people out was as important as ruling them in.

Now I cut to the chase with Wilma's little sister. "You were in town when Harriet vanished. Wyatt, too."

She turned on me. "So what? You think I had something to do with some wacky old woman disappearing? Believe me, I stay out of what goes on in this town. It was bad enough growing up here. Now I've gotten away, what do I care?"

It was a common small-town story. One kid makes good, leaves and never comes back. But Fran *had* come back; did so regularly, in fact, despite her apparent contempt for the place. She whipped a cigarette pack and lighter from a stylish leather bag.

Down in the boat basin, men in rubber boots traded banter and tools as they worked to keep their means of livelihood afloat another day.

"Bunch of losers," Fran commented scathingly.

Right, I thought, wanting to smack her. And getting busted for receiving stolen property was truly classy, wasn't it? On the other hand, there's a slant-roofed little shanty on a rocky hill up in coal country that I've never returned to at all.

"Why *do* you come back?" Ellie asked Fran reasonably.

"You saw Wilma," she replied. "I can't abandon her and if I only send money and don't visit her feelings get hurt. She *is* my sister."

I had a feeling that wasn't the whole story but I let it go for now. "So you went to work for Wyatt Evert because you knew if you did, the job would bring you here. That way, it wouldn't feel to you as if you *were* visiting home. It would be just that you were here on a business trip."

Fran glanced resentfully at me, crushed the cigarette under the heel of her smart boot. "Which even if it were true is none of *your* business," she retorted. "What do you two want from me, anyway?"

Implying that nothing about yokels like us could be of any interest to a smart, snazzily reinvented person such as herself. Gosh, I love it when somebody gives me an opening like that.

"Wyatt Evert's a crook and you're his accomplice. You're on the run—that's why you've changed your name, isn't it?—and unless you talk to us right this minute I'll make sure you go to jail on the Florida probation you're violating just by being here."

Fran's face sagged in shock, telling me I was right about one thing, anyway; she'd run out on the Florida probation order. "I have no idea what you're talking about," she said, recovering swiftly.

Maybe it was on account of her faithfulness to Wilma that I took pity on her. Or maybe it was that shanty I've never had the guts to revisit. Fran came back often, and when she did she stayed at Wilma's wild kingdom.

"Fran, I'm not trying to jam you up, or Wyatt, either. Not unless I have to, and I hope I don't."

She eyed me mistrustfully as Sam appeared on the breakwater, once again pushing Maggie in the wheelchair, full of news. "Hey, Mom, you're not gonna believe it."

"Sam," I began firmly; when it comes to manners a boy's best friend is still his mother. "This is—"

I turned to Fran, intending to reintroduce her so he could shake hands, say it was nice to see her again, and hope that she was enjoying her stay in Eastport.

But he didn't wait. "Wyatt Evert," he told me excitedly, "just punched Tim Rutherford in the nose. There's blood all over the sidewalk!"

From her seat in the wheelchair, Maggie peered closely at me while Fran reacted to Sam's report.

"Oh, god. *Why* did he punch him?" Fran asked.

"Dunno," Sam replied, "but—"

"Your eye looks better," Maggie told me. "The bruising is going down. The contact lens isn't bothering you?"

I was still wearing the lenses and surprisingly, I'd begun getting used to the green. It gave me a jolt of "who in heck is that?" in the morning right after I first put them in, but that was all.

"They're fine," I said, turning to Sam again.

"—asking something about nonprofit," he was saying. "And then, whammo."

"What else did you hear?" Fran questioned him intently. "I mean, before Wyatt punched the reporter."

Sam frowned. "I wasn't really paying attention."

But Tim must've asked Wyatt *something* fairly pertinent, which to me just reinforced the notion that maybe there'd really been something to the nonprofit angle Tim talked about, on our trip to Machias.

"Seems our friend Wyatt's a tad sensitive on the subject of his business dealings," I said when Sam and Maggie had gone on, Sam's curly head bent charmingly to hear what Maggie was saying.

He'd traded the gauze arm-sling for a red bandanna that made him look dashing, as if he'd been injured in a sword fight; also, the last time I had seen my son so fascinated by a conversation, Bert was confiding a secret to Ernie on Sesame Street.

Sam was in *close* mode. Later: *push away.* I had no illusions my little pep talk about Maggie had altered anything.

Fran tried to change the subject: "Wyatt's feeling nervous. He says you think he might've killed the old battle-axe. And Roy McCall says you think maybe *he* had something to do with that dancer who died, Samantha."

She colored at my inquisitive glance. "Roy and I have had a few drinks since we met at your house," she explained grudgingly.

And more, her face said clearly, not that I cared. But she was trying to divert me so she went on, piling one messy detail upon the next.

"I've been sneaking away with him, actually," she confessed with sly defiance. "There's plenty of empty rooms in Eastport. A crew member's room at the motel or in a B&B during the day. Roy can borrow one when he wants. They all borrow each other's rooms, no one cares."

Which was way more sociology than I wanted to learn. "But you've got *him* wrong too," she added. "Roy's in *more* trouble than before. The replacement for Samantha, the dancer who's coming in? Tonya some-body? *Well.*"

Happily, she prepared to deliver news that might take the spotlight off her. "Tonya, it turns out, has stood around in some shoots in front of cameras. But that's all."

Commercials, Roy McCall had said. A toothpaste ad. But now I realized: the days of dancing toothpaste tubes were long gone.

"She'd never actually *danced* in a production. She's *awful.*" Fran's eyes shone at the memory of trouble that wasn't her own. "So now the guys footing the bills are mad at him for letting the *first* one get killed."

She was on a roll, thinking her ploy was working. "That's very interesting," I replied, trying not to react to the fact that all the motives I'd thought up–lovely, bloody-minded motives like vengeance in Wilma's case or defense against ticked-off Mob guys, in Roy's–were crashing and burning.

"Now, about Wyatt and his supposed nonprofit organization," I said. Whereupon she sensibly realized she'd run out of subjects to divert me, and gave in.

"I just found out, myself." She was suddenly defensive. "I knew Wyatt was bent but he swore up and down this time he was on the level, that there was money enough in playing it straight not to need any stealing."

Sure, and pretty soon zebras would be wearing polka dots. "What's the crooked part? And how did you find out at this late date?"

She rolled her eyes. "I was cleaning out the van. I found a ledger stuffed way down in the upholstery, under a seat."

"And?" Fran didn't only look defensive; she looked scared. So considering her history, I suspected what must be coming next.

"It's just like the one I use for keeping Wyatt's financial records. For the tour business *and* the–"

"Fran," I interrupted, "have you ever filled out forms to register a nonprofit organization? Don't try to tell me you don't remember."

As a project, registering a nonprofit is like writing *War and Peace.* By the end, you're lucky if your writing arm's not tied up in a sling like Sam's.

"No. I haven't. And Wyatt wouldn't have. I do all that stuff," she said. "Or I thought I did, but now it looks like he keeps records, too. Only the numbers are different. Bigger," she emphasized, "numbers."

Starting a nonprofit is simpler, of course, if you do no paperwork at all, just tell people you're benefiting something and take their money. By the time anyone figures it out, you're out of town with a new name and new racket somewhere else.

So maybe Tim Rutherford had been right. Maybe the tour operation was just a good way to identify the fattest pigeons.

"You don't handle the money or make solicitations yourself, though?" I quizzed Fran. "Or deposit checks into any account that has your name on it anywhere?"

"No. I never even knew about any bigger money. All I see is my pay. And it's not," she added bitterly, "enough, if it turns out I go to jail. I was on the pier trying to figure out what to do when you two came along."

"You're going to do nothing. You're going to sit tight until we see how this all shakes out," I told her, getting up. "Maybe if you're telling us the truth, you can be gotten out of this."

A second set of account books: real numbers for a fake nonprofit, so Fran wouldn't realize she was only getting crumbs from the table. If she was being honest about that it was possible she could be saved from the wreckage.

But as Fran headed forlornly up Water Street toward Wilma's, I was already less sure than I'd been. "Ellie, what if the guy who drowned found out somehow what Wyatt's up to? Fran might've figured she had as much to lose as Wyatt. She is on probation. Wyatt could've held that over her. Threatened her, so she'd help him get into the guy's room."

"So Fran gets her cousin the motel landscaper to steal a key, maybe. Wyatt wrecks the boots, makes sure the guy ends up in a deep part of the marsh," Ellie mused. "But while Wyatt's at it, Harriet sees something compromising from her window?"

". . . and being Harriet, she confronts Wyatt. That's what the argument with Wyatt could've been about. And . . ."

Across the street, Tim Rutherford headed for La Sardina, a red-stained handkerchief pressed to his nose and the desire for a good stiff orange soda clear on his face.

He hadn't seen me. But at the sight of him, mental lightning struck: newspaper reporters. And . . . newspapers.

"Hang on a second," Ellie said before I could tell her about my epiphany. She crossed the street, collared Timmy, and listened intently to him once she'd asked him a question.

When she returned, I was still hot on the trail of my own insight. "Ellie, what if Harriet already *knew* who Harry was? All the old newspapers she kept stacked in her hall. She took clippings from them. So maybe she actually *read* them."

Ellie caught on nimbly. "So Harry walks up to the porch and introduces himself. The name rings a bell, Harriet digs out the old newspapers where she's seen that name, to check? And she's got them out, maybe right there in plain sight, when Wyatt shows up?"

"Which Wyatt *would* do, if Harriet had called him to say she saw him up to mischief in that tourist's room. Forrest said he'd seen them arguing *at her house*."

"Harry said he'd talked to Wyatt back when Harry first got to town. Wyatt would've recognized the name if he saw it again."

"Newspapers with Harry's name, the whole ghastly story, and maybe even Harry's picture. That gives Wyatt a brainstorm."

"Get rid of Harriet. But don't just hide the body. Hide it with an old story about Harry. So if it *is* ever found . . ."

"Wyatt couldn't have been sure, then, that the tourist guy's drowning wouldn't be investigated as murder even without Harriet raising the alarm. And George had mentioned those boots to him, too. So he was in a panic, wanting to direct suspicion in some other direction in case someone *else* got snoopy."

"He couldn't have known in advance that cellar wall would collapse," Ellie said. "That would've been just good luck, for him. But he'd've intended all along that if the body *was* found . . ."

"It wouldn't just fail to suggest some connection with Wyatt Evert. It would point straight at Harry," I finished.

Oh, it was lovely, thoroughly wacko just like Wyatt Evert himself, and even the fact that it still had miles of loose ends—we did not, for instance, even know how Harriet had died—didn't spoil it, at first.

But there was one thing wrong with it. It wasn't simple. And I'd already had one complex theory do the house-of-cards act on me that morning. As a result, I couldn't get Bob Arnold's words—Victor's, too—out of my head: *The simplest explanation is usually the truth.*

So my happiness began collapsing swiftly, and what came next didn't help. "What were you talking with Tim about?" I asked as we jaywalked past the art gallery and the dime store. The big windows previewed summer: in the art gallery, bright watercolors and whimsical sculpture, in the dime store, squirt guns and American flags.

"Something I just wondered. Tim's from here, too, and he's about the right age. So I thought maybe he'd been in Fran's high school class."

"So what if he was?"

She'd learned something, I could tell, but she didn't look any happier than I felt. "I thought when we were at her place that Wilma must be watching some of those kids for other people," she said. "But not in day care, or foster care."

Eastport did have its own day care center, run by a pleasant, efficient woman who I thought must take atomic vitamins. Faces washed and noses wiped: when she brought those kids into the IGA they followed her up and down the aisles quietly and obediently, like well-behaved ducklings. None of them looked as if, behind their smiles, their teeth had been filed to sharp points.

By contrast: "One glance at Wilma's house and the state would be chartering a fleet of vans to take those kids away," I said.

"Uh-huh. The thing is, though, if you add a lot of kids to the fact that Fran comes back to Eastport often, even though she doesn't like it, here. *And* sends money. Well, you wonder . . ."

"Why." Fran's behavior *was* curious, and her feelings for her sister didn't quite explain it.

"And the answer is, they are *all* Bounce kids," Ellie went on, "but they're *not* all Wilma's. Nieces, nephews, all kinds of relations. Tim says some of the parents are away working, haven't got the wherewithal to take care of the kids. Or they're in the military, or whatever. Wilma just takes 'em all, no questions, overnight or long-term."

Drat; there went the rest of my disdain for Wilma. "And Tim knows this because . . ."

"Because he was going to do a story for the *Tides* about how great it was of Wilma to do that. Until she pointed out what you said, that the next thing you know she'd have inspectors on her doorstep. So Tim decided it'd be better to let Wilma go on flying under the radar, and he killed the story."

Good old Tim. BB guns or not he'd thought foster care wasn't necessarily better for those kids than Wilma. And having been in the equivalent of foster care myself, I had to agree; I was well aware that there exist many dedicated, devoted foster parents.

But I also knew every kid wasn't guaranteed a foster family from heaven, and that you upset people's applecarts—even the creaky, one-wheeled variety—at your peril.

Tim Rutherford had apparently learned that somehow, too. My regard for him rose another notch. "And the bottom line is?"

Ellie sighed. "One of those kids is Fran's."

Oh, for heaven's sake, of course. I mentally smacked my own forehead as Ellie went on. "Tim said Fran dropped out of their class as a junior, six months pregnant. No one knew the father. I doubt that matters now, who he was."

Suddenly getting Fran off the hook looked even less like a cakewalk, and more like a fire walk. "You know what this means, though. If Fran knew all along Wyatt Evert was a crook . . ."

"And it's one thing to support your sister but it's a bigger ball game to support your own child. *And* stay out of jail, so you can keep seeing your kid."

"So if someone else, like maybe Harriet, found out about Wyatt's scheme—*if* he had one—Fran had just as good a motive as Wyatt to get rid of that person," Ellie said. "Maybe better."

We headed uphill; me walking, Ellie striding. "Slow down, will you?" But she didn't.

"Probably most people here didn't recognize Fran, and she changed her name to keep the Florida probation people off her trail." Ellie was thinking aloud. "That's why I didn't tumble sooner to who she is. But there's another thing bothering me."

Oh, terrific. "What?"

"You told me you'd locked all the doors the other night."

"Yes."

"So let's say Roy really was in Portland. If he was, he wouldn't have wanted it, would he?" She turned to face me. "The key, I mean. Your house key, that you told me Roy had. He wouldn't need it, wouldn't even notice if it was gone probably. So who might've stolen it, used it, sneaked it back onto his key ring?"

"Fran," I said. "She implied she'd had a rendezvous with Roy since he got back from Portland. Today, maybe. It's how she knew we'd asked him questions."

"And Fran's clever," Ellie said thoughtfully.

"Yes. She's had to be, to survive."

The question was, how clever? As if in answer, a detailed picture of a motel-room dresser top rose in my mind. Loose change from the pockets; wallet, cell phone, too, probably. And . . .

And a ring of keys.

Chapter 9

Back at my house, all was peaceful except for the racket of the men beavering away at the cellar project. But I regard noises made by other people working on my house as music, so that didn't bother me.

"I'll be back," Ellie said. She wanted to find out where Wyatt Evert had gotten to after his poke at Tim, maybe try to float some story whereby Wyatt would agree to talk to us. I had a date with Wade that I didn't want to break, so I let her go.

At the door she peered at me. "You sure you're all right?"

"Fine," I said firmly. The bruise on my face had faded to an exotic greeny-lavender color, and my shoulder only clicked a little bit when I moved it. The swimmy feeling in my head was a constant, mildly annoying backdrop, but it wasn't getting worse. When she'd gone I took ibuprofen instead of the aspirin I would otherwise have chosen; if the

197

wooziness I felt meant my brain was getting ready to hemorrhage, I didn't want to encourage it.

Then I returned to the hall, where the old floor lay sanded to the bare wood. I'd run the vacuum over it since otherwise the dust would've smothered us all; now I ran it again.

Or rather, I started running it, using the soft dust-brush attachment to clean carefully in the spaces between the flooring pieces and in the corners formed by the baseboard trim. Halfway through, though, I realized: the machine's roar obliterated other sounds, such as for instance the back door opening.

The thought made my heart lurch. Switching off the machine I stood there with my head pounding and my ears ringing, feeling the presence of someone standing in the hall behind me.

Slowly, I turned to face . . .

No one. No one at all. Cat Dancing sat watching me with a smirky look on her furry features. "Scat," I told her and she got up disdainfully and stalked away, uttering some feline oath.

And then, unable to help myself, I went around locking doors and windows again; Wade showed up before our appointed time and caught me latching the door from the ell to the yard. He raised his eyebrows, followed me inside, and closed the door behind us.

"Feeling a little vulnerable, are we?" he commented.

"Yep," I replied shortly. "Not like before, but . . ."

After some thought, earlier that morning I'd waited until I saw Mr. Ash through the kitchen window in the yard with the dog. Then I'd put the Bisley into a secret hiding place in the kitchen mantel; not even Sam knew the sliding door was there, installed when the house was built 200 years ago.

Carrying the gun made me feel even more anxious and paranoid, as if it were a magnet for trouble instead of a tool to fend it off. I would carry a weapon, I'd decided, when I was alone in the house. The rest of the time I could get to it in a heartbeat if need be.

"I keep waiting for the other shoe to drop," I went on. "You know that feeling?" I handed Wade a tack cloth. "Anyway, thanks for helping me with this." We knelt side by side, began wiping.

The first pass of my cloth brought up a thick coat of dust from the vacuumed surface. A paintbrush loaded with polyurethane would bring up even more, then deposit it again in hard, finish-coated beads to give the floor a cobbled appearance.

"Wilma Bounce didn't pan out?" Wade said. "Or Fran?"

"I don't know yet about Fran," I said. "But I'm pretty sure about Wilma."

I turned the tack cloth over; the first side was already clogged with wood dust. "That she didn't, I mean. I suppose if you wanted to, you *could* still make the case against her."

We moved forward in tandem, me wiping the left side of the floor and Wade the right. "But now it turns out her cat wouldn't have wandered as far as Harriet's house, and Wilma knew it."

I summed up my visit with Ellie to Wilma's and our chat with Fran Hanson. "She's not quite the unredeemed character I thought, either. Wilma, that is."

I added the kid-care details. Wade wadded the tack cloth and pushed it under the old cast-iron radiator.

"How about a case against Wyatt? Or Wyatt and Fran together?" he suggested, dragging out heaps of dust the vacuum hadn't been able to reach.

"I guess it's possible. But that would be awfully detailed, too, wouldn't it? Making it work right so they didn't get caught at any of it, *and* making sure it stayed linked to Harry Markle."

"Complicated things do happen sometimes," he pointed out.

"Sure. It would also hinge on the tourist's having found out about Wyatt's racket, though, and threatening to expose it, which I have no way to confirm, either. And after that . . ."

After that a whole string of things would have had to line up;

improbable things like Wyatt happening to see Harriet's newspaper and pay attention to it while he was upset about something else.

"Ellie and I still plan to talk to Wyatt. But I don't have high hopes. As for Fran, that theory's got other problems."

Such as how could she be *sure* she would get my key back to Roy before he noticed it was missing? "I hope she's *not* involved. Just being hooked up with Wyatt, that girl's in way over her head." A sigh escaped me. "Maybe Harry Markle's got the right idea after all, and it *is* all about him. Now, *that* would be simple."

Like puppets on the same pair of strings Wade and I turned, opened new cloths, and started back. "Harry's still working on that?" Wade asked.

"Uh-huh. I guess. But he hasn't said much about it and I've got to believe that means he's not getting anywhere, either, any more than we are."

"Paint after this?" Polyurethane, he meant.

I nodded, sighing again. "Wade, I'm starting to think the only way anyone will get to the bottom of this is if some culprit walks up and *confesses* to killing Harriet. And to the rest of it, too."

Meanwhile when you already have a headache the best thing to do is open a can of polyurethane floor finish. That way, at least you've got an excuse. "Is it hot in here?"

I pulled off my sweater and hung it on the radiator. Wade reached out and laid a hand across my forehead.

"No. But you look sort of pale. Maybe you should let me put the first coat on."

I'd already opened the can of poly and was stirring it with a paint stick. The sludge at the bottom was fudgey-thick, and you can't have it shaken at the paint store; it puts bubbles in it.

"Uh-uh. The first coat dries too fast, so you won't be able to keep a wet edge if you're working by yourself. Gad, it stinks." The fumes rose up medicinally.

Wade went to open the door, feeling that the last thing I needed was chemical brain damage, and in fact when you are finishing a floor it's a good idea to do it outside. But like so many aspects of do-it-yourself home repair, this is impossible.

Finally the polyurethane was stirred. Also we'd taken the brushes outdoors and gotten the loose bristles out of them (me taking breaths of fresh air, trying not to let on how nauseated I felt) which meant there were only about a zillion loose bristles still left in the brushes.

And we'd locked Monday and Cat Dancing in Wade's shop where Monday could sleep and Cat could amuse herself by, I imagined, learning to load, aim, and fire a variety of deadly weapons. At last we knelt at the end of the hall, the polyurethane can open between us and brushes in hand, like runners on their marks.

"Ready?" Wade asked. Finishing a floor is a sprint; it takes only a few minutes but while you're doing it, you can't stop.

"Ready," I replied. I loaded my brush with the watery stuff and applied it to the raw wood in long, even strokes as Wade did likewise. The dull, pinkish-white surface glistened and came alive; the old wood glowed richly, pale radiant gold.

Which naturally was when urgent knocks sounded first on our front door, and then on the back. Both phone lines began ringing and a *ping!* came from Sam's computer, signaling e-mail.

Also, Mr. Ash chose that moment to climb the cellar steps. "Ahem," he said, or something ominously like it. "We have a small emergency in the cellar."

"Oh," I said clearly, watching the light-shards sparkle in the scimitar-shaped panes of the fanlight over the front door. I was thinking how *interesting* they were, really *interesting*.

And then I passed out.

"I'm fine. Utterly fine. I'll shoot anybody who tries saying otherwise."

Focusing on Ellie, I attempted a grin, meanwhile realizing that for a moment I'd forgotten I didn't still have the Bisley bulking in my sweater pocket. Or the sweater, either.

Not a good sign. The *yes* or *no* question is the crucial one about gun possession, I feel, including any that are in my own possession. But never mind; they thought I'd meant it as a joke.

Now my head was clearing except for the odd noise I kept hearing. "I was only out a few seconds. You'd think I'd been in a coma for a month, for heaven's sake."

Wade frowned down at me. "You're sure it was just the smell of the polyurethane?"

"Of course it was." I looked away. "What about the hall?" I'd forgotten that, too. And I felt dizzy; fumes, I decided.

"Mr. Ash and one of his guys are finishing it," Wade replied as he ran me a glass of water. "Here, drink this."

I gulped it, heedless of the chlorine flavor, eager to do whatever he asked so as not to be sent to the clinic. Our recent run of medical emergencies had impressed Wade with the idea that Victor's professional skill made up for his many personal sins.

But the only time I wanted care from Victor was if I needed actual neurosurgery. Otherwise I'd prefer some wild-eyed quack who spoke in tongues and handled live rattlesnakes on Friday night.

"I found Wyatt," Ellie told me. "Or I think I have. Talked to Fran, again, and she told me where he said he was going. Jake, you look ghastly."

"Oh, thanks." All that knocking I'd heard had been Ellie at the back door and Mr. Ash at the front; he'd finally gone around and entered from the yard, through the open Bilco door, and come up through the cellar.

"What emergency?" I asked him now. We'd deal with Wyatt Evert later.

Mr. Ash cleared his throat, readying himself to deliver bad news.

"Old water main was behind a foundation stone. One of the fellows, he smacked that stone with a big hammer."

Suddenly I identified the sound I kept hearing: roaring, but not in my ears. "An *empty* old water main," I said hopefully.

" 'Fraid not," Mr. Ash said. Now came another sound: trucks. Big ones, the kind the city sends when a water main gets broken. A backhoe rumbled off a flatbed, thunderingly. Through the screen door I glimpsed its toothed yellow blade, ready to bite.

"You deal with that," Ellie told Wade decisively, gesturing toward the backhoe, "while we go up to the Calais emergency room and have Victor check on Jake. Just to be on the safe side," she added, looking meaningfully at me, and I agreed at once.

For one thing, if I didn't, Wade was going to haul me there kicking and screaming. "I'll be fine," I assured him.

And for another, Victor wasn't in Calais, today. He had a regular schedule and this afternoon it put him at the Eastport clinic, no need for a car trip.

And Ellie knew it.

Five minutes later we were headed out of town. "So you know where Wyatt is right now?"

"I do, indeed," Ellie said. "If he went where Fran Hanson said." We passed Bay City Mobil where the fellows had Joey Robley's old Dodge on the lift, peering into it; Joey had 200,000 miles on the car and said he would drive it into the ground, after which he intended to go there, too. And Joey was ninety-six so the Bay City fellows took him seriously on this.

Ellie pushed the accelerator. It was low tide, and on either side of the causeway acres of clam flats lay sparklingly exposed. Moments later we were on Route 1 heading north through the woods, Ellie as usual passing any car that didn't match her exotic speed.

"Well," I demanded, "are you going to tell me?"

"Wyatt's up at the Moosehorn. He spotted us talking to Fran and had a fit about it, she said, and he knows she told us about the ledger. He *said* he was going up to collect some things he'd left at the ranger station."

She ripped past a lumbering dump truck; my heart only stuttered a little. "But he could be at the marsh double-checking, to be sure there's no evidence to tie him to the boots incident," she added. "And then he would skedaddle."

Suddenly, talking to Wyatt felt urgent again. "And if he leaves, experienced scam artist that he is, we'd never—oh god—find him again."

She swerved back into the right-hand lane a good millisecond before a highballing log truck barreled by on our left. "That's what I thought. So I hope you're telling me at least a little of the truth about your fainting episode back there."

That I'd passed out on account of the fumes, she meant. "I *think* I am. But Ellie, I can see a doctor later if need be. Right now—"

She turned to me. "You promise to go to the hospital right afterward and get looked at. We told Wade we would, so . . ."

"Ellie!" Doom roared at us in the shape of a driver whose notion of proper passing space was even smaller than Ellie's.

She yanked the wheel and put both right tires suddenly into the shoulder, soft sand inches lower than the pavement. The car did a buck-and-wing, fishtailing slipperily out of danger before Ellie jounced us expertly into the travel lane again.

". . . we're going," she finished, unfazed.

Just at the moment I'd have agreed to go to Borneo if only I didn't have to go there on this death trap of a road.

"I do not see why," I babbled anxiously, "when the southern Maine Turnpike is being widened to, I gather, about thirty lanes, at a cost of approximately a hundred million billion dollars, we cannot be given the measly few bucks it would cost to put a paved shoulder on Route 1. There are roads in *Afghanistan,* traveled by *donkeys,* better treated than . . ."

"Okay, okay," Ellie said. "I've been driving this road my whole life, you know." Still, she slowed down and so did my heart rate, and for a while the trip proceeded in relative calm.

But ten minutes later I was losing my breakfast into a ditch, in the middle of the Moosehorn Refuge.

"I don't get it," I moaned, splashing my face with water from Ellie's jug. A true Maine native, she kept her car stocked for everything short of nuclear winter. "Maybe it isn't paint fumes."

"Hmm," she said, eyeing me narrowly. "Well, we're here so we might as well go on. But I'm telling you, the minute we're finished with Wyatt . . ."

"I know," I grumped miserably. "Let's get it over with."

Back in the car, I checked my eyes in the visor mirror. The green lenses were still in, by some miracle. But the world kept spinning gently unless I tipped my head back and then it lurched. Dizzily, I rode alongside Ellie, into the swamp.

We found Wyatt Evert in his van, a big white Econoline with the words *Evert Wild Natural Excursions* emblazoned on the panels. Inside, the van was fitted with custom bucket seats featuring pockets for maps and binoculars, drinks holders, fold-down lap desks, and individual overhead reading lights. The upholstery, I noted, was luxurious enough to have had a ledger hidden in it.

Also, that van had enough heating power to melt the polar ice caps, as I discovered when Wyatt opened the door and a burst of tropical air blew out at me. It wasn't even a particularly cold day but he was sitting inside with the engine running so he could keep his surroundings toasty.

Which was typical of Wyatt. He talked a good game but when it came to action, George had been right on the money about him: Wyatt was a whey-faced stinker with a politically correct line of crap, meant not to save the earth but to line his own personal pockets.

"What do you want?" He hadn't been retrieving any tourist-tripping snares or anything else odd that I could see in the van.

"Couple questions. Beautiful here," I said, waving at the flat water spreading away smoothly.

I didn't have the Bisley. Wade wouldn't have swallowed the going-to-the-emergency-room story if I'd stopped to retrieve the gun. Now I noticed how empty the marsh was: beautiful and remote.

Cattails thrust up between lily pads near the shore; water birds skimmed so near you could see them glance brassily at us, knowing we couldn't shoot them. In the Moosehorn Refuge the birds were aware of their protected status; you could stand by the side of the road and watch eaglets emerging from their eggs.

Wyatt scowled, seemingly unaware of the adult eagle descending now to a nesting platform fifty yards off. On the platform was a nest so huge, just seeing it convinced me that birds had indeed descended from dinosaurs. I slapped at a bug biting my cheek, another on my neck. Apparently the blackflies were descended from carnivorous monsters, too.

Correction: they *were* the carnivorous monsters. I slapped at another one. "So, the guy who drowned," I said, feeling suddenly that I wanted to keep this conversation short; if I didn't get out of here soon I'd be getting a blood transfusion at that hospital. Also, I remembered again how allergic to blackflies I was. "Did he have any idea what a lowlife crook you are?"

Evert blinked, recovered swiftly, and opened his mouth to lie. Then he got a look at my face.

It was wearing my patented lie-to-me-and-I'll-disembowel-you expression. I'd found it useful, back in the city, when one of my money-management clients wanted to keep something a secret: say, a numbered bank account in the Bahamas, or a second set of books like the ones Fran Hanson swore Wyatt was keeping.

Also, without the Bisley, my hard-nosed expression was the only weapon I had. I only hoped Wyatt wasn't as savvy as the birds.

"No," he said evenly. "He didn't. I'd never met him until he came on one of my excursions. And he wasn't a plainclothes cop or anything like that, if that's what you're thinking."

I had been. Somebody already on Wyatt's crooked trail posing as an ordinary tourist . . . it was a possibility. Trouble was, there were so many possibilities.

"He was a retired shrink from New York. Check all you want, you'll find out I had no motive to kill him. Or anyone else."

"You didn't sabotage his boots, and send him out here alone to drown?"

A small smile twitched his thin lips. "Let's see, and then I killed Harriet Hollingsworth because she saw me sneaking into the guy's motel room." He frowned thoughtfully. "Got hold of that newspaper page, too. And then maybe I killed the dancer Harry Markle was hot about, to make it look even more like Harriet's death was part of some other situation?"

Scam guys were always quick on the uptake, so I wasn't surprised he understood so much. Knowing how other people think is a big part of the scam guy's bag of tricks. They never look or sound guilty, either; just the opposite, if they're good.

Wyatt was good. A dozen or so blackflies landed on my neck and bit. "Damn," I uttered, recalling the last time I'd been bitten by a few of them: fever, swollen glands.

I tipped my head back carefully to meet Evert's snakelike expression, but a wave of dizziness still made my gut turn over.

"What was your argument with Harriet about?" I asked him. "And before you answer, Wyatt, let me just tell you I know a fair amount about your past. So don't waste time trying a snow job on me, okay?"

He didn't. Instead, he surprised me utterly. "Harriet knew it, too. All those newspapers she collected in that shambles she was living in?" A disgusted expression crossed his face. "The old bat read them all and she recognized *me* from a picture in one of them, a story about a little action I had going back in the city. A fund-raising effort."

He smiled reminiscently. "God, it was sweet."

"Until you got caught?"

The smile vanished. "Yeah. Tabloids made a big deal of it, ran a mug shot. So this Harriet woman sees me just walking by her house, gives me a look like she's shooting me through the heart, and the next thing I know my phone's ringing in my room at the motel." He shook his head. "You can plan for everything but that, you know? A stupid coincidence that screws you royally. Someone who knows you."

"You went to Harriet's house. You argued with her."

He nodded. "Absolutely. I've got a good thing going here, I didn't want her messing it up. I offered to pay her. She played it tough: hit the road, Jack, or she's calling the cops."

I glanced at Ellie, who was listening with keen interest. The black-flies were making a bloody picnic out of me but this was too good to cut short. "And?"

"And I believed her. I was going to leave the clients here, just disappear into the sunset. Hell with 'em."

"But you didn't," Ellie said. "Why not?"

"Because first that damned idiot in the rotten boots went and drowned himself in the marsh, and I couldn't cut out on that or people would think maybe I'd had something to do with it," he said impatiently. "You think I'm stupid?"

He had a point. If he'd gone just when George and Bob Arnold were feeling suspicious about those boots, Bob would've put the alarms out for him instantly. Wyatt's past would have been exposed, and his scams crossed state lines so the FBI would have gotten involved.

"Then the old woman just vanished. Poof, like my wish was granted," he said. "So what the hell? Nothing to do with me. I forgot about it and went on with life."

He looked momentarily pleased. But then he remembered that we could still queer his pitch. Or Fran could.

I was remembering something, too: that you didn't get to be a career scam artist by being a bad liar. But so far, I thought I believed him.

"So," Evert asked, "you going to mess me up? Me," he added, "and Eastport's sourest little sweetheart, Fran Hanson?"

"That depends," I countered as more flies bit hard. "Are you going to mess her up?"

Maybe Wyatt was lying through his yellowish teeth and he was a murderer with or without Fran Hanson's help. But if neither of them had done anything deadly, I wasn't completely sure I wanted to upset their applecart. Fran's, especially.

"Does Fran still have a job?" I asked pointedly.

By now I'd lost something like a quarter of my blood volume to the swarms of vampire insects inhabiting the Moosehorn Refuge. It was time to clear out whether I intended to let Wyatt off the hook or not.

He nodded resignedly. "Guess I don't have much choice, do I? If I fire her, she'll be testifying before the dust clears."

"And mail fraud is an annoying charge," I agreed. "It could turn into all sorts of complications."

Money laundering, interstate commerce fraud, racketeering; for a minute, I was happy for Fran. Assuming, I mean, she didn't turn out to be a bloody murderer, herself.

But then I noticed that blackflies had gotten into my hair and were feasting on my scalp. "Ouch. Ellie," I said, "grab the hairbrush out of the car, will you please? I've got to . . . agghh."

"Better get some bug dope," Wyatt observed, "before they eat you alive." Behind him another eagle lifted from a nesting platform, its shaggy white legs hanging beneath it like dinosaur drumsticks.

Or maybe it was another blackfly. All I wanted was to go home, take a shower, and slather on a gallon of calamine lotion. "Forget the hospital," I said, back in the car. But it came out, *"fgh hshpshtl."* My tongue felt thick.

"Ellie," I began in alarm. It came out *"Eglegl."* She looked at me, said a word I'd never heard from her before, and hit the gas. Five minutes later, Victor said the very same word as he saw me in the ER entrance of the Calais Hospital.

Drat, what was he doing here? *"Hglgl,"* I said, trying for nonchalance and failing. It seemed that nonchalance, along with any hope of coherent speech, had become unavailable to me.

But I didn't have much time to resent this; the next thing I knew, the ceiling was whirling and I was being wheeled down a tiled corridor. No one was paying any attention to my objections. Instead, they were cutting my clothes off: never a good omen.

Somebody slapped a plastic mask onto my face and a needle into my arm. Victor was speaking tersely in what I knew from the bad old days as his get-the-crash-cart-*now* voice, so penetrating it could liquefy bone marrow. Also, that's what he was saying:

"Get the crash cart. *Now!*" Chills wracked me as hives rose on my body like some fast-forwarding nature film documenting a hideous biological process.

Which this was. Even in my seriously befogged mental state I recognized it: anaphylactic shock. I'd known I was allergic to blackflies, but I'd never been bitten by so *many* of them before.

Distantly, a creaking sound penetrated my consciousness; after a moment I realized it was me, wheezing. My lungs were closing, swollen by the allergic reaction.

"Victor," I mouthed, looking up into his eyes.

But I could make no sound and he wasn't listening, anyway, his eyes darting from cardiac and blood pressure monitors above my head to the plastic IV bags hanging above my right arm.

"... Benadryl," he said. I shut my eyes, the sense of purposeful activity around me fading fast.

Fading and gone.

Victor glared at me. "Nausea. Ringing in your ears. And this dizziness ... what is it like, and when does it occur?"

"When I look up. Like this . . ."

I tipped my head back and was rewarded by a wave of vertigo so intense I had to grab the gurney rails.

"Mm-hm," Victor said, looking unimpressed. "Let me guess. It also happens when you turn over in bed at night."

Maybe he wasn't impressed, but I was. "How'd you know that?"

"Never mind. It's my job to know that."

I was in an observation room off the main area of the ER. No more IV, no more cardiac monitor. The clock on the wall said I'd been here an hour, although it felt like a year; no clock in the world moves slower than the one in a hospital emergency room.

"What're you doing here, anyway?" I asked Victor.

He scribbled in my chart. "Car-moose collision," he replied distractedly. "Cracked his skull. The driver, not the moose."

Ellie was outside, rummaging in her car trunk for a set of clothes in which interesting slashes had not been cut by hospital scissors. Also she had the green contact lenses in her purse; in the last act I could remember clearly, I had popped them out when my eyes started itching, back at the marsh.

Victor held up three fingers. It was the gesture he once used when my coffee failed to meet his standards. One, filter the water. Two, grind *fresh* beans . . .

Three, dump the pot over his head. On the other hand, he had just saved my life. It was getting to be another of his annoying habits, short-circuiting my disasters.

"One, you had a recent blow to the head," he recited, "but you're not showing any neurological signs at all. Two, you had a bout of allergic shock, but we've reversed that completely. And three, you absolutely don't show any symptoms of anything else."

"So there's nothing wrong with me?" I didn't see how that could be true, though the hives were gone completely as if they'd been, as Sam would've put it, Fig Newtons of my imagination. I could breathe again, too, and the awful panicky feeling was gone.

And Victor didn't seem particularly concerned about me at all. Still, I was gearing myself up for a battle. Just because Ellie was bringing in clothes didn't mean Victor was going to let me put them on. Also, I was worried about what he might say next. Maybe he was saving the worst for last, and he was about to tell me I'd have to stay for–terrifying phrase–"a few tests."

But the battle didn't come.

"It's BPV," he said. "Benign positional vertigo. You jolted your inner ear the other day when you fell." He picked my chart up again, glanced through it, and tucked it under his arm.

"You can get it from a sinus infection, too, but yours is traumatic. It'll go away if you don't coddle it. Don't drive till it's been gone for two weeks, that's all."

"That's all?" I repeated. Relief surged through me. When you are being examined by a brain surgeon, you can't help knowing he could flap up the top of your skull if he wanted to.

Or if you needed him to. But: "Uh-huh. Let's just get a last set of vitals–"

Vital signs: pulse, temperature, and blood pressure.

"–and then you can go home."

For a moment I thought the hangover from the Benadryl he'd pumped into me had me hearing things. "Huh? You mean . . . I can just leave? Just like that?"

He turned from the door and I could tell from his eyes that his thoughts were already miles away.

"Jake, you had a bad allergic reaction. But we've reversed it—you didn't require resuscitation, that was just a precaution—and I expect no further trouble. The dizziness . . . as I've told you before, the simplest explanation is usually the correct one. In your case I'm sure of it. Go home."

That phrase, again: *simple*. Victor went on as he noted my expression, misinterpreted it.

"Call me if the nausea from the dizziness gets worse, I'll write you for something stronger than the Benadryl I'm sending along. But I warn you, the hangover'll be worse, too."

Phooey. I already felt as if I'd drunk half a gallon of Old Peculiar. Not nearly as peculiar, though, as when I'd come in.

"Victor," I said. My attitude was less combative, suddenly. Much less. It would be a shame, I thought, if the clinic lost Victor.

But he was gone before I could even thank him.

Riding home, I felt shaky and uncertain, which I guessed was normal considering that I had just missed being fitted either for a pair of wings or a little pitchfork.

"Darn it, I'd actually started getting used to myself with green eyes."

Ellie whizzed us down Route 1 through Robbinston and Red Beach, in and out of pine groves. "Never mind," she said. "Victor may be a twit but his advice on that particular topic is right on."

He'd forbidden them, said that with my immune system revved from the allergy attack I might react badly to contact lenses.

"Don't even dream of putting them in until you're completely better," Ellie decreed.

213

"I guess," I sighed reluctantly. "I really wanted to help Maggie somehow, though. The poor thing, all the word games she's played with Sam, waiting for him to really notice her. But she's not getting through to him. Not the way she wants to, at least."

It had been that way with Sam's father, also: You can want all you want but you just can't get there from here. "And now my *blue* eyes look . . . I don't know. Strange. Unfamiliar. But I guess that's probably normal, too."

A wave of tiredness washed over me, and I was cold. Ellie switched the heater on and I huddled shivering in the passenger seat as we made the turn onto Route 190.

"You didn't call Wade, did you?"

"No, of course not." Off the causeway to our left spread the pastel-blue expanse of Passamaquoddy Bay, a big black-and-orange container ship plowing massively in toward the freight terminal. Beyond, Deer Island lay between blue water and sky like the sweep of a green paint-brush.

"I figured I'd only tell him something if I needed to," she added.

So Wade hadn't been scared unnecessarily. Like I said, Ellie didn't panic. "Thanks."

We passed the City of Eastport sign, daffodils massed around it. "Wyatt's not our problem either, is he?" Ellie asked.

"No. I wish he were." The houses and church spires of town spread before us. "It's just too big a stretch, him hurting Samantha to cover killing Harriet and that tourist. It's like Wilma, you could *make* it fit, but . . ."

"But you'd be forcing it," Ellie agreed. "And when we found him he didn't look as if he was doing any evidence cleanup, did he? Just sitting there."

"Making plans for his next move, I'll bet, now that Tim's sniffing around. But that isn't a crime. Or for him no more criminal than usual."

We turned onto Water Street. The bustling business district with its old redbrick and wood-frame buildings, the shops with their snapping banners and the swept-clean sidewalks shone watercolor bright in the afternoon sun.

Beyond, wooden boats bobbed in the harbor, the tide moving slowly up the dark-brown pilings of the fish pier. "And have you noticed how calm things have been, lately? Except for just now, of course," Ellie added. "But that *was* an accident."

When my house came into view I gazed at it with gratitude through a swim of ridiculous tears, just happy to be alive. My romp through the emergency room, along with the drugs and fluids that had been pumped into me, had roiled my emotions up. Nobody home, thank god.

"I should come in with you." Ellie pulled into the driveway.

"Uh-uh." I got out, closed the door firmly. Mr. Ash's truck wasn't here, either, nor any vehicles of the guys on his crew. "I'll be fine."

A sigh escaped me. "But Ellie, our suspects are evaporating. Roy, Wyatt, Wilma, even Fran . . . she's a tough little hustler, but you know darned well she didn't commit murder. Just the idea of being caught on a probation violation scared her to death . . . she tries to be a hard case, but she's too much like Roy. She doesn't have the nerve to be a killer. And right now, I just want to get some sleep. We can talk about it later. Okay?"

Wade would be back soon; he wouldn't have gone far until he heard the results of my medical visit.

"Okay," she gave in. "But I'm going to call you in a little while. And you'd better answer the phone or the next thing I'll be calling is an ambulance."

She put the car into reverse, checked the rearview mirror. I stood a moment, watching her go, feeling the chilly breeze shift with the storm yet to come, riffling the spring-green leaves. Then I dug my keys out, took a deep breath of the fresh salt air, and let myself into the house.

Inside, late afternoon sunlight lay in gold bars on the old kitchen floor.

Monday's nails clicked in the hall, alarming me for a moment until I realized the polyurethane must be dry now. Curled atop the refrigerator, Cat Dancing eyed me with her usual mixture of mischief and scorn.

I pulled off the jacket Wade had pressed on me before I left and replaced it with my cardigan, still on the radiator. I'd already decided to put the Bisley back in the pocket and leave it there, but at the moment I couldn't summon up enough energy even to open the compartment behind the mantel, much less lift the big weapon, load it, or—god forbid—fire the thing.

Then I saw the three notes on the kitchen table: one from Sam. He and Maggie were out on the sailboat for a final spin before the storm put them in port for a while. One from Wade: he was at the Federal Marine office, would be back soon.

And one from Mr. Ash. I looked out the kitchen window. The door leading from the cellar to the yard stood open; I made a mental note—if this kept up, I was going to have to get some sort of Rolodex for my brain—to hook the hall door leading to the cellar. Monday padded over to me, her tail wagging anxiously.

"That's okay, girl," I whispered. "Everything's fine. Go on and lie down. We'll go out later."

Uncertainly she obeyed, circling in her dog bed, while Cat yawned expressively as if to say human affairs were a terrific bore and by the way, where's dinner?

Then I read Mr. Ash's note again: *I left you something.*

Another home-repair gift, I supposed; more insulation or a gravity-defying ladder. But just now I didn't care: too tired, too discouraged. I put the kettle on for tea, walked past the hall door before I remembered to go back and hook it, then trudged upstairs to wash.

The shock-sweat clinging to me was noxious, bitter as old grease. The spot on my arm where the IV had been ached, and the way I felt inside was worse; jangled and debilitated in the extreme.

The notes also reminded me unhappily of Jemmy Wechsler; I'd

sent an e-mail thanking him for his help. He should have replied, letting me know the e-mail address I had for him was still good. But he hadn't.

And on top of it all I felt like such a fool. Whoever thinks money experts must be smart doesn't know me very well, I thought. Running around chasing down harebrained notions and hitting dead ends . . .

But Ellie always swears most problems can be helped by applying enough good hot soap and water, so I applied them and as promised did feel somewhat improved afterwards. A shower would have been better but I didn't have the ambition for that.

Besides, I couldn't take the Bisley into the shower, and now that I was awake I intended to head right back downstairs for it.

Later, I promised the shampoo bottle, splashing water onto my face. Then, glancing into the mirror over the sink, I was hit with a realization so shattering it made me stagger:

Blue eyes.

Chapter 10

I gripped the porcelain. The face in the mirror was not the lean, angular one I usually saw there. It was plumpish and puffy with fatigue, eyes made round by anxiety and remnants of shock. It was a child's face staring from the mirror.

A child with blue eyes, as they had been long ago on the day when a young cop pulled her from the smoking ruins of a town house explosion. Lifted her, carried her from the blasted wreckage of bricks and boards, gazing earnestly into her face and talking all the way, telling that child the big lie, the one all children are told: that everything would be fine.

Gazing into her eyes, which had been blue. Not green. Harry Markle had remembered everything about that day, more than I had. He'd been an adult, or nearly so; very young, then.

Yet when we'd remembered it together, I'd been wearing green contact lenses. Thin, invisible, not brilliant green but a nice, normal, every-day shade of eye color. To look at them, you'd have thought I was born with those green eyes.

But I hadn't been. I turned off the faucet without looking at it, keeping my gaze fixed on the mirror and the upstairs hall behind me. From where I stood I could see the newel post of the stairway balustrade, and some of the balusters. Sam had taken his sling off, replacing it with the red bandanna, and tossed the gauze one onto the newel post. Beyond, the oblong panes of the upstairs hall window shone golden with afternoon.

Nothing moved. The house was silent. Wade was at the terminal, Sam was out on the water and Ellie was at home. All quiet on the downeast front.

I decided I could still get downstairs, to the Bisley in its hiding place in the kitchen mantel. As I reached the upstairs landing, the kettle I'd put on began to whistle piercingly.

And stopped. Someone had taken it off the flame.

Wade? I wanted to call, but the word choked in my throat. No toenail-clickety dance of joy from Monday, no grudging meow from Cat.

Just footsteps padding slowly over the fresh polyurethane in the hall, soles squeaking on the new surface. He was already looking up the stairs as he came into view, his face divided into moving rectangles by the white-painted balusters.

"Hey," he began. "Hope you don't mind. I heard the kettle, thought you'd forgotten it, so I came through the cellar door and turned the burner off."

But the cellar door had been hooked shut. "Harry," I said, amazed I was able to make any sound at all. "Or . . . not." He'd already seen it in my expression, that I knew.

He smiled, a little shamefaced. *You got me.* "Yeah. Not."

He put a foot on the bottom step. All the possible actions I might take sped through my mind, all useless.

"All those accidents," I said. "You engineered them." The emergency fire-escape ladder in the bedroom closet, I thought desperately . . . but he'd be on me before I could get it deployed.

"They were to reinforce the notion that *you* were a victim. To keep the 'someone's after Harry and his friends' idea alive."

The attic . . . maybe I could make it there ahead of him but I couldn't keep him out. I'd just be a sitting duck higher up off the ground than before.

"Victims," Harry said, "are so unlikely to be villains. But I was amazed, myself, that being a victim worked so *well*."

Yeah, just dandy. "Memory," I said, trying to buy time, but for what? "Memory is a funny thing. I guess I should have known when you remembered so *much*."

He grinned lazily. "And I should have known you'd figure it out sooner or later." He shifted his weight confidently.

"Sooner, now, though," he said. "Those print checks on me'll come back any minute. I had it fixed so I'd get a heads-up if someone ran me. I made sure Harry's forwarding address and phone were always mine, just in case of something like that."

"Harry's dead?" But the NYPD didn't know it; probably no one did. And at the NYPD, Harry Markle was still one of their own. So they'd alerted the old cop, as a courtesy, that someone was running his fingerprints. And whoever this guy at the foot of my stairs was, once Bob began checking on him he'd known his time here was running out fast.

"What happened to the real Harry?" I asked.

He hadn't forgotten that child's blue eyes. He'd never seen them. And who else would know so much about Harry Markle *and* the killer Harry had been tracking except . . .

A shudder went through me as I understood the rest of it and how thoroughly I had been fooled.

How fatally. "When," I asked, "did you kill Harry?"

Small shrug: "Just before I left New York. No one missed him, believe me. Living in a room full of old clippings and notes, all his old cases. Going over and over them, that's all he did. And going through a fifth a day. By then, Harry wasn't the kind of guy anyone would miss."

Sure, after this guy had broken Harry by killing the women he loved and loading Harry with guilt. Grief made my throat close. Meanwhile the house continued silent: nobody home.

Just us chickens. "Then, though," the man below me went on, "a funny thing happened." He shook his head with remembered wonder. "It turned out *I* missed Harry."

A smile of pure pleasure, charming and bright. I recalled how unlike their cartoon stereotypes the bad guys always are. The man looking up at me with such happiness in his eyes might have dropped in just to recall old times.

Instead of to kill me. "Harry gave me a purpose in life," he said. Shockingly, he spat on the new floor, and when he looked up again his eyes were dead coals.

"Useless, lazy, drunk son-of-a-bitch. Supposed to be the goddamn hero, ace freakin' detective."

Uh-oh. Things were trending uglier. "He failed you somehow?" I guessed, taking a step back. But he looked up, caught me at it.

His right hand was behind him. I eased forward again and his arm relaxed. "Goddamn right he did. Big explosions, cute little kid, get in the papers. Get his picture on all the front pages." Deep breath. "Oh yeah, he loved that stuff. When it came to your ordinary cop grunt-work, though, couple nobodies happened to be in the wrong place at the wrong time, killed in a stickup, I guess that wasn't *glamorous* enough."

Bob Arnold had been right when he said it all probably started with a grudge. And this guy had already told me about it; I just hadn't understood what he was really saying.

"They were your folks, weren't they? The nobodies who died in a stickup that Harry didn't solve."

"Didn't *try* to solve," he corrected. "Didn't *bother* to. He got it as a cold case, sure. Part of a routine housecleaning. Still, at first it gave me hope. I understood that it was a long shot that he could solve it after so long. But did he even *try*? No. Good working people, not famous. Not *important*. Just my parents."

"So after your hopes were dashed yet again, you decided to show him what it's like. Him and the rest of the cops. By killing people *they* cared for."

What would happen, I wondered, if I just walked down the steps and past him? But the way his dead-coal eyes had begun smoldering again made me decide not to try to find out.

"The story you told me . . . it happened. But it was *you* pushing that woman off the roof. You taunting Harry, getting away."

The thought sent a chill through me; shivering, I plunged my hands reflexively into the pockets of my heavy old cardigan. And was astonished by what I found there:

I left something for you.

It was a gun, a .25 or maybe a .32 semiautomatic pistol. I'd handled them enough so I could tell by the feel of it.

Where the hell my old buddy Mr. Ash had gotten it, or what he'd been thinking when he left it in my sweater pocket, were questions for another day. My question now was: loaded? Or not?

Please, god. "The other night, you made the prank call from the pay phone. And it was you in the kitchen, you came in through the hole in the foundation in the cellar wall, didn't you? Up the cellar steps. You left the knife with the fake blood on it, and the note."

A new thought hit me. "But how'd you get in? I locked up and the cellar door was hooked, just like today."

Like a magician he produced a thin strip of celluloid: the kind that still comes in the collars of new dress shirts. Keeping my face blank, I found the gun's safety, thumbed it. I needed to shoot him where he stood, or try. Take a chance on the gun being loaded; my only chance.

But even as I thought this, his own hand came out with a gun in it, too. I stared at it, hypnotized.

He waved it, breaking the spell. "Let's get this over with."

Getting this over with wasn't on my to-do list. "You haven't told me why, yet. What got you to Eastport? And why me, now?"

He studied me as if this were the stupidest question he'd ever heard, waited for me to come up with the answer for myself. When I didn't, he said:

"You made a big impression on old Harry. Even while he and I were doing our little dance together, back in the city—"

Where this bastard was killing people, murdering them just for spite, and Harry was desperately chasing him—

". . . he never gave up on the other thing. All those clippings in his room? Notes and a diary of his hunt for some old dead guy he had a bug about, didn't believe the guy was really dead. And that guy's daughter, that kid who Harry'd made such a big deal of saving."

The kid being me.

"And afterwards, with Harry gone, hey, I had a lot of time on my hands."

That charming smile again, a little gesture as if appealing to my common sense, as if this were the most reasonable thing in the world. "So then I started looking for . . ."

"For my father." I finished his sentence crisply. The pieces fell together like glass in a kaleidoscope.

"You picked up where Harry left off," I said. "Did your homework, thought my father might be here because I'm here. That was why you came to Eastport, wasn't it? But once you arrived . . ."

Ellie's words came back to me: *He had a reason at first. But now . . . now he's doing it because he* likes *it.*

So this was probably not a fruitful conversational angle. Meanwhile, the little gun felt like a cannon in my hand but it wasn't. Even if it turned out to have bullets in it, I'd have no time to get it out of my pocket. And I'd thought Wade had exaggerated about needing a large caliber to put a guy down, in a situation.

But looking at this guy now, I thought I could've parted his hair with a bullet and he wouldn't've flinched. Slowly, he began mounting the stairs. *No time . . .* I took a wild guess:

"As for Harriet, her problem was never what she wrote, all those letters to the *Quoddy Tides.* Her problem was what she *read.* Old newspapers . . . When you told her who you were, she knew better. Just like she'd known Wyatt. She'd seen the real Harry's picture in the tabloids. She *knew* you weren't him."

He stopped. "Very good," he said in faintly mocking tones.

"And the tourist . . . a shrink, Wyatt Evert told me. A retired psychiatrist from New York. Could he have been . . . Harry Markle's psychiatrist? The tourist didn't know you, but you knew him. And for you, that was enough."

Now that I knew so much, the rest was easier to figure. "The boots were just misdirection. Just something to confuse the whole picture, assuming anyone even paid attention to them. You never got into his room. You followed him to the marsh. You found him alone and you drowned him."

His face said that I was right again. But he couldn't resist bragging a little more about it, letting me know how smart, how *superior* he was.

"The damn boots were the only hard part. The switch for my own, which I'd messed up in advance so they'd look sabotaged. Same size, but I had to struggle in the marsh getting them on him. Him not being able to help me and all. Now, stop stalling and come down here."

Not on your tintype, buster. Stalling was the name of the game, at the moment.

"How'd you kill Harriet? No wounds, no poison . . ."

But just then Sam's gauze sling on the newel post caught my eye again. At the sight a vivid mental picture rose up, of the night he'd gotten it.

Of the ambulance technician punching Sam in the chest to get his heart started again. But it was a punch in the chest that had stopped it, too, from the broken steering column.

"Your fist," I said. "You punched her in the chest? You didn't know it would kill her outright. But you were . . ."

"Lucky," he finished. "Yeah. I just wanted to put her down, shut her up until I could figure out a good way to do it. Turned out I didn't have to."

"The blood on the porch?" It *had* been there, I realized; the gossip—about that much, anyway—had been right.

"Scalp wound, when she fell." He shook his head impatiently. "Got people talking before I noticed it myself and got it cleaned up. That, and that damned boot *she* was wearing."

Harriet's boot, the one that had been found in the compost heap. "Dragging her through backyards in the middle of the night," he went on. "Freakin' thing fell off, I couldn't find it in the dark. Although"—he brightened hideously for an instant—"it *was* exciting."

Yeah, the risk of getting caught with the corpse of a harmless old woman you'd just murdered must've been a thrill. I felt a strong urge to punch this guy, myself, right in the nose.

"Why'd you put that paper in her hand? And . . . where the hell did you get the mortar to put her in the wall?"

He shrugged carelessly. "Men painting the Danvers' house left a window open to air it out. I just spotted it, climbed in. I dragged her in the cellar door and closed it behind me." He was enjoying this. "The mortar was a stroke of luck, it was down there already, couple bags. I didn't know she'd be found so soon, but that turned out to work pretty well, too, didn't it?"

Uh-huh. Just ducky. He came up another step. At this range he could put a hole the size of a Pontiac in *my* chest, and if I turned to run it would be all over instantly.

And I still didn't know if my gun was loaded.

"As for the newspaper, well, I'm always the funny man. I just couldn't resist the joke."

Hilarious. So while we'd been working up one theory after another, he'd been winging it, improvising day by day, trusting in his wits and a benevolent universe to pave his path.

"It was fun while it lasted," he went on expansively, "but now . . . happier hunting grounds, that's what I need. There's plenty of small towns where I'd fit right in, don't you think?" His eyes were fixed on mine. "Move in, do my thing, and—poof!"

He smiled brilliantly. "Here today. Gone tomorrow. After I finish up here in Eastport, of course. Your son, his girl, your husband. And that friend of yours, that Ellie."

His voice lingered on their names, touched their images in my mind with a filth-dipped brush. He was getting disorganized, unraveling at the edges; it showed in the way his face changed so fast, in his jittery energy. And in the way he kept slapping new names onto his victim list: *somebody likes it.*

Not that it was going to help me any, that his emotions were running haywire.

Somehow I had to look down long enough to make sure something more than a dry-fire would come out of that damned gun if I shot him through my sweater pocket. And I had to do it without him figuring out that I had the thing.

There was also the interesting little matter of shooting a person at all. Now that push had come to shove, I saw the difference between me and this guy. He was hardwired for killing people; I wasn't.

On the other hand, Sam would be home soon, with Maggie. Wade too, maybe with Ellie and George.

None of them knowing what I knew. They'd all walk right into the house. Into my death scene, and then into their own.

Unsuspecting. I breathed in quietly, centered myself.

Focused down, as I had on the shooting range. Praying that the damned thing was loaded; begging heaven, because it was my only way out of this.

"Yeah, good old Harry," my opponent reminisced. "Kept a diary, Harry did. And you were on every page. It was all he wanted in life, to find your old man. He wanted to tell you the truth about what happened back then, and how it all turned out. 'Cause he figured you *deserved to know.*" He gave the words a sour twist. "Damned old fool."

The thought kept nearly dropping me: the notion, previously unimagined, of a life lived in service to the child I had been. But while he'd been talking, the monster before me had also been climbing the stairs, and now he was nearly on me.

I could almost hear his heart beating, feel his short, hot exhalations on my face. Then the cellar door opened, metal latch clicking; not hooked anymore, I realized. Because this guy had already come through, slipped the hook with his handy-dandy strip of celluloid.

At the click he turned alertly, scuttled back downstairs, the gun in his hand. "Make a peep and I'll shoot whoever it is in the face," he grated, and moved out of sight across that newly finished floor.

Without thinking I rushed down the steps after him, in time to see him backing toward me again, hands raised, the gun now dangling from one of them. Coming toward him was Lian Ash, the weapon in *his* hand the twin to the one in my own. *I left something for you . . .*

But Lian had kept something too; good for him.

Suddenly his meeting with Wade took on a new meaning. Lian had bought the guns from Wade. Suspecting . . . or had he known? "Get out of the way, Jacobia," Mr. Ash told me. "Quick, now."

But not quick enough. A second later my personal nightmare had an arm around my throat; his other hand pressed what felt like the end of a cannon barrel to my forehead. Worse, when he turned, he slammed me against the wall hard before he dragged me partway up the stairs again.

And that was bad, but much worse was the whole world tilting abruptly, whirling and spinning, so that without warning, six images of Lian Ash turned like a nightmare Ferris wheel at the foot of the stairs.

"Hi," I gasped, trying and failing to make the images one.

"Hi," said the turning wheel of faces. So *dizzy* . . .

Still halfway up the stairs and in the madman's grip, I felt myself being held at arm's length like a rag doll and shaken. "Shut up! Get up here, old man, or I'll–"

My captor shoved me against the wall, my head smacking it so hard I heard plaster crack, then flung me away. By then I had such vertigo I could barely tell up from down.

"I said come here!" he shouted at Mr. Ash. He was losing it.

But I wasn't; losing it, I mean. Even then, to my own immense surprise, I was still in the game. Hill country, tenements, waitressing, numbers running, getting Sam out of the city, even Victor: sometimes all you can do in this world is hang on. Just . . . hang on.

I'd gotten into the habit. And I hadn't taken all that target practice for nothing. The question still was, was the damn gun loaded?

Screw it. If it went off when I fired it, we would know. Six whirling faces and pairs of eyes saw the gun in my hand, widened startledly, narrowed in scornful amusement.

"Okay, hand it over." As I'd thought, it was a .32 semiauto, nothing special but plenty for my purposes. Only I couldn't . . .

Six hands reached out, the whole world whirling.

"No." I couldn't get the damned thing level, couldn't even figure out which direction *was* level.

"Go on, now," I gasped, "don't make me–"

But he wasn't having any. To him, I must've looked ridiculous. "I'll have the last laugh, you know," he smirked. "It's too late, now."

Somehow he was above me on the stairs; I must have fallen when he flung me away from himself. He took a step down toward me, and another. In my dizzy vision his shoe was huge, as if it might crush me. I could see through the spinning balusters to the other faces, too, tumbling below.

"You look like your mom," said the voice at the foot of the stairs. Ash, I remembered. Lian Ash.

The inside of my head whirled anew, words forming out of the sound of the voice and from some memory I couldn't quite catch. And then I could, the recollection crystalizing in a burst of all the word games I'd been hearing Sam and Maggie play for so long.

Scrabble, anagrams, synonyms and homonyms. Words spinning. Falling together, mingling with that voice in a dizzy rush.

Lian . . . lean. Tip. Ash . . . tree. Tiptree.

Six guns materialized, inches from me. "Bitch," someone said. No soul in that voice. "Little bitch."

"No," Jacob Tiptree said. I'd found him at last.

"You," I whispered.

Alive . . . But I'd found him, I knew with a rush of drowning sorrow, in the moment before my death.

Soundlessly the world exploded.

Hot. Wet. Red.

The sound I didn't hear blew into my head like a cleansing wind, scouring away nausea, dizziness, everything, leaving in its place a huge emptiness that hung there for a moment, sharp and pure.

Then the world rushed in: the man who had said he was Harry Markle crumpled onto me, bleeding. I pushed him away hard and he rolled off. His right eye was gone, and that is all I am going to say about that.

But I'd never fired at him. Someone else had. A voice came from below; gratefully I focused on it. "Just like your mother," the voice said, as footsteps mounted the stairs. "You have her eyes."

A long, ghastly sharp straight razor slid from the sleeve of the crumpled man who had called himself Harry Markle. An NYPD gold shield lay on the stair by the body. Number 1905. Lian Ash picked it up as he shoved the body aside, stepped over it toward me.

The weapon in Ash's other hand matched the one in my own. He had fired the shot, I realized belatedly, not me.

The razor's glint disappeared back up the sleeve as the body on the stairs lurched once, convulsively, and tumbled. The sound was like a sack of something heavy and wet thumping end-over-end. Turning from it as Mr. Ash helped me down step by step, I flashed back: *Lifting me . . .*

But that was then and this was now, as we reached the foot of the stairs and the man standing in front of me realized: I knew who he was. "I saw you through the kitchen window," he told me, "when I was out in the yard. You were putting that big gun away in the mantel."

Releasing me, he stepped back to look at me assessingly. "Unwise, I thought."

"Yes." There was an understatement. He was good, I realized, at understatement. I let a breath out. "I guess it was dumb, huh?"

Which was when it hit me that I'd had it all, as Sam would have said, bass-ackwards. "Did you," I asked slowly, "ever send me any cards? Or a hundred dollars in an envelope, once?"

He looked strangely at me. "No. I didn't. Never anything at all."

"I see. No, don't apologize. I just needed to know." So it was true, the idea of a life lived in service to that child. And to the woman I was now. The man called Lian Ash wasn't the last surviving important person in Harry Markle's sad life. I was. The monster had been hunting me.

"You knew the real Harry was dead?"

He shook his head. "I knew he wasn't active, not why. We old fugitives tend to keep abreast of these things."

Yeah, I'll bet. Like Jemmy Wechsler, who kept his ear to the ground so obsessively, it was a wonder it didn't sprout roots.

"Once Harry was out of the picture, I figured it was safe to get a little closer to you." He winked at me. Then he grew serious again. "Till then he was probably watching out for guys like me who might show up in Eastport, try to make contact. From what I heard he'd made quite a hobby out of me. So I stayed in Machias, laid low."

"And you knew this guy *wasn't* Harry Markle?"

"I didn't at first. Scared the heck out of me when I heard somebody by that name was around. I thought he must've found out I was here, after all. Didn't want him to see *me*, of course."

"Then why'd you buy those guns from Wade, if you weren't suspicious?"

He shrugged. "One for me, and one for my old landlady, Mrs. Sprague. Always figured she needed one around. Opportunity came up so I took it."

His eyes met mine. Blue, like mine. "Later I made a point of getting a look at him. *Then* I knew it wasn't Markle, but if I said so I'd have to say *how* I knew. Besides, the only thing I could think of, he was another cop, and it was some kind of trap for that *other* fellow Markle had been chasing."

He glanced toward the motionless man in my hallway. "I thought he was one of the good guys, whoever he really was. And I was wrong."

"Yeah. Me, too." Boy, was I. "When were you planning to tell me the truth about yourself? Or did you ever intend to?"

"That's what I came back to do," he replied quietly. "I'd been afraid to, you see, for so long."

That I might reject him? Or turn him in to the authorities, maybe. "And you weren't anymore?"

A short laugh. "Oh, yes. I was afraid. But driving away this afternoon, it occurred to me, I'd just put a gun in my daughter's hand in case she needed it." His tone darkened. "I left my little girl alone to fend for herself. And I ran. Just like before."

"So you came back." A silence between us. Then: "Give me the other weapon, please," I said. "Please—"

What should I call him—Dad? I didn't think so. "Jacob, give me that gun. We need to go out to the kitchen and put this—"

The second weapon, the one I hadn't fired. ". . . away."

My mental processes were kicking in with a vengeance, maybe because my body was getting used to shocks: mental, physical, and emotional. I took the gun from his hands, wiped it and gripped it as if I were firing it.

An excess of caution, probably. No one would question the story I was planning to tell. But I wasn't taking chances, now. Stepping over the motionless man, I made it almost to the kitchen door before a sound made me turn again. The man on the floor rose with nightmare smoothness. In his bloody hand, a razor . . .

And that face. Half the brain behind it is gone, probably. A layman's diagnosis, not the way Victor would've phrased it at all. But accurate phrasing was the smallest of my worries as I stood staring, momentarily paralyzed with fright.

But *he* wasn't paralyzed. More to the point at the moment, he wasn't *dead.*

Yet. The face twisted in despairing triumph, the ugliest thing so far because it showed he knew *yet* was the operative term here. But I guess when half your head is demolished inside, if you know anything it's that *nothing to lose* has become your motto.

Or slogan. Or theme song. Whatever. *Damn it, Jake, will you* do *something?* a voice in my head yammered uselessly.

The razor at my father's throat glinted fierily in a shaft of late-afternoon sunlight. Then I noticed I still had the guns, the recently fired one in my hand, the other in my pocket again.

That's me: always the last to know. It struck me that quite a number of important things had failed to dawn on me in a timely manner lately, but this was no time for self-recrimination.

I knew what I wanted to do, but the blood-drenched, half-demolished figure with the razor gripped impossibly in its fist kept moving, bobbing and weaving. If I fired, I might hit . . .

"Come on, give it here." The voice dripped contempt, mixed bubblingly with blood, the remaining eye rolling whimsically in a way that would have been cartoonish—any second it was going to pop out on a spring, or a stalk—if it hadn't been so awful.

"Come on, girlie," he wheedled. "You ever even held a gun before? Come on."

In that moment I'm not sure which I hated more: being called girlie, or the fear on Lian Ash's face.

I dropped that sucker where he stood.

When we reached the kitchen I put the gun from my sweater pocket into the hiding place with the Bisley, tucking the small weapon in beside the massive one.

"We need to call Bob Arnold," I said, rubbing my icy hands.

Too many years, too many questions. Where should I start? Did I want to? The baggage I'd carried around for so long seemed lighter than what I confronted: him. In the flesh.

But he didn't go to the phone. Instead he spoke again in reply to my final question. The one, after all the rest had been answered, that I was afraid to ask.

"I didn't kill her," he told me quietly. "I know it's what you always thought. Everyone did. The police, the FBI—they still think so. That I killed your mother and the rest of them."

The explosion had half-leveled a city block. Jemmy Wechsler had told me later that a lot of it had been stolen Army ordnance, the kinds of things civilians never get their hands on.

Aren't supposed to get their hands on, for reasons that were obvious on that early morning years ago, when they all went up at once like a Fourth of July celebration in hell.

A kind of fury seized me. "Why should I believe that? And why, if you didn't, did you run? And leave me . . ."

The ashes of the wood fire from the shack in the hills were cold in my mouth. Poverty and grief, neither of which I'd earned, and the people they sent me to, my mother's folks, hating me because I was half him. Watching me every minute for signs that I was like him; finding them regularly.

"Because it was set up to look just exactly as if I did kill your mother," he responded quietly. "And you. By a fellow who'd learned everything from me. But then he decided that I wasn't radical enough to lead anymore. Because I wouldn't kill innocent people for the cause. So he decided I'd gotten too old." Small laugh. "I was twenty-four. He's dead now. Last I knew he was a law-abiding husband and father paying taxes and covering his butt with the best of them."

His smile was bitter. "But at the time he was good. Didn't miss a thing. If I were to walk into an FBI office today, noon tomorrow I'd be in a federal prison. Your mother's death was the cherry on a very big cake, Jacobia. Once I was in, I'd never come out again."

"You ran before you knew if I was even alive."

Contradiction in his eyes; that didn't jibe with what he thought. "What's the first thing you recall after the explosion?"

"Screaming." I remembered it too well. "Sitting there under that big piece of sheet metal, screaming my head off."

"You're sure?" he insisted. "Nothing before that?"

"No. Well . . ." Doubt crept in as I ransacked the old memories. "Floating. Flying through the air. The blast blew me into the yard, sheet metal must've fallen on top of . . ."

He shook his head. "Jacobia. There wasn't a scratch on you."

That was true. But how did *he* know?

I'd heard many times what a miracle it was, in voices sour with the unspoken wish that it had been me blown to bits and not her. They'd loved my mother, the relatives who'd taken me in, or had felt what they identified as love, once she was gone. That's the definition of a saint: dead, so you can't blow your image. I by contrast was very much alive, and what they did know about me, they didn't like a bit.

"Do you seriously believe you could be blown through the air," he persisted, "then land under the convenient shelter of a piece of corrugated sheet metal?"

First the explosion. *Then* into the yard. *Floating*...It was corrugated metal, grooves like waves on water, glittering.

The lightbulb went on. "You carried me there?"

He nodded slowly and I realized with a shock that I believed him. It explained why I'd been unhurt. It didn't fix things. But it stowed them in a section of old baggage I knew wouldn't have to be opened again.

"I thought you murdered her. That's what they all said." My mother's people: to them, her husband's name had been a curse word. "But killed yourself, too. Burnt to ashes that blew away on the wind."

The bloodthirsty, satisfied tone when they said it: I'd been tasting those blown-on-the-wind ashes all my life.

"So you've been watching me from afar? And when you were satisfied Harry Markle wasn't on your trail anymore, you moved up here to be closer. You answered my ad for a mason to get nearer still. But you never—"

Of course he hadn't. After so many years, why should he risk his freedom on what I might do?

"I'm sorry," he said. "I wish I could talk to the young fool I was. I wish I could bring your mother back. But I can't."

He looked squarely at me. "I can't do so many of the things I wish I'd done. And I'm so sorry," he repeated. "For all of it, Jacobia. For everything."

Which was when Bob Arnold rushed in without knocking, found me covered in blood with a gun on the kitchen table in front of me. He'd come to tell me he'd just gotten the fingerprint report.

But he stopped when he saw us. "On the stairs," I managed to say, and he went, whereupon I burst into sobs. I despise crying in front of people, always have, but now I thought I could weep for a year and not be done with it, that they'd have to set up a saltwater intravenous to replenish my tears. Then Wade arrived, took one look at me and one at Mr. Ash.

And comprehended utterly, the way he knows what weather is coming out on the water: not the details, maybe, but enough of the drift to know just what to do.

"Hey," he said kindly to me. "You don't need this." He took the gun, which I'd picked up again.

"Hey, yourself," I said gratefully, hating the way my voice trembled.

After a little while Bob Arnold came back looking grimly resolute. "I need to know what happened here, Jacobia."

By then George and Ellie had arrived, too, summoned by Bob. I said the man we'd called Harry Markle had come into the house and surprised me, that he'd attacked me.

That Mr. Ash—I was still calling him that, of course—heard the struggle, rushed upstairs just as I'd fired the little .32 semiauto I had been carrying in my sweater pocket when I was alone in the house.

That I'd shot my attacker twice when he wouldn't back off. He'd fallen on me, and then down the stairs: end of story.

And although I could see in Ellie's eyes she was skeptical, and Wade figured out that something else had happened, and Bob Arnold knew I'd been carrying the Bisley, not a .32, they all took my story as gospel anyway. Why would I lie?

Two shots fired, two bullets missing from a recently fired weapon. The only part missing from my story was two shooters and I wasn't telling that. If I brought Lian Ash into it, Bob might feel it was necessary to look into his background.

So I shut up, glancing around dazedly. But when I did, a new terror struck me: Sam wasn't here. Maggie, either.

After I finish up here in Eastport.

Your son. His girl.

Chapter 11

"W here were they going?" I demanded, jumping up. The world only wheeled a little bit, then straightened. "Did they tell anyone?"

Wildly I ran to the door, yanked it open, peering out to the street and the driveway. But they weren't there, either.

"Wade?" I turned helplessly. It was dark out now.

"I'm on it," he called, already at the telephone. "I'll try Victor. Maybe Sam talked to him lately."

But when Wade got through to the hospital they said Victor wasn't available. A man had come in earlier in the day asking for him and the two had gone off urgently together. A man with close-clipped greying hair, wearing a leather jacket.

"He's got them," I said. "He's got them, he's done something to them, and he's dead. I killed him." *The last laugh* . . .

"I killed him . . . so now, *he can't tell us where.*"

"Harriet's house," Ellie said decisively, already halfway out my back door. "He *wants* us to know."

As soon as she said it I knew she was right. Finding bodies wouldn't be bad enough, cruel enough, for *his* last laugh. No, he was setting us up for something worse than that.

Much worse, as we discovered upon walking into his place: Prill was unconscious. The big dog's breathing was shallow and fast, her eyes rolled back in her glossy, reddish-gold head.

That son of a bitch. "Call the vet," Ellie told George, "and can you get someone to take her out there, right away?"

George nodded grimly, grabbed the phone and found it dead—another joke, ha-ha—and hustled out to his truck's cell phone.

"Poor thing," Ellie was crouched by the animal. "He must have poisoned her."

Wade and Bob Arnold were in the kitchen, searching it for a clue to what this mad evil bastard might have had in mind for us. But I didn't have to search. Deep down in the coldest place in my heart, I knew where to look.

"There," I said, waving miserably at the map of Eastport on the corkboard over the mantel, at the murders and accidents we'd suffered marked on it.

In reality of course he'd been keeping score. There was his own house with a cute little smiley-face drawn on it; looking at it made me want to put my fist through it. And there the Danvers' house elaborately decorated with two horrid stick figures, eyes fatally x-ed in, to represent Harriet and Samantha; jagged lines of waves for the water in the cellar, inked-on lightning bolts.

"Guy was an artist," Ellie commented acidly, looking over my shoulder.

From the Moosehorn Refuge: cartoon bubbles and a balloon-captioned word: *glub!* Dear heaven.

There was even a receipt tacked to the map, from an on-line weird pet dealer called Captive-Raised Invertebrate City. The receipt was for a dozen brown recluse spiders—*Loxosceles reclusa*—via FedEx.

Oh, this guy was hilarious. The spiders were a real hoot. I felt their legs on my arms again as I went on scanning the map.

A word captioned over my own house: boom! A sketch of Sam's speeding car flying downhill . . .

Okay, you son of a bitch, I thought, my fury growing.

I see how clever you've been. Now tell me—

"There." Ellie pointed to a mark that I'd taken at first to be a printed icon: small, neat, unlike the cartoonish scrawls of other annotations.

But upon closer inspection the icon was inked in: a small, round, black object with a fuse burning at the top of it.

"Wade . . ." He was at my side in a heartbeat.

"They're down at the boat basin," I said. "Sam, Maggie, and probably Victor, maybe with explosives."

Over in her dog bed, Prill sighed heavily and didn't breathe again. "Oh, no," Ellie mourned.

But then the dog took another sighing, shuddery inhalation, just as a big bearded guy I didn't know rushed in, some friend of George's, lifting the dog as tenderly as a baby, cradling her.

"I'll take care of her," he promised, his hugely muscled arms wrapped protectively around the animal, and went out again.

Peering out after him, I saw he was tucking her into the sidecar of a Harley-Davidson motorcycle, which ordinarily I wouldn't have been in favor of at all, but now I had no choice.

Not to mention no time. "We can all go there in the back of Wade's truck," I said, "and . . ."

We moved in a rush toward the back door, which was nearest. All but Lian Ash—I still called him that, in my mind, and I had a feeling I would be doing so for a long while, maybe forever—

—who hung back alertly. "Wait."

His command could've cut through lead sheathing. We halted as he stepped in front of us, leaning down toward a length of something barely visible stretched across the doorway opening.

"Trip wire," he pronounced. So we all went out the front again, feeling a good deal more nervous than when we had arrived. But not as nervous as we were about to be.

Not by a long shot.

"**It's a bomb,** all right," Mr. Ash said ten minutes later.

The cloud-filled sky had darkened early. We stood on the finger pier, gazing along a flashlight beam into Sam's boat, where Sam, Maggie, and Victor had been tied up on deck.

Seeing them, I felt my heart go dead in my chest. Their eyes were closed and for a moment I thought they'd been given whatever Prill had, only a lot more. Then I spotted Sam's chest moving.

"Alive . . ." Wade squeezed my shoulders. Bob Arnold was going around under the big lights that made the dock resemble a stage set at night, talking to boat owners and Coast Guard guys, asking them to get the vessels out of the boat basin, onto open water.

Wisely, he'd decided not to tell them that if they didn't, a bomb might blow them all up; as it was, the scramble of activity that resulted began making me anxious: engines, and boat wakes.

"I can't stand it," I said, "I'm going aboard and—"

A big hand stopped me. "Hold your horses."

Lian Ash assessed the contraption tangled under the wooden deck chairs the three prisoners sat on. "Let me think about this a minute," he said calmly.

"What's there to think about? It's a—"

Victor's eyes opened. "Bomb," he snapped viciously. "It's a clock and some explosives, any *moron* can see that it's a—"

"Correct," Lian Ash interrupted mildly. "An old-fashioned alarm clock with two brass bell-domes by the winding stem, hooked to a wire tied to four sticks of good, old-fashioned dynamite."

For a moment it was a toss-up which would explode first: my ex-husband, or the device. "*Do* something about it, you big—"

"Don't move," Mr. Ash said sharply. "What's wrong with this picture?" he added, echoing my earlier thought. Then:

"Got it. It's that stuff he's tied you up with. And the material that's under the dynamite. Was it there when you got here, do you recall? Also, how much of it was there? Say, a cupful? Or more?"

Another boat motored out past the concrete mooring dolphin, sending another wash of waves glittering under the lights into the boat basin, rocking the pier we stood on and the boat we were peering into.

"Hey," Sam protested, waking, trying to get his hands free. "What—?"

"Oh," Maggie moaned groggily.

"Stay still, everything's fine. Do as I say, please," Victor told them, and they obeyed at once: that voice of his. I thought I despised it.

But now I'd have fallen on my knees and thanked God for its instant effectiveness, if the backwash from the parade of exiting boats weren't threatening to knock me off the finger pier.

"What do we do now?" The water was the deep, pure blue of fountain-pen ink, the breeze off the waves fragrant with cold sea salt mingled pleasantly with a whiff of diesel. No stars, and the smell of rain drifting with the other scents, but you just couldn't believe anything could go wrong on a night like this.

"Det cord," Lian Ash said to Wade and George. "It looks like colored clothesline, but . . ."

The Coast Guard crew was setting up barricades at the end of the fish pier, the sawhorses yellow in the lights from Rosie's hot dog stand.

A hundred yards away on Water Street, folks were beginning to gather under the streetlamps, their shapes mere dark silhouettes against the lighted store windows.

"It's the cord they use to set off explosives," Wade told me. But I already knew that, and the picture of what had been put together here was coming horridly clear.

"So cut the cord," Victor grated. "What's hard about that?"

"It's not that simple," Lian Ash answered. "For one thing, it's not fuse cord, which is what you're probably thinking of. Safety fuse burns slow, thirty or forty seconds per foot and doesn't explode. It's designed that way, to be less volatile." He frowned. "Detonating cord has an explosive core that goes up at twenty-five thousand feet per second, flame ball around the cord about eighteen inches in diameter. And that's not the half of it. See that mound of grey stuff, sort of clayish looking, by the fake bomb?"

"Fake bomb?" Victor began apoplectically, and started to get up, whereupon Wade fixed him in the pale-grey stare he's been known to use on guys bigger than he is.

"Sit your butt on that chair and pipe down," he said.

Victor did so.

"Fake by comparison, I meant," Lian Ash clarified. "Anyway, I'm pretty sure that grey stuff's C4," he went on quietly. "Commonly known as plastique. Cord's in a ring, little length leading from it to the explosive." He shook his head slowly. "Bottom line is, I'm not sure what all booby traps are laid for us here. Do something wrong, whole dock would go. Lot of other stuff down there, too. I see an M14 land mine, for one thing."

"What'll it do?" Victor asked. "How *do* we get out of this?"

"Well, it could be complicated," Mr. Ash said. "In order to activate the M14, the safety clip is removed and the pressure plate is rotated from its safety position to its armed position."

Somehow he seemed to understand that the details would calm

Victor. He went on: "There are letters on it, A for armed and S for safety, on the pressure plate. You align an arrow to arm it."

"And then?" Victor demanded.

"Once it's armed, pressure can cause the mine to detonate. When pressure is applied it pushes down on the Belleville spring underneath the pressure plate."

"Oh," Victor said faintly.

"The spring pushes the firing pin onto the detonator which ignites the main charge. In this case, it's probably tetryl."

"So what *do* we do?" Bob Arnold asked. It hadn't escaped him: Lian Ash was smarter about high explosives than your average stonemason.

Deep, contemplative breath from Mr. Ash. "Well. Nothin' for it, I guess, but to get down there and undo it."

"Wait a minute," Victor piped up, "I'm still not so sure I want you down here fooling around with this stuff."

"Dad," Sam put in quietly.

"How do I know," Victor demanded argumentatively, "that *you* know anything about this at all, that you're not just some fake with a big mouth and a fancy line of talk, just trying to impress people?"

"Dad, shut up," Sam said again as Maggie's eyes, alert until now, drooped alarmingly.

The sight sent a fresh pang of anxiety through me: What had that bastard dosed them with?

"How do I know," Victor ranted unstoppably, "you won't blow all *three* of us to *kingdom come?*"

Sam groaned, and for a moment I recalled being his age, and feeling so immortal. Being tied up over a bunch of explosives was bad enough, apparently, but now his father was embarrassing him.

But Lian Ash didn't seem the least bit affronted by Victor's question. Instead, a beatific smile spread on his lined face as he bent to answer Victor's question.

"First sensible thing you've said since we all got here," he replied. "And the answer is . . ."

He stepped down onto the deck of the little boat, bobbling dangerously for a moment until he got his sea legs under him.

". . . the answer is you don't. And till we're sure I *haven't* blown you up," he added uncomfortingly, "neither do I."

He frowned at his task. Maggie was unconscious again, beads of sweat on her lip and not much color in her face.

"Wade," Lian Ash said, "can you come down here with me? It'll take more than one pair of hands to untangle all this rat's nest."

Despite the clear danger, Wade moved forward alertly. He'd have stepped in front of a freight train for Sam.

"Just a minute," Bob Arnold put in. The boat basin was empty now and the dock swept clean of people and vehicles, the barriers all up at the entry.

"Bomb squad's in Augusta. Take them a while to get here. But they're coming, and what I want to know is this," Bob told Lian Ash. "They've got the knowledge, experience to handle all this kind of stuff. No doubt that if we give 'em time to get here they can get these people out of the fix they're in."

That last part for my benefit. There was plenty of doubt but he wanted to give me hope. "What I want to know is, are *you* that good? All by yourself?"

It was the question he'd been putting together in his mind: Who was Lian Ash, that he could do it too? Was he, for instance, a man into whose background Bob Arnold should look deeply once this was all over? A man with odd secrets, even a wanted man, perhaps?

Or, as Victor had suggested, was Lian Ash just going to make everything dreadfully worse? He looked up from where he crouched.

"First of all we don't have that time, for the bomb squad to get here. This clock, dynamite, they're not the main show but the clock is ticking. It's a timer. It'll set the rest off, we give it the chance. I don't know when." He took a deep breath.

He could say no. He could back out.

He could stay free.

"The answer to your other question," he said, "is yes."

Bob digested this. "All right then," he said gravely. "I'll want to talk with you afterwards." He turned away.

Wade looked up at me. "Jake. Go on, now. You and Ellie, too, George. Get away from here, we'll just do what has to be done and we'll be with you shortly."

All of us, his eyes said. I had no choice but to believe it.

Lian Ash whistled softly. "Huh. Look at that. It really is a Claymore. Don't see those much anymore. And bags of ANFO pellets. Looks like about sixty pounds."

"Which means?" Victor quavered.

"Powder factor, that's how much it takes to do a job, is a pound of explosive per cubic yard of rock broken up enough so you can dig it with a front-end loader."

Victor did the calculation in his head. "Not," he groaned, "what I wanted to hear."

Me either. Wade glanced at me. "Jake, unless you've got some practical activity to contribute here . . ."

I understood. They weren't going to do it until we left. And the longer we hung around the closer that clock got to zero hour. Whatever that was.

"Right. See you later," I told Sam more confidently than I felt. George was guiding Ellie up the narrow metal gangway to the pier. Turning away I felt an axe of misery chop through my heart, but I had no choice. Staying wouldn't help anything.

The gangway's serrated metal steps were agony under my feet but by the top I felt weightless. As if, were I to let go of the rail, I might sail up balloonlike into the night sky: disembodied with fear, with the near-certain imminence of a final loss.

Which was how I knew for the first clear time what Lian Ash had felt, all those years ago, when he was going away from me.

On December 6, 1917, two ships collided in Halifax Harbor, a few hundred miles northeast of Eastport as the crow flies. It was during World War I and one ship carried benzine, TNT, picric acid, and gun-cotton. The other, a Belgian relief vessel, does not figure prominently; it could have been any ship. What mattered were the explosives.

And the result: The blast killed 1,600 people outright, the munitions ship's half-ton anchor crashed to earth two miles from the explosion, and a three-mile-high mushroom cloud rose over the emptied bay, the water blown away.

The Halifax blast, still famous around these parts, was the largest human-caused nonnuclear explosion in history and back in my kitchen I tried very hard not to think about it.

Instead I let Monday out of the workshop and she made a beeline for her water bowl; Cat Dancing followed, heading for the hall but coming back at once, shaking her paw at what she still smelled there.

While we were out an ambulance had taken the body away. But I could still feel it there, too, as if it had been drawn on the floor with invisible chalk.

The phone rang again and I took it off the hook. Everyone in Eastport wanted to know what had happened, how I was, and—this of course was the important part—what in the world was going on, down on that finger pier?

But I didn't feel like telling them.

Numbly, Ellie and I began fixing dinner. I'd tried calling Maggie's mother but there was no answer; now I stood rigidly at the counter peeling potatoes, feeling that if I stopped, I would probably fall to the floor screaming.

The peeler slipped, taking a slice of skin from the end of my index finger. Two drops of blood. I put the peeler down. Outside the kitchen window: black sky.

Please, I implored it. *Oh, I am begging you.*

Ellie put her hand on my shoulder briefly, then went back to shaping Swedish meatballs and lining them up in a Pyrex dish: two dozen meatballs each the size of a toddler's fist, enough for all of us and more, bless her heart.

When the men went out on the water, you never knew for sure that you'd see them again. Anything could happen: equipment. A rogue wave. A freighter. There was no end to the things that could go wrong. You dealt with it. I picked up the peeler and it took another thin skin-strip immediately.

Monday came over and pressed against my leg. *Please.*

"I think," Ellie suggested, "twenty potatoes are probably enough." She took the peeler from my hand, or tried to.

After a moment I allowed my fingers to open.

These two would be here, I realized. George and Ellie, no matter what. But that thought I absolutely could not allow myself to take any further.

"Lian Ash seems okay," George said expressionlessly. He was intuiting more than I would ever have expected of him. Now some of the notes and papers from Harriet's house, that the impostor known as Harry Markle had left there, lay on the table in front of him as he frowned into a spiral notebook.

"What's this, do you think?" he asked. "I know it's a map. But not of anything around here. I don't recognize any of this."

Ellie and I peered over his shoulder at the neatly drawn diagram on a sheet of blue-lined paper. "A cemetery," Ellie said, pointing at the

sketch of an old-fashioned grave marker, the letters RIP inked in miniature on it.

But no other markers. And the topography did look familiar to me.
Brooklyn, I thought, and there was Manhattan, and the shoreline of
New Jersey. "No, not a graveyard," I said. "Will you get out the atlas,
please, Ellie?" She hurried to fetch it.

"George." A new thought hit me. "Will Bob know he needs to get
people away from the windows? The glass?"

I left the rest unspoken: Halifax. All these years after the event,
most people in the United States didn't even know that it had happened. But in Halifax, just a few hours away via ferry, an army of people had been blinded by flying glass that day.

George nodded seriously, not wanting to say it either. "Bob knows,"
was all he said as Ellie returned with the atlas.

But suddenly I couldn't stand it anymore. "I'm going to the third
floor, maybe from there I can see . . ."

What? But I couldn't just sit. The stairs creaked ominously, each
riser groaning an alarm echoing the ones in my heart. The third floor
windows, their ancient panes wavery antiques, looked out over the
rooftops of town to the harbor.

Traceries of new eaves obscured my view of the dock, but the boat
basin was visible under the big lights, empty now except for Sam's
boat, its little mast like a finger pointing at heaven. The boat was moving away from the pier, coming around in the basin between the dock
pilings and the big concrete mooring dolphin jutting from the water.
Due east; I couldn't see who was at the helm or what was happening
on the small vessel.

But someone must be there. Human hands turned the rudder, ran
the throttle of Sam's little Evinrude, kept her heading steady in the
glare of the big dock lights.

I stared, transfixed, my fingers grazing the windowpane. All the
other boats were moving away, out into deeper water, all speeding at

full throttle, I could tell by the faint disturbance of their wakes. Footsteps creaked up the stairs behind me, but I dared not turn away. *Who was on that boat?*

I glanced at my wristwatch. It was just past seven o'clock. Or as Sam would have put it, 1900 hours, now going on . . .

1905. "Dear god . . ." Harry Markle's badge number.

Turning back to the window as George and Ellie came into the room behind me, I had a final, mercilessly clear view of a small boat bobbing ghostlike in the fading illumination of the dock lights behind it. Something went over the side, quick as a fish.

Then, without warning, a ball of orange flame expanded from it in the ghastly millisecond before the boom arrived, a sound from some vast, damned thing's yawning maw, like a roar of defiance rumbling up straight out of the bowels of hell.

The windowpanes *bulged* inward. Shingles flapped and sailed from the roofs of the houses nearest Water Street, flew away like startled birds. My heart gave a *thud* in my chest.

When the flash faded, Sam's boat had vanished and bits of stuff floated down through the dock lights.

I sat slowly down on the floor of the attic room, my face in my hands. If I moved, it would be true.

So I didn't move. I don't know for how long. Not until . . .

"Hey." A hand touched my hair. I looked up, disbelieving.

It was Wade. Behind him stood Sam.

"You'd better come downstairs," Ellie told me. "Victor's here, too." I stood shakily, still unable to believe my eyes.

"And," Ellie added, smiling through her tears, "he's in the kind of bad mood I'm afraid only *you* can do something about, Jake."

"I don't suppose there's a drink around here," Victor asked bitterly, rummaging in the cabinets.

Ellie went to find him one as Sam looked on. He was chomping at the bit to get back to Maggie, who was still at the dock being looked at by the paramedics. But I needed him here where I could see him as Monday danced joyously around us, toenails clicking, and even Cat Dancing gazed down benignly—well, benignly for her—from her perch atop the refrigerator.

"How did he know?" I whispered into Wade's shoulder. "The badge number . . ." I'd explained what must have happened.

"Not sure," Wade replied. "He got them out of the det cord first." Sam, Maggie, and Victor, tied up with the explosive, red "clothesline."

". . . and up off the pier." Wade went on. "Bob Arnold grabbed them, took them past the traffic cones, he'd gotten everyone else back, too, by then."

Another benefit of small town policing as performed by Bob Arnold: he never lied, not even to the bad guys. So when he said *move,* everyone had, and he'd gotten people away from the glass hazard, too.

"No eye injuries that we know about so far," Wade confirmed, avoiding the main issue, which was what had *he* been doing all that time, he and my father, while Sam, Maggie, and Victor were being whisked to safety.

"Every window on Water Street'll need replacing, and lots of them uphill," he said. "Guess folks getting ready for the weather taped a lot of the old glass, though. Guy must've been stockpiling those explosives. Probably stolen."

Sure. It was why he'd been traveling, I supposed: a gravel pit here, a road project there, a National Guard storage depot somewhere else. All the loot piled up in the U-Stor-It he'd mentioned, on the mainland till he needed it. Wade came across with the rest of the story.

"I stayed to help defuse the stuff, we thought we were going to be okay with it," he said. "But all of a sudden he—"

Lian Ash. Jacob Tiptree.

"—he asked Sam what time it was, Sam told him, and a funny look came on his face," Wade went on. "Next I knew he was shoving me off the boat, firing the engine up. Said to tell you he'd see you later, and he was outta there like grease through a goose."

Military time. And Harry Markle's badge number. No fool, my old man. He was a professional.

And he knew his bombs. "He didn't say anything else?"

"Um, yeah. He said, 'Shame on me.' "

Fool me once, shame on you. My heart clung stubbornly to the memory of that shape going over the side, just before the blast. So quick, I barely glimpsed it, but surely it had been there.

Surely it had. Not that going overboard would guarantee anything.

"I'm sorry, Jacobia," Wade said. "The Coast Guard guys went in there just as fast as they could afterwards, got the searchlights on to see if maybe . . ."

If maybe he'd survived, by some miracle I didn't deserve. I clung to Wade, torn between gratitude for what had been saved and a kind of grief I'd never known before.

And then we heard it: Bob Arnold, calling as he came up the back steps. "Somebody want to take a damned fool off my hands?"

The back door opened. Bob marched in, looking about as angry as any of us had ever seen him, before. "I got things to do, you know, every god damned alarm in this town is goin' off like blazes, bunch of bomb experts be here any minute now, full of pee and vinegar and mad as all hell 'cause there is not one freakin' thing left for them to do about anything . . ."

Oh, he was wired, our police chief, his round face pink with a combination of fury, exertion, excitement, and remembered terror, little round beads of sweat standing out on the skin above his rosebud lips.

Behind him, dripping wet and resembling the ghost of some ancient shipwreck, stood my father. "Won't go to the hospital," Bob told us disgustedly. "I figured maybe Victor would take a look at him."

His eyes were huge and haunted, his face full of pain, and he kept shaking his head as if trying to clear it. But when he saw me he rushed toward me and in the next instant his cold arms wrapped around me, his body shaking with chills from the icy water and with his emotion.

Fool me twice, shame on me. "Coast Guard fellows found him floating," Bob went on. "His eardrums are broken, they think. Anyway, he can't hear. Blast, probably. I don't know what else."

He shrank from my embrace, wincing. "Broken ribs, I'll bet," Victor diagnosed, seeing this.

Wade nodded. "Shock wave broke 'em," he agreed. "Or slammed him against some ledge. Drove him right down against it, I would imagine."

"Lucky it didn't slam his skull on it." Victor took a large swallow of his whiskey. "C'mere, let me see him."

Now that he wasn't in danger of being blown to kingdom come, my ex-husband was getting his wind back. He led his patient to the dining room where the light was better, bending solicitously to him, and I recalled again how kind Victor always was to his patients, as if their need were the medicine he needed himself.

I turned to Bob. "I don't get it. How'd he live?"

Bob shrugged. "Coast Guard guys said they saw him go over the side with his toes pointed, I guess that'd carry him deeper, and then he must've just swum like a son of a bitch, far as he could get, prayed for the best."

George spoke up slowly. "Sometimes a guy, he's done all the right things, everything he should've but he drowns. Another guy, water'll spit him back out even though by all the rules, he's the one who ought to've gotten made into fish food."

He looked toward the dining room where Victor's voice went on in a low, reassuring murmur. "That guy, what turned the trick for him was, it just wasn't his turn to go."

Thank you. Another siren went off somewhere, joining the cacophony of car alarms, bank alarms, smoke alarms, and all the other alarms that howled steadily as people struggled, mostly without success, to get them turned off again.

Bob looked around at us. "Gotta go." His eyes met mine. "You tell the old fellow in there—"

His head angled toward the dining room, ". . . that I guess we won't be needing to have that conversation, after all."

About bombs, he meant. About who knew what about them, and why.

I felt my throat close again in gratitude; if a sparrow fell in Eastport, Bob knew it. Did something about it, if need be; all in good time.

But if not, then not.

Soon after Bob had departed, Maggie arrived, struggling up the porch steps and gamely insisting she was fit as a fiddle. She had refused another trip to the hospital. "But my mom's not home yet," she explained, "so I thought I'd come here . . ."

She put a pale hand on a kitchen chair to steady herself, as Victor returned to fill a new glass of whiskey and refill his own. "Young lady," he told her, "please step into my consulting room."

My own head was clear, ears as soundlessly normal as they'd been before I tumbled off the ladder. Victor paused to peer at me.

"I'm fine," I told him calmly. "No ringing, no dizziness."

He took my chin in his hand, turned my head gently. "Hmm. I think when he manhandled you, it jolted your ear again. I always said you needed a good smack. I suspect the vertigo won't come back."

"Oh," I said. He took his hand away. "Victor . . ."

Don't go, I wanted to say. Which was ridiculous, of course. So I said nothing and after a moment he took his glasses of whiskey and went into the parlor with Maggie and Sam.

"Here," Ellie said a little later, holding a tray out to me. Lian Ash was in the dining room alone. "Why don't you take it in to him?"

I'd said nothing to her about who he was. But she'd seen us

together, our two faces side by side, each illuminated with its own new knowledge. And it was Ellie, so all she'd really needed to know was in her generous heart. On the tray she held out were a small silver coffee pot and cups trimmed with a pattern of blue forget-me-nots.

He'd told me some lies. He'd hoped I would check them. The story he'd spun that day at the kitchen table about mistaken identity; the grammar book, the biography, and the handbook of explosives:

All clues. He'd known me well, as he should have. He'd been watching for years, afraid to approach. Hoping against hope that I would find him, somehow. Fearing it, too.

Like me. Outside it was raining, the spring storm roaring in suddenly as if to make up for the long wait with the violence of its arrival, gusts lashing the torrents through the dark streets.

He'd never been incarcerated, of course. Another lie, some bad stuff up front so I would trust him; as I said, he'd known me well. But a man with his past couldn't afford crime. So he'd never seen the inside of a cell, other of course than the one he'd inhabited, that he had built for himself. And from that, only I could release him.

The decision was easy.

"Thank you," I said, taking the tray from Ellie, and went in to sit with my father.

Chapter 12

Summer did come, and it seemed only a heartbeat later autumn did, too, green leaves igniting in an explosion of yellow, burnt orange, and crimson against the pointed firs.

Sam aced the underwater demolition test for the seminar with coaching from his grandfather, whose identity he did not know even now but seemed somehow to understand. It was as if, in the days after the storm and over the summer afterwards, all the things I'd been so afraid to say got said anyway.

Or didn't need saying. In September, we gathered at camp to view Roy McCall's music video, airing it on a battery-powered VCR.

"Jake," Ellie said as the film began with a swooping aerial overview of Eastport and the bay. "It's the whole town! They must have shot it from a helicopter."

Streets and harbor, sea and sky, the boats tiny scale-model versions and the people too small to be seen. As a camera panned serenely over rocky cliffs, glittering inlets, and back to the miniature buildings of Water Street again, you would never guess there were people in Eastport at all, much less that some of them were being murdered.

A yellow leaf pinwheeled from a branch onto the mirrorlike surface of the lake. At the dock's far end, Prill and Monday lay gazing at the water and dreaming, I supposed, of floating Milk-Bones, while Cat Dancing prowled the cabin's foundation pillars, demolishing—at last she had found her true calling—mice.

"Ain't no wharf there," George objected to the picture on the television screen. *They-ah*: the downeast Maine pronunciation.

McCall's minions had employed creative license in cutting the video, rearranging Eastport's geography to suit their needs. Roy was back home in Los Angeles, now; he'd been cordial enough for the rest of his stay, here, but I doubted we would see him again.

"Nevah has been," George went on indignantly. "No lobstah boat nevah came intah the habbah that way, neithah."

And more in this deliberately exaggerated accent, as an idealized version of our small world unreeled. Eastport had never looked so polished nor bounced so exuberantly to such noise as the sound track blared. Even Maggie, who liked *all* music, winced, then turned the sound down.

She was going to Bar Harbor in a few days to take courses at the Jackson Laboratory, and work at a paid internship she had set up for herself, there. She'd dated Tim Rutherford once or twice but nothing came of that and anyway, Tim was gone to the news desk at the *Boston Herald*. She needed, Maggie had told me calmly, some time away.

"You heard from Wyatt Evert lately?" Wade asked. We sat on the deck, glancing back into the cabin now and then to see what new fiction McCall had perpetrated on us. At the moment, six cat-costumed dancers were boogaloo-ing down an improbably prosperous-looking Water Street, to a reggae beat.

"No. He's into whales now. It's a wealthier demographic." Or so

Fran had told me, calling to report also that Wilma's cat had reappeared as mysteriously as it vanished.

Fran came back to Eastport, still, but only to visit Wilma. Fran and her daughter lived in Portland now, in a group house with other single women who also had children. She'd straightened out her Florida probation situation, and she sounded well.

"You know who I wish I'd hear from, though?" I added, but Wade answered before I could finish.

"Still no Jemmy, huh?"

I shook my head. "I wrote to him about the graveside service in case he wanted to come."

The NYPD had found Harry Markle's body in a shallow grave in Brooklyn, from the map left in his killer's notes. And since Harry had no family, I'd been able to claim it, have it shipped here to Eastport for a proper burial. I'd thought it was the least I could do.

Now his remains lay in Hillside Cemetery under a granite marker I'd had cut for him: *Ever Faithful.* I had wanted to keep the shield as a memento of him, but in the end we pinned it to his dress uniform, which was buried with him.

A person's interment was, after all, a special occasion. "It would be just like Jemmy to show up: blitz in, blitz out," I ventured, looking out at the lake's still water.

The dock was brand-new, glowing yellow-pine-colored in the slanting light of early evening. The spring storm had taken six boats, a dozen roofs, scores of trees and a vast amount of other property along the coast and on the mainland, including Wade's dock.

It had also taken the rest of the siding from the back wall of my house. The Shingle Belles were repairing it: the siding, *and* the structure beneath the siding.

"Maybe he still will," Wade said. "Jemmy, I mean. Show up."

I didn't think so, though. It was a problem: where Jemmy was, why he wasn't in touch. And what, if anything, I should do about it.

But a problem for another day. "Sleeping any better?" Wade asked.

"Some," I lied. White nights, seeing it all again.

Behind us Victor came into the cabin, began complaining: couldn't the road here be paved? Why wasn't electricity run into this place? And . . .

In the end, Victor had decided to stay in Eastport. At his nattering, Wade chuckled; somehow it just wasn't a party without Victor. You could always count on him to bring the whine.

Then: "You had to do it, Jake. The guy could've killed us all. And he *would* have, if not for you."

Once my attacker's fingerprints were linked to the New York homicides and a severely edited story of the rest of it was told, what I'd done was ruled self-defense. Tim Rutherford was still here, then, but surprisingly he didn't call to ask about it, and never probed into the past of Lian Ash.

Or maybe it wasn't surprising. Tim was quick on the uptake, not so quick to upset applecarts if he sensed they shouldn't be.

Sunset spilled onto the water. "I know," I said. "Trouble is, when I did it, that wasn't why. It wasn't that he would have killed me."

The moment flooded back, freshly hideous. "Or my father, or anyone. I did it because I was angry. So I shot him. That's all."

I took a deep breath, willing the pain away, but it didn't go. "In the minute when I was doing it, I was as bad as he was."

"No," Wade said with surprising vehemence. "The idea that it's how you *feel* about something, makes it good or bad—that was *his* mistake, too. But Jake, it's not the thought that counts. In this world, it's the action that counts. And the result."

"So, Maggie," Victor said from inside, patronizingly. "How's that little job of yours working out? Meet any new boys?"

Glancing back I saw Sam roll his eyes exasperatedly, over his father's head. "Dad, it's not a little job. She's going to be helping to develop new eyedrops for allergic people."

The psychology experiment had died after I couldn't stand to wear the lenses anymore. But Maggie had turned lemons to lemonade as usual; now she smiled tolerantly at Victor. "No," she told him. "No new boys. Can I get you anything? A drink?"

Victor harumphed, annoyed at being handled so skillfully, while my father sat watching the music video roll to its end. *For Samantha*, the dedication line read.

"Blown up any boats lately, old fellow?" Victor needled him. Victor's opinion, come to in leisurely, after-the-fact fashion, was that a *good* bomb man could've kept that boat from blowing up altogether.

No reply from my father. I hadn't been aware of him for all those years, but he'd been aware of me. *Acutely* aware; in fact I gathered he'd been quite the well-informed little watchbird.

It was how he'd known about Sam's dyslexia—that grammar book—and my dislike of heights, which he'd been aware of long before he ever came here. And back in the city Victor's behavior had been so bad, the nurses at his hospital had voted him the surgeon whose body was most likely to be found stuffed in a car trunk.

So I wasn't expecting much friendship between the two, and in this I was correct: The old man looked at Victor. His hearing had come back. "You're welcome," he said, and his eyes said more.

At this, Victor got up to find himself another drink, his hands trembling. And when you have made a brain surgeon's hands tremble, you have impressed him; take my word for this.

Satisfied, I turned back to the lake where it was now nearly dark. Monday and Prill climbed the deck steps, lay by our feet as inside, better music began playing: Chet Atkins' *Stay Tuned*.

"So, listen. I was wrong, what I said about putting down old baggage," Wade allowed quietly. "Advising you to, I mean."

My turn to contradict. "No. You were right. It's good to put it down, if it's too heavy."

I smoothed Prill's ears. She'd recovered entirely from her overdose

of sedatives, which was what Victor, Sam, and Maggie had been dosed
with, too: no lingering effects. As for all the times the dog had stepped
between me and the man I'd unwisely given her to . . .

Well, she hadn't been protecting *him.*

And she was ours, now. "You'd just better know what's in the baggage," I added. "Before you put it down."

Inside, my father and Maggie were dancing, him light on his feet.
Sam's hand rested on Victor's shoulder. A trick of lakeside acoustics
brought Sam's words to my ears:

"Don't worry, Dad. The past . . ."

The sound faded but Sam's lips kept moving. I wondered what he
was going to do without Maggie.

I wondered if he cared.

". . . the past is provolone."

But not all of it, unfortunately; the *don't ask, don't tell* policy that Bob
Arnold had chosen to apply to my father couldn't last forever. It's a
funny thing about secrets; the good ones may lie low for a long time,
maybe even forever. But the bad ones always fester into something
ugly, sooner or later.

And my father was a proud man. I only hoped he wouldn't be too
stiff-necked to let me help him, when the time came.

Wade got up. "Coming in?" Delicious smells floated from the
cabin: lasagna, garlic bread. Salad with the last of Ellie's red garden
tomatoes.

The last for this year. "In a minute."

After he'd gone I sat watching the stars fill the night sky, their glow
turning the lake to a milky glimmer.

In it I saw that young cop's face again and wished he could know
how it all ended, that the questions he'd asked his whole life on my behalf had at last been answered. I wondered if he did know, in some way
perhaps that living people cannot fathom.

A loon laughed, out on the lake.

About the Author

SARAH GRAVES lives with her husband in Eastport, Maine, where her mystery novels featuring Jacobia Tiptree are set. She is currently working on her seventh novel, *Mallets Aforethought*.